REDEEMING REPUTATION

Book one
Redemption Tales

George H McVey

This is a work of fiction. Names, characters, places and events are products of the author's imagination or are used fictitiously. Any resemblance to actual persons, living or dead, locales or events is entirely coincidental, or used in a purely fictitious way.

ISBN-13: 978-1475247183
ISBN-10: 1475247184

DEDICATION

This book is dedicated to the memory of my father, Shelby Wayne McVey, who introduced me to the movie cowboy. Many a night I was force fed equal amounts of Bonanza, the Rifleman, and the Lone Ranger, to name a few.

Saturdays weren't spent watching cartoons but Riders in the Sky and movies featuring Roy Rogers, Gene Autry, Clint Eastwood and of course the most famous of movie cowboys, the one and only Duke, John Wayne.

Dad died as I was writing this novel, but my love for the Old West is his fault. So thanks, Dad, and tell Gene and Roy I said Hey, Howdy Hey.

Acknowledgements

As anyone who writes knows, no book is totally written by one person. Yes, the ideas and words are mine, but there are several people who made them and this book better. I want to take the time to thank them here. If you helped and I forget to mention you, don't think your help wasn't appreciated. Just realize my memory is faulty.

First is my wife of twenty-six years, Sheri. She is my first beta reader. She fixes the glaring grammar issues and encourages me to keep going. She puts up with me talking about my characters as if they're real people.(They are to me) She allows me to ignore her without complaint when the story is flowing. I love you, darling, and couldn't do this without you.

My daughter Valerie is also an early reader for me. What her mom doesn't catch she usually does. I love her help and am proud of the woman she has become. To do what I ask of her, plus take care of an autistic child, amazes me more than I say at times.

To my sons George and Alfred, who listen to my plot ideas and pretend to think they're good ideas, go my next thanks. I know you think the old man is bonkers, and you might be right.

My mother-in-law Greta, gets special notice too. She does the final proofreading for me. She is also a constant cheerleader for me in my writing endeavors.

Next is my writing partner, Sophie Dawson. Sophie and I challenge each other to write more and to write better. She is the person I bounce ideas off of and know she will tell me what she really thinks. Sophie, I look forward to a continued friendship with you and to writing Redeeming Cottonwood together.

I have to give a nod to all my friends at CIAindie.freeforms.org I have learned so much from the writers there. They have helped and encouraged me to improve my writing on a regular basis.

Several people read this book and the last and gave me feedback. Amanda, Kendra, Travis, Molly and the rest of my beta readers, thanks for your help. This book is better for your input.

My editors, Karen, Mary and Diane, thanks for your help too. All these people have made this book better. Without them it would be full of mistakes. Any that made it through all their help are purely my own fault. (I probably tweaked something after they were finished with it.)

Finally, to you who are reading this little tale of mine, I appreciate your time and choosing my book to read. If you like it let me know. Leave feedback for me at Amazon.com and tell your friends about my books. Ok, if you're still reading by now you can relax. It's time to grab a sarsaparilla, your sixguns, and "Go west, dear reader. Go west."

Chapter One

"Nobody move! This is a hold up!" Those words woke David Nathaniel Ryder the Third from a deep sleep. As he opened his eyes, he saw two men with bandanas covering the lower parts of their faces. Each had a sixgun pointed at one side or the other of the train car Nathan and his fellow travelers occupied.

"Now this will all be over in a minute if no one tries to play hero. I want you to take any weapons you have on you and put them in the bag my partner is coming around with. Then take everything of value that you have and place it in this bag. Just do as you're told and we'll all get out of this without a problem."

The shorter of the two began to walk up the aisle collecting weapons from the men in the passenger car. When he got to Nathan he stopped. "Come on, gambler, I know you have a gun somewhere. It's either in an arm holster or a hidey on your arm."

Nathan held up his Bible, "I believe you are mistaken, sir. I am not a gambler. I am a Minister of the Gospel on my way to the New Mexico Territory to work on a circuit."

"If you're one of those Bible thumpin' preachers, why are you dressed all fancy like a gambler? I weren't born yesterday, mister. I may not be a church goer, but I seen a few preachers and they dress plain and simple. Who you tryin' to fool? Now hand over your piece." The outlaw thrust the gunnysack at Nathan.

"I assure you I am indeed a preacher. These are the clothes I left New York in. I have not yet had a chance to change my attire into something more western."

"You assure me, do you? You talk like one of those rich businessmen from New York. Maybe you're carrying a lot of money."

The taller outlaw noticed the commotion. "What's the holdup, Shorty?"

"This here fella claims to have no weapon. He dresses like a gambler or fancy businessman, but says he's a preacher headed for the territory. I think he's a lying, Slim."

The taller outlaw, called Slim, stepped closer and looked Nathan up and down.

"Well, Shorty, I agree he don't much look like a preacher. What's your name, Preacher?"

"David Nathaniel Ryder the Third."

"That name sounds familiar to me. I think I heard about a rich preacher in New York named Ryder."

Now it was Nathan's turn to sigh. He had hoped not to have to admit to being the son of the most prominent preacher in New York. "That would be my father."

"Shorty, he really is a preacher. He don't have a weapon on him, but I bet he is loaded with cash. How about it, Preacher? Don't your Bible say something about giving to the poor? I think you should hand over your money to us poor men right now." Slim held out his gunny sack while pointing his gun straight at Nathan's face.

Nathan reached into his jacket pocket and pulled out a money pouch filled with gold double eagles. He opened the pouch and showed the contents to the outlaws. "This is all the money I have in my pockets. I will give it to you under one condition. You take it and leave all these other people alone. After all, this is more money than you will probably get from all of them combined".

Slim looked Nathan in the eye and laughed. "I don't think you understand the situation here, Preacher. I'm in charge, not you. Now put that money bag in my sack and sit down before I put a bullet in your noggin."

Nathan thought about it for a minute. He knew with the training his grandfather had given him, he could defeat these two. However, he wasn't sure he could do it without causing one of the other passengers to get hurt. He slowly put his money bag in Slim's sack and sat back down.

Slim turned away from him and took in the other passengers. "Well, the good preacher has made his contribution to our poor box today. Now it's time for the rest of you to do so. I want all jewelry, cash and anything else of value put in this sack as I come to you."

With Shorty standing by the door just behind Nathan, Slim approached each passenger. They slowly dropped their valuables into the sack. Everything was going perfectly until Slim got to a pretty, dark haired mother and her young son. As he was collecting her money, he noticed a gold cross necklace she was trying to hide inside her dress.

"Lady, I said all your valuables. Now give me that necklace."

Slim reached out to yank it off her neck and as he did so, her son, seeing the masked man reaching for his mother, reacted. "Leave my Mama alone!"

He grabbed Slim's arm and bit him on the hand as hard as he could. Slim reacted without thinking and slammed his sixgun up against the side of the child's head. The blow sent the boy flying, to land two seats down the aisle. Blood began pooling under the child's head.

Shorty stepped towards the action, his pistol moving back and fourth, looking for any reactions from the passengers. Nathan watched in anger as the mother gave up her necklace and rushed to her son. He knew he had to do something. Just as he was about to rush Shorty, one of his Grandfather Nate's stories came to his mind. It was a story about using Indian stealth and cunning to outwit several outlaws who wanted his gold.

He stood slowly and walked towards Slim. "You do not listen too well, do you, hooligan?"

Slim spun toward him, thrusting his gun at Nathan. "Whatcha talking about, Preacher?"

"I told you that was all the money I had on me. I never said it was all the money I had. I am escorting an offering to the New Mexico Territory from my father's church for a mission project to the Mexican people.

"Why don't you and your companion come with me, collect that strong box and leave these people alone?" Nathan motioned towards the baggage car behind him.

Slim, greed shining in his eyes, motioned to Shorty. "Well, Shorty, since the eastern preacher is so willing to part with his cash, why don't you just take him to the baggage car and empty that strong box of its contents?"

Shorty motioned for Nathan to proceed to the baggage car. Neither outlaw saw the smile that played across Nathan's face as he walked calmly out of the passenger car. No sooner had he entered the baggage car than Nathan dropped down on all fours and swept Shorty's legs out from under him. As Shorty fell Nathan stood and used his right hand to knock the outlaw's gun from his fingers. With a powerful left uppercut, Nathan knocked Shorty unconscious. Nathan dragged him farther into the baggage car, grabbed some of the rope netting that secured the passengers' bags, and tied the outlaw up.

Nathan retrieved Shorty's sixgun, then slipped his coat and shoes off. Running quietly to the far end of the baggage car, Nathan exited and climbed up on top of the car. He cautiously proceeded back to the far end of the passenger car. He dropped as stealthy as an Indian back down to the entrance to the passenger section.

He silently opened the door and rushed Slim but the padding of stockinged feet must have reached the outlaw. Slim turned straight into the flying fist of the young preacher. His feet flew off of the floor and he landed hard on his back. The sixgun in his hand discharged harmlessly into the ceiling. Before he could bring it back to bear on his attacker, Nathan wrenched it from his grasp and smashed the grip down between Slim's eyes, rendering him senseless.

Nathan handed the gun to the conductor and informed him of the other outlaw tied up in the baggage car. He proceeded toward the place where the mother held her child's head in her lap. Another male passenger turned to him and whispered, "Preacher, I'm a doctor. I've done all I can, but that little boy isn't going to make it."

Nathan dropped to his knees beside the child and did the only thing he knew to do. He placed a hand on the child's forehead.

"Oh, God, we cry out for mercy and healing for this child!"

As the astonished passengers' watched, the bleeding stopped and the knot on the side of the boy's head slowly shrank. The child's breathing became less labored. Nathan thanked God aloud for his healing touch and smiled at the mother. She just nodded her head and continued to love on her child.

Nathan stood and announced to the doctor, "Sometimes, Doctor, you just have to appeal to the Greatest Physician to do what only he can." He turned to help the conductor drag the stunned outlaw to where his companion was tied up. Returning to his seat, he settled in to await the next stop and a lawman.

Chapter Two

The train pulled into Moberly and the conductor headed for the depot office. Not long after the man returned with the sheriff and a couple of deputies in tow. After a few minutes the sheriff and conductor entered the passenger car. The conductor pointed Nathan out to the sheriff.

"Excuse me, Reverend Ryder, would you please accompany me to the sheriff's office?" The sheriff gestured towards the door of the train.

"You need a statement, of course. If you would permit me, I need to get my horse out of the cattle car and my belongings from the baggage car. After that I would be glad to meet you at your office."

"That would be fine, Preacher."

David Nathaniel Ryder the Third quickly gathered his things and his horse, Sunrise. Once finished, he headed straight to the sheriff's office. As he tied Sunrise up in front, he heard the train pull out of the station heading onward, south and west towards Franklin.

Upon entering the office, Nathan, found the sheriff and his two deputies reading over the statement the conductor had given them. Seeing Nathan, the sheriff motioned him to take a seat. He grabbed a pen and a piece of paper and started his interview. "Reverend Ryder, will you state your name for the record."

"David Nathaniel Ryder the Third".

"It is my understanding that you are a man of the cloth. Is that correct?"

"Yes sir, I recently graduated from seminary and received my ordination."

"Why were you on the train today, sir?"

"I am heading to Franklin to meet up with my grandfather. We'll be continuing to the New Mexico Territory for my first ministry assignment. I will be riding a four church circuit based out of Redemption."

"I see. Will you please take a look at this statement given by the conductor about the events in which you participated on today's train."

Nathan looked it over and handed it back to the sheriff, "Yes, that looks correct to me."

"Preacher, I have to ask. What made you, a minister and easterner, decide to take matters into your own hands like that?"

"Honestly, Sheriff, I was going to let matters play themselves out until Slim pistol-whipped that child. His actions angered me."

"Ok, but why not a straightforward attack?"

"I was going to do just that. But a tale my grandfather used to tell me suggested a more successful approach; subterfuge and stealth."

"I'm sorry, what?"

"Excuse me, I am still stuck in New York mode. Hmm ... trickery and playing sneaky Indian."

"You say your grandfather told you a tale that gave you this idea? Who in the world is your grandfather?"

"Obviously, his name is David Nathaniel Ryder, but you might have heard him called Nugget Nate Ryder."

"Nugget Nate is your grandfather! I would love to know what tale he told you that led you to separate and knock them two owl-hoots out like that."

Nathan quickly told the story of how his grandfather had been saved by Indians once because of their willingness to lie to an enemy and then use the element of surprise to overcome superior numbers. "I just figured if I could get one of them to follow me to the baggage car I could get the jump on him. After that it was a walk in the park to sneak over the top and surprise the other one from the far side. It worked much better than I hoped."

The sheriff and his deputies just looked at this man who was dressed like an eastern dandy. They still found it hard to believe he was kin to one of the most famous mountaineers in the west. If that wasn't hard enough to swallow, the fact that he had the sand to try such a daring plan was beyond them.

The sheriff faithfully wrote down all that David Nathan Ryder the Third had told him and handed it over to be signed.

Nathan signed the statement. "Am I free to leave now?"

"Sure, I don't see any reason to keep you. These two statements will be enough for the judge when he gets back around this way. Until then, I'll keep them two locked up."

"Thank you, Sheriff, I'm going to pick up a few supplies at the general store and then head to Franklin. I expect if I ride hard I'm only about a day away from Franklin, which will still get me there ahead of my grandfather."

"Actually, if you don't stop for supplies and ride hard you should reach Franklin by sunset. It's a hard ride, but only about six hours away, if you push it."

"Well, thank you for the information." Nathan shook the man's hand and exited the office. He quickly saddled Sunrise, moved his gear from his luggage to his saddlebags, and placed his now overstuffed saddlebags on the back of the horse. Mounting, he set off at a gallop for the railroad tracks heading toward Franklin.

A hard, hot, six hours later, Nathan reined in his golden palomino just outside the city limits of Franklin, Missouri. As he sat there looking toward the town, words of his grandfather came to him. "*Never ride into a western town unarmed, my boy. It'll mark you as a greenhorn or an easterner, neither of which receives much respect here in the west.*"

Nathan reached into his saddlebag and pulled out the old, worn holster and shiny new Colt Peacemaker his grandfather had given him when he headed west for his ministry assignment. He climbed down off Sunrise and strapped on the belt, settling it just right. He left the leg-string untied. *"No need to look like a gunfighter, but maybe having this rig on will keep a repeat of the train from happening here in town."*

He pulled the Colt from the holster a few times to make sure the new gun didn't catch in the old leather harness. Finally, he checked to make sure the gun was fully loaded, then dropped it back into the holster and engaged the hammer thong to keep the gun firmly in place as he rode into town. Then he pulled his Sharps rifle from the saddle boot, made sure it was also loaded, and replaced it in the boot.

The sun was just starting to set. Nathan loved the way the sinking orb turned the sky and the prairie a hundred different shades of red and gold. It was almost enough to cause him to sit and enjoy the show God was putting on; but he wanted to arrive before dark.

He patted Sunrise on his neck. "Well, ol' boy, we've spent a long and hard ride getting here. How about you and me stay in town for a few days? A stable and some fresh hay for you, a real bed and meal for me, plus time to relax before Nate arrives."

The golden head and blonde mane bobbed up and down in agreement almost as if the big stallion could understand what his rider said.

"Well, that settles it then." With that Nathan swung back up into the saddle and rode into Franklin. Little did he know a telegram awaited him that would change his entire life.

Chapter Three

Nathan rode into town and right down Main Street. Reaching the center of town he saw the Cattleman's Saloon and Hotel and tied up at the hitching rail. He entered the hotel and approached the desk. "Welcome to the Cattleman's, sir," said the young man behind the counter. "May we offer you a room?"

"I would love a room and a bath if you have one available."

"Right away, sir. I have the Presidential Suite which has a large copper tub right in the room. It's only twenty dollars a week."

Nathan knew that price was a bit steep and would eat into his travel money. Seeing as how he had almost lost it all anyway, it wasn't that big a deal. After climbing across the top of a train, fighting two outlaws, followed by that fast, hard ride to Franklin, a copper tub of steaming hot water would be just what he needed. "I'll take it. Can you have someone start filling the tub for me while I get my horse to the livery?"

With a big grin the desk clerk turned the hotel's ledger for David to sign and took his double eagle. "Of course, Mister Ryder. Are you David Nathaniel Ryder the Third, sir?"

Nathan was a bit shocked that this man would know his name as he had just signed Nathan Ryder on the ledger. "Yes, I am. Have we met before?"

"No, sir, but the telegraph agent came by three hours ago asking if a David Nathaniel Ryder the Third had checked in here. He said that he had an urgent telegram for him and was told you would arrive at any time. He stressed the matter was urgent, Mister Ryder, so you may want to visit the telegraph office before you go to the livery. It is just up the street across from the bank. The livery is on the other side of town."

Nathan handed the desk clerk a quarter as a tip. "Thanks for all the help. I'll do that. Please ask them to fill my tub and keep it hot 'til I return. I wouldn't think it should take me long."

Yes sir. Thank you, sir!" The clerk replied as he slipped the coin into his pocket.

Nathan left the hotel and rode down the street to the Western Union office. "Just a few more minutes, Sunrise, and we'll get you all settled in." He patted the trusty horse on the neck and turned to enter the telegraph office. He wondered as he did so who had sent him a telegram, and why. Only his parents and his grandfather had known he was planning to stop in Franklin on his way to Redemption, and his grandfather was meeting him here. *Well, I reckon I'll know what is so urgent in a moment and who sent me a telegram.*

Nathan entered the room and saw an old, silver haired man bent over the telegraph machine, taking down a message. The clicks of the machine clattered in the otherwise still room. Nathan waited patiently, knowing that to speak to the man now might cause him to miss part of the message he was receiving. After a few more seconds the man put down his pencil, tapped in a return message, then turned towards Nathan.

"Thank you for being so patient youngster," the old-timer smiled. "So many of my customers just barge in talking like they're the only thing I got to do in this here place."

"Well sir, it was obvious to me that you were copying a message and I knew if I interrupted you it would just take me longer to get help."

With a chuckle the man seated himself at the counter. "Right you are, sir. How can I help you today? Need to send a telegram or want to mail a letter? We're the Wells Fargo office too, ya know."

"Actually, sir, I was told at the Cattleman's that you'd been looking for me, something about an urgent message. My name is David Nathaniel Ryder the Third."

The old-timer's face fell and became serious. "Yes, sir, I do have a message for ya. Hold on just a minute." Then he got up, walked to the desk, and picked up the yellow form of the Western Union telegram. Walking back over to Nathan he handed it to him. "I hate to be the one who has to give someone so young and pleasant news like this, but here ya go."

Nathan took the telegram with trembling hands and read.

To: David Nathaniel Ryder the Third STOP

From: The Offices of Smythe and Jones, Attorneys at Law, New York, NY STOP

Mister Ryder STOP

Regret to inform you that your grandfather passed away this morning STOP

It is imperative you meet our agent in two days' time STOP

END MESSAGE

Nathan dropped the telegram back onto the counter and wiped one single tear from the corner of his eye. With a voice full of emotion Nathan spoke to the telegraph agent. "I believe I need to send a couple of telegrams after all."

"I figured that, son. Are you ok? Do ya need a few minutes?"

"I'm fine. It was a bit of a shock and I wish there had been more information but I do understand the cost of a telegram so I will send a note to my parents to find out what happened. Let's get the telegrams sent, and then I need to get my horse stabled."

"All right, Mister Ryder. Give me your first message."

Nathan picked up the telegram and looked at the name of his grandfather's attorneys again. As he thought of what to say to them the memory of his grandfather's enjoyment of picking on them came back to his mind.

Nugget Nate might have been one of the richest men in America, thanks to a lucky mining strike and a business sense that was way sharper than the old mountaineer looked; but he loved stirring up his blue-blood lawyer. He refused to pronounce the man's name properly, no matter how many times the lawyer corrected him. "Look here, Lawyer Smith, I don't care how fancy you spell it, you still got the second most common alias for a name and your partner has the first."

"Nate, you know that my name is Smythe not Smith and you know that my ancestors came over on the Mayflower. You're just being ornery again."

Shaking himself out of the memory with a smile, Nathan took a pencil and wrote out his message to Mister Smythe.

Smythe and Jones, Attorneys at Law New York, N.Y.

Personal attention Mr. Smythe

STOP

From: David Nathaniel Ryder the Third STOP

Your telegram received informing of grandfather's death STOP

Waiting at Cattleman's Hotel Franklin until your agent arrives STOP

END MESSAGE.

Nathan handed the message to the telegraph agent, who took out a red pencil and began counting up the words. As he worked on calculating the cost of the telegram, Nathan began one to his mother.

Mrs. David Ryder 1330 Park Ave. New York, NY STOP

From Nathan STOP

Got word of Nate's death Mother what happened? STOP

Not in poor health when I left New York. STOP

END MESSAGE

"Well youngster, the first message is gonna cost ya twenty five cents. Give me just a second and I'll figure up the second one." The telegraph agent took the second message and began marking that one too. "Second one's gonna cost ya about fifteen more cents, so forty cents in all. I hate to charge ya anything considering the nature of your messages, but the company insists."

Nathan laid a silver dollar on the counter and said "I'm going to get my horse bedded down over at the livery. Then I'm going to the Cattleman's for a hot bath and something to eat. Can you send any replies for me there? You can have what's left for a delivery fee or to hire a runner to bring them to me."

"All right, young feller, ya go ahead. I'll send my grandson to the hotel with the replies when ya get them. Again, I'm mighty sorry to be the one who has to bring ya such terrible news."

"Thank you, sir, I appreciate it."

Nathan left and took Sunrise to the livery at the end of town. He bedded the stallion down and spent a bit extra to make sure he got washed, brushed and had a bit of sweet corn mixed with his grain. Then he walked to the Cattleman's and retrieved his key. Once in his room he stripped and sunk into the still warm bath. He washed off the trail dust and the ache of news he hadn't expected to hear for several more years.

Chapter Four

Nathan, freshly bathed and in clean clothes, headed down to the café across from the Cattleman's Hotel. As he crossed the lobby to the exit, a woman's voice caught his attention. "I said take your hands off of me! I don't know what you're talking about!"

In response to the voice, Nathan turned to the swinging saloon door that separated the hotel lobby from the saloon next door. Nathan saw the striking figure of a woman in a dark, forest green dress and long curly locks of the deepest red struggling to get away from an obviously inebriated cowhand. Who was attempting to drag her towards the saloon.

"I know it's you, Emerald. I ain't ever likely to forget them purty green eyes and red hair as long as I live. Now come on and quit teasing. I got my ten dollars right here."

Struggling and losing ground, the woman continued to cry, "I keep telling you I'm not this Emerald you're talking about. My name is Grace Hopewell and I'm a school teacher, not a… a… saloon girl."

Nathan quickly looked around. Everyone was watching but no one moved to do anything. His hand fell to where his Peacemaker should have been and realized that just like a tender-footed, greenhorn easterner, he'd left it in his room after his bath.

Well, that would never have stopped old Nate from doing the right thing, so he wasn't going to let it stop him either. He approached the struggling lady from an angle so the cowpoke could see him coming. "Excuse me, miss, but is this gentleman bothering you?"

The cowboy, anger and lust in his eyes, turned to Nathan, "Why don't you just mind your own business, ya dandy? This ain't no lady. We're ol' friends, and about to become better ones, so beat it."

"I wasn't talking to you, mister. I was addressing the lady. It seems to me that you don't want to be this fellow's escort. Perhaps you would be willing to allow me to escort you to dinner over at the café instead." With that, Nathan held out his hand like a true eastern gentleman escorting a lady to the dinner table at a garden party.

"Why, thank you, kind sir, that seems a much more appealing invitation than the one I just received," the lady said turning to accept his arm and smiling. Nathan felt his heart skip a beat in his chest.

Standing before him was the most beautiful woman Nathan had ever seen. Even in her distress, the skin of her face flushed from anger, she was more radiant than any of the young ladies his mother had paraded through their home the last few years.

Her skin was like alabaster and her eyes were the color of polished emeralds. The smile she gave him seemed to light up the entire room. Her small dainty hand came to rest on his arm and he turned her towards the door of the hotel, the cowboy all but forgotten.

"I'm sorry Miss, let me introduce myself. My name is David Nathaniel Ryder the Third, but you may call me Nathan. May I inquire as to the name of my radiant dinner companion?"

With a blush that started below her modest neckline and rushed to the roots of her lovely red hair, the young lady said, "Nice to meet you, Mister Ryder, my name is Grace Hopewell. I would be delighted if you would call me Grace."

"Only if you'll call me Nathan. Mister Ryder is my father."

"Now wait just a minute!" Came a roar from behind them. A heavy-gloved hand gripped Nathan's shoulder. "I don't know what game yer a-trying to pull here, but that there is Emerald Dawn. She was a saloon girl I met last year in New York, and I got my ten dollars for the night, so she's coming with me."

Nathan turned and faced the cowboy, who was working himself into a real storm of anger. "Cowboy, this lady has told you more than once in my hearing that she is not this Emerald person. She is not going anywhere with you."

With that comment, Nathan grabbed the cowboy's hand by the thumb. With his thumb and forefinger Nathan applied just enough force on a pressure point in the cowboy's hand to let the drunk know he meant business and then released him. "Why don't you go back in the saloon and get another drink? Better yet, partner, go somewhere and sleep off the ones you've already had."

"Why, you greenhorn dandy, you don't know who yer messin' with. I'm Kid Cody and I don't back down from no eastern dandy." With that, the cowpoke loosed a roundhouse punch at Nathan's head.

Nathan blocked with his right and tried once more. "Last warning, my friend. You're in no condition to continue this. Go sleep it off."

Nathan's words only seemed to enrage the drunk more. The Kid's right hand streaked to his six-shooter.

When Kid Cody slapped leather and found no gun, he was surprised. He looked down at his holster to see it was empty. He looked back up, right into the barrel of his own gun, held firmly in the steady hand of the eastern dandy. His last conscious thought before the butt connected with the top of his head was, *Maybe this guy ain't such a greener after all.*

As the cowboy hit the floor, Nathan opened the cylinder of the six-shooter and emptied out the cartridges. Turning to the shocked desk clerk, Nathan handed him the gun and ammunition.

Smiling at the bewildered stare the man gave him, Nathan said "You might want to send for the sheriff and have this man locked up until he sobers up. I expect when he wakes up he is gonna have quite a headache and not be in a very good mood."

Then he turned to Miss Hopewell and said, "Miss Grace, I hope all this violence didn't spoil your appetite. I tell you, I'm so hungry I could eat a bear." Taking her hand and returning it to his arm, he opened the door and ushered her into the night.

Chapter five

Nathan escorted Grace across the street and into the café. After getting settled at a table that looked out the big front window, Nathan turned his attention to his dinner companion. "I realize you accepted my invitation to get away from that cowboy. So if you aren't hungry don't feel obligated to stay."

With a twinkle of mischief in her eyes, and a slight exaggeration of her southern accent, Grace looked at the young man who had come to her rescue. "Why, *Sah,* are you saying y'all don't want to have dinner with lil' ol' me?"

"Oh, no, ma'am, I can't think of anything I want more right at this moment."

Again that unique blush covered Grace's face. "Well, then, how can I refuse such an invitation?" Her look then turned serious. "However, I must thank you. If you hadn't stepped in when you did, I shudder to think what might have happened."

Nathan thought he could have listened to Grace's southern drawl all day, "Glad to be of assistance. If I may ask, what is a lady such as yourself doing out west alone?"

"I am on my way to the New Mexico territory. I graduated from teacher's college last month and a friend of my father's set me up with a teacher's job in a town there. I am supposed to meet him here so we can travel together to Redemption for introductions to the town council."

Nathan's mouth dropped and he was about to comment on the fact that he too was heading to Redemption when a portly woman with a jovial attitude appeared at their tableside.

"Welcome to the Franklin Café folks. I'm Sue. My husband and I run this place. Here's our menu. Take your time looking it over and let me know when you're ready to order."

Nathan turned his attention to her. "Thank you, Sue. While we are looking this over can we get a pot of coffee?" Then, realizing he knew nothing about Grace's tastes, he turned to her. "I just realized I don't know if you even like coffee. Forgive me for assuming you did."

Grace, once again blushing, said, "There is nothing to apologize for. After what you did for me I feel like we're old friends. Coffee sounds absolutely perfect."

"You mean to tell me you two don't even know each other? The way you were setting here talking I thought you must be a young couple headed west with dreams of a home and family."

Blushing even harder, Grace smiled at her, "Oh no, Mister Ryder here is my knight in shining armor, having just rescued me from the clutches of a wretched ogre in the hotel lobby."

Now it was Nathan's turn to blush as Sue shot him a quizzical look. "Oh, he wasn't that bad. Just a cowpoke who had a little too much whiskey and made the mistake of thinking the lady was someone else."

"Don't let him fool you, Sue. The man was a beast who was insisting I was his for the night for the price of ten dollars, and no one else was prepared to do anything about him. If it wasn't for Nathan's quick thinking and quicker hands I don't know what I would have done."

Sue looked back and forth between the two of them. "My, it seems that you two have had quite an adventure tonight. Let me get you that coffee, and if you don't mind fried chicken and mashed potatoes, Ol' Momma Sue will bring you some good western comfort food, on the house."

Nathan laughed and said, "Fried chicken and potatoes sound great to me, but I insist you let us pay you. After all, this is how your family makes its living, I'm sure."

"Honey-child, don't you worry about that. Does it look like I've missed any meals lately?" Sue placed her hand on her ample belly and giggled like a schoolgirl. She turned towards the kitchen and yelled, "Harold, two chicken specials and make it quick." Then she wobbled off to get a pot of coffee and some cups.

Just as Nathan was once again preparing to tell Grace that their destinations were the same, the bell over the door signaled the entrance of someone else into the café. Nathan turned and saw a tall, thin man with a silver star on his vest look around the café, until his eyes fell on Grace. Then they focused on Nathan, and the town sheriff walked right up to their table. "Mister Ryder, is it?"

"Yes, Sheriff, can I help you?"

Hooking his hands in the top of his gunbelt, the sheriff said, "I need to ask you and the lady some questions. Would you mind if I sat down for a minute?"

Grace said, "How rude of us, Sheriff. Please, have a seat."

"Thank you, ma'am." Pulling out a chair from the table behind him the sheriff turned it around backwards and straddled it like he was sitting on his horse.

Mister Ryder, I hate to impose on you, but the people over at the hotel told me a very interesting story. I need to verify it if I can. They say that you disarmed and incapacitated a drunk in the lobby, a drunk who was practically abducting the young lady here. Is that correct?"

"I guess you could say that. I just provided a way out of the situation for Miss Hopewell here. She took it. The cowboy wasn't too pleased and tried to stop me, so I applied a bit of pressure to a nerve in his hand which made him let me go. Then he tried to hit me. I blocked it and told him to go sleep it off. Instead, he tried to shoot me. So I took his gun away and helped him get to sleep."

The sheriff, head cocked at a funny angle, smiled. "You took his gun away and helped him get to sleep. 'Way I heard it was you outdrew him with his own gun, and then pistol-whipped him with it."

Grace joined the conversation, "You should have seen Mister Ryder, Sheriff. I didn't know a man could move that fast. One second the drunk was going for his gun. Then, he was looking at it in Mister Ryder's hands."

"Yes, ma'am, that's what everyone's told me. So, Mister Ryder, my question to you is; are you a gunslinger?"

"What? No, of course not. I am the furthest thing from it, Sheriff. I, well to be honest, I'm a preacher."

Shock was evident on both the Sheriff's and Grace's faces. The sheriff was the first to respond. "You're a preacher. Well, I must say I have never heard of a preacher who could out-draw a known gunfighter like that."

Now it was Nathan's turn to be shocked. "A known gunfighter? I thought he was just some drunken cowboy."

"Mister Ryder, are you telling me you don't know who it is that you knocked out over there in the hotel?"

Nathan shook his head. "No, he told me his name was Kid Cody, but that didn't mean anything to me."

"So not only are you a preacher with fast hands, but you captured Kid Cody, leader of the most wanted gang of outlaws in Missouri. All without even knowing who you were facing? Preacher, I don't know much, but I think that God was looking out for you tonight. Not only that, I think you got more sand than any other preacher I ever met. However, I'm not sure if you got any *l*uck at all. I got just one more question for ya. How soon ya planning to leave my town?"

"Excuse me?" Nathan said, looking the sheriff in the eyes and noticing the concern and fear there for the first time. "It sounds almost like you're saying I'm not welcome in Franklin anymore."

The sheriff chuckled. "Mister, you're welcome here. I'm just worried. See, when the Missouri River Gang hears that an eastern preacher is responsible for putting their leader in jail they are gonna come after ya in full force. I hear you're fast, but I'm not sure you're that good."

"My original plan was to leave in the morning, but I received a telegram today asking me to wait for my grandfather's lawyer here."

"Why would you need to wait for your grandfather's lawyer?"

"He passed away, and they need to bring me something things to sign about his estate."

"His estate? Who was your grandfather?"

"His name was David Nathaniel Ryder Senior, but you may have heard of him as Nugget Nate Ryder."

Grace gasped and her hands flew to her neck. "Uncle Nate is dead? But that's not possible."

Nathan turned to look at the young woman. "Uncle Nate? You knew my grandfather?"

As tears rolled down her cheeks, Grace nodded. "He was my father's friend who arranged for my teaching job in Redemption." Then she burst into tears and sobbed. "Now what am I supposed to do? He was going to meet me here, escort me to Redemption, and introduce me to the rest of the town council."

Nathan reached his hand across the table and placed it on Grace's hands. "Don't worry, Miss Hopewell. If my grandfather thought you were the best candidate, then I will make sure the city council honors his contract with you."

The sheriff cleared his throat and stood. "Well, I'll leave you two to your supper. Mister Ryder, when you've gotten Miss Hopewell settled, will ya come by my office? There is the matter of some paperwork, so that your reward can be paid to you in the morning."

"Wait, Sheriff. What are you talking about?" Nathan called as the sheriff walked away.

"Didn't ya realize, Mister Ryder, when ya knocked out that 'cowboy', you earned a thousand dollars for capturing Kid Cody alive? If ya had shot him ya would have gotten five hundred. Missouri loves its hangings." With that, the sheriff tipped his hat to Grace and exited the café.

Sue brought out their dinner and they tucked into it. Conversation was centered around their shared grief and individual memories of the likable Nugget Nate Ryder. Neither one of them was in a hurry to end but soon enough the last dish was empty, dessert consumed, and the coffee gone.

Nathan settled up with Sue, who tried to refuse until he mentioned the reward he was about to collect. Then he escorted Grace back to the hotel.

As they entered the door the desk clerk called to them. "Mister Ryder, the telegraph agent's grandson dropped off this telegram for you." Nathan went to the desk and retrieved his message.

To Nathan Ryder STOP

From Jefferson Smythe Attorney at Law STOP

Arrive Franklin two days STOP

Meet to settle grandfather's estate STOP

END MESSAGE

Nathan carefully folded the telegram, put it in his pocket, and turned to Grace. "It seems that I am stuck here for at least three more days to settle my grandfather's estate. I know that you're overwhelmed and at a bit of a loss right now. Why don't you get some rest and we'll talk tomorrow."

Grace nodded. "All right. I'm kind of tired and still in shock about Nate. I have to figure out what to do next. I was expecting him tomorrow. I don't have much money left and now I have to make a plan to get to New Mexico in the next three months."

Nathan took her hands and looked her in the eyes. "I told you, Grace, I will see you to Redemption. My grandfather would come out of his grave and whip me good if I didn't."

"We'll talk about this tomorrow. I need to get to my room before it gets too late, and you need to get over and see the sheriff."

With that she turned and started toward the saloon door.

"Where are you going?"

"To my room."

"Why are you staying in the saloon rooms?"

"They were the cheapest rooms they had, and all that I could afford."

"Absolutely not!" Nathan turned to the desk clerk. "Is there another room with a tub on my floor?"

"Hmm, yes sir, the room adjacent to yours is called the First Lady Suite and is a duplicate in every way."

"Great. I want you to give Miss Hopewell the key and send the bellhop over to her old room to retrieve her belongings. If I hear she had to set foot in the saloon again you and your staff will answer to me. Do we understand each other?"

"Yes sir! May I ask for how much longer the two of you be staying?"

Nathan could see the nervousness in the clerk's eyes and knew he was remembering the speed with which Nathan had drawn the outlaw's own gun earlier.

"What's your name?"

"It-it-it's James, Mister Ryder"

"James, I'm not Mister Ryder, that's my father. I'm just Nathan." Nathan smiled and drew a money pouch out of his boot and pulled out two gold double eagle coins.

"That should take care of us for the next four nights. The extra you split between yourself and the bellhop. I'll expect the two of you to keep a close watch on Miss Hopewell for me. I don't want to even think there'll be a repeat of what happened to her tonight. Understand?"

James looked at Nathan for a second and gave a slight nod of his head. Then he reached behind him and took a key off of the wall. "Miss Hopewell, I hope you'll forgive me, there seems to be some mix up with your room. We are moving you to the First Lady Suite for the remainder of your stay. I'll send a girl up to draw you a hot bath before bed, and Mark will transfer your bags for you. We have been given explicit instructions that you're to have no more contact with the saloon. So if you'll allow me, I'll escort you to your suite."

Grace turned to Nathan with tears flowing down her face. "This is too much, Nathan. I can't allow you to do this. It is too expensive a gift to give."

Nathan pulled the handkerchief from his jacket pocket and wiped her tears. "No, it isn't! First off, I'm not doing this for you. I'm doing it for my grandfather, who obviously believed you were worth his time and reputation. Secondly, if thinking of this as a gift is uncomfortable for you, then consider it part of your cut of the reward I'm going to collect. If it hadn't been for you I wouldn't be collecting it. So, no obligations here. I owe you more than this. From here to Redemption you will not feel obligated to me; this is your cut of the money. Now go enjoy yourself. I need to run to my room for a second, then go get our reward."

Nathan headed up the stairs and looked back to see Grace hand her old key to Mark the bellhop. As he entered his suite he saw his holster hanging on the bedpost and heard his grandfather's voice in his head. *"You're in the west now, son. That was stupid earlier and could have cost you your life. That shootin' iron means life out here. Don't go out without it again."*

"I hear ya, Nate. It's time to stop thinking like a New York socialite and start acting like you taught me."

Then he put on the holster and, unlike last time, he went ahead and tied it down low. After all, the sheriff had made it plain that Cody's gang might be calling on him soon. Nathan knew he needed to be ready.

So before he left he went over to his saddle bags, pulled out the extra ammo for his Peacemaker, and filled half the cartridge belt. Digging to the bottom, he pulled out his first sixgun, Nate's old Colt Navy. He stuck it in the gunbelt on the left side facing right, as a backup.

Nathan filled the other half of the cartridge belt with the 34 rounds for it. With one thought he drew the old navy, opened the cylinder, and made sure all six chambers were full. Grabbing his Stetson from his bag, he shook it out and placed it on his head. With that done, Nathan headed out to collect his unexpected windfall.

Chapter Six

Nathan quickly exited the hotel and walked down the sidewalk to the sheriff's office. He noticed the sheriff take in his change of attire, specifically the tied-down holster and extra six-shooter.

"Mighty funny look for a preacher there, Nathan."

"Sheriff, you made it very plain to me that trouble was gonna come looking for me soon. I figured I should be ready for it. After all, you heard me earlier. I've got to look out for Miss Hopewell until I can get her to Redemption in the New Mexico territory."

"Fair enough. I just hope your speed and luck holds, because if you don't know how to use those shooting irons you're toting, I'm afraid we'll be burying you."

Nathan smiled a hard smile. "Sheriff, I saw your recognition of my grandfather's name at dinner. Do you really think Nugget Nate Ryder would allow his grandson to come west without teaching him how to live in the west?"

"You know Nathan, I think I'm just gonna quit assuming anything about you. I have to remind myself your grandfather was one of the most famous mountain men in the high lonesome, and it appears he taught you what he knew."

"That's true, Sheriff. He did. I plan to make sure everyone sees me as a westerner as soon as the general store opens tomorrow. This will be the last day for my eastern clothes. There'll be no more forgetting where I am. Come morning I'll reorient myself to the cowboy my grandfather let me be in the summers of my youth." Nathan yawned, "Now, what do you need from me for this reward you were talking about? I figure I'm gonna need that money to get Miss Hopewell out to New Mexico. I had planned to just trail-ride but I can't do that with a single lady along."

The sheriff pulled out a hand-written account of the capture of Kid Cody and a pencil. "Just sign this-here account of what happened in the hotel, affirming you knocked the Kid out and left him to be taken to jail by the authorities. That's me. Then I'll give you a bounty voucher that you can cash in at the bank in the morning."

Nathan signed the report and the sheriff signed the voucher. Each handed the other the paper in his hands. The sheriff stuck out his hand and Nathan shook it.

"I'll let you go. I'm sure you want to get back to the hotel and get some rest. Just do me a favor and make sure you lock your door tonight. I know some more of the Missouri River Gang is in town somewhere. As much as I appreciate you catching Cody I don't want to see a bunch of gunfights in my town."

Nathan nodded. "I fully understand, sheriff. I heard from my grandfather's attorney tonight. He's planning on being here in two days' time and concluding our business the next, so in four days time I'll be out of your hair, I believe."

"No offense, Preacher, but good. I mean, you're a nice enough fella but I won't rest easy 'til you're long gone. Hopefully, after you leave and the Kid is sent to the capitol, the Missouri River Gang will leave us alone."

"Understood. You have to do what's best for your town." With that Nathan bid the sheriff goodnight and headed back up the sidewalk to the hotel.

He hadn't made it halfway when three men with bandanas covering the bottoms of their faces stepped from the shadows and faced him.

"They say you outdrew Kid Cody tonight, Greener. Is that true?" asked the one in the middle.

Nathan looked at the three and noticed that all three had their holsters tied down low and no hammer thong on their guns. It was obvious they had been increasing their courage with some rot-gut whiskey. "Listen, fellas, I got lucky. Cody was really drunk and wasn't at his best. I'm just a simple preacher on his way to the New Mexico territory for a circuit to ride."

"Well, Preacher, I don't believe you coulda outdrew Cody drunk or sober. Ain't no way some eastern dandy like you coulda taken the Kid, and my two buddies and I aim to prove it. So I suggest you step out in the street here and prepare to meet that God of yours."

"Gentleman, I concede that you're better gun-slingers than me. There isn't any need for any of us to meet God tonight. What say you go have another drink and let me go on my way?"

The guy on the left approached Nathan and shoved him toward the street, "Preacher, one way or another you're gonna have to face us, either here and now or when you least expect it. Now, get out in that street and prove you ain't some yeller eastern dandy like you look."

"You tell him Sam," the one from the middle moved towards the street while the one on the right pointed at Nathan. "He's wearing an iron low and tied so he must know how to use it. Not only that but he's gotta backup on that gunbelt."

Nathan realized there wasn't any way out of this unless the sheriff came along soon. Since the few people on the street had already run for shelter he figured that he was going have to face them or die here without lifting his gun. *This is not New York, kid. You can't back down out here.* " He heard ol' Nate saying.

Nathan sighed. He let his right hand slowly move down to his hammer thong and slip it off as he walked out into the middle of the street. Just as he reached the street he looked up and saw the silhouette of Grace Hopewell in the window of her suite, watching what was happening.

"Gentlemen, I implore you one last time let this go and we can call it over. I don't want to send anyone to hell tonight. Please let me buy you a drink and talk about your eternal souls instead of a gunfight that someone is gonna lose. What do you say?"

The three outlaws looked at each other and laughed. The one in the middle said, "We say it's time to say your prayers, Preacher, and prepare to meet your God."

Nathan shook his head in sadness and set himself. "Okay, boys, make your play."

Everyone who saw it couldn't believe what happened next. The three outlaws moved and their hands streaked for their pistols. But before even one of them touched metal the Peacemaker that seemed to materialize in the Preacher's hand boomed three times. Three sinners lay in the middle of the street as their souls suddenly stood in the presence of the God they'd just laughed about.

Nathan quickly opened the cylinder on his Colt. He pulled out the three spent shell casings, dropped them in his pocket, placed three new bullets in the empty holes, clicked the cylinder shut, and holstered his gun. As he did, he heard footsteps running up behind him and quick as greased lightning he spun towards the sound, gun jumping into his hand as he turned.

"Easy, Preacher." the sheriff slowed his pace and held his hands away from his body, showing he wasn't a threat. "I see you didn't quite make it back to your room."

Nathan, with a deep sigh and tears on his face, holstered his weapon. "No, I didn't." He watched as the sheriff walked over to the three men and pulled the masks off their faces. "I tried to talk them out of it, Sheriff, but they were determined to draw me out. Why did they want to die so bad? I even offered to show them a better way. All they wanted was to see who was faster."

The sheriff walked over to Nathan just as they heard someone running from the direction of the hotel. This time it was the sheriff who spun, reaching for his weapon, but Nathan stopped his hand before it reached the gun. "It's Grace. Can you send her back to her room? She doesn't need to see this."

The sheriff, turning back to Nathan, shook his head. "If she is determined to go teach in the Territory she better start getting used to seeing quick draws and dead men. It'll be a part of her life from time to time there."

"I guess you're right." Nathan said. "I just hate that the first dead bodies she has to see were killed by my gun."

Grace threw her arms around Nathan's chest, pinning his arms. "I saw the whole thing. I was so scared. I thought they were going kill you!"

Nathan looked down at her perfect face and was shocked by what he saw. Fear and loss were written there for all to see. No one would ever know they had just met a few hours ago. Anyone who saw her run up would think they were a couple, if not married, from the way she reacted. What surprised Nathan even more was that he didn't really care what people might think. "Hush, Grace, its okay. I'm fine. It's ok, really. They didn't hurt me." Nathan pulled an arm loose and stroked her hair as she sobbed into his chest.

Just as suddenly as she had grabbed him, Grace seemed to realize what she was doing and where she was. Her hands dropped and she stepped away from Nathan. She wiped her face and looked around to see who-all had seen her display. "Well good," she said. "I'll, umm, see you in the morning, then." Without another word, or a look at the three men lying in the street, she turned and walked back toward the hotel.

"Well Preacher, I think you got more troubles than just an outlaw gang to deal with," the sheriff chuckled. "Come on. We need to go and do some more paperwork. Looks like you just made another seven hundred dollars."

Nathan looked at the three men he had shot. "What about them?"

"Oh, the undertaker will be here shortly. I saw the doc heading over to his place on my way here."

Nathan followed the sheriff to his office and signed three more reports of capture. These marked DEAD across the top and he received three more bank vouchers totaling seven hundred dollars. Then, without a word he walked back to his room almost too dazed to know where he was and what he was doing.

He came to himself sitting in the big brass tub as the bath attendant poured another kettle of hot water into the almost-full tub. *I just sent three men to hell. How did my life go this direction? All I wanted to do was show men the path to a relationship with God and the forgiveness of their sins.*

Before he could slip too far into despair he again heard the words of his grandfather come to him. "*In the west, Nathan, iffen a man insists on drawing down on you then you gotta beat him to the draw. Don't matter if you're a preacher or not. Iffen you don't draw fast and shoots to kill, you'll be dead. Then how you gonna help those who want to know Jesus if yer living in heaven with him?*"

He had always known Nate was right, and that was why he had let Nate teach him to draw and shoot. It was the reason he'd practiced all those summers. He'd just never thought about it in a real sense until now.

Nathan bowed his head and thanked God for a grandfather who was both wise and stubborn. He went on to thank God for keeping him alive to continue his real work. He asked for peace with what he had done. He got out of the tub and got dressed for bed. Nathan gathered up his eastern clothes, walked over to the fireplace and after emptying his pockets, tossed his eastern suit into the fire.

As the suit burned to ash he felt the final eastern refinements slip to the background of his mind. The western training his grandfather had drummed into him moved up and settled in. Nathan walked over to his saddlebag and pulled out his other outfit, a pair of dungarees and a pale buckskin shirt. He laid them on the chair for the morning. He got down on his knees and reached under the bed. Pulling out his Sharp's rifle, he made sure it was loaded and put the safety on. He leaned it against the headboard of the bed.

Finally, he retrieved his gunbelt from the bathing room, walked over to the door, and made sure to lock it. . He placed the belt over the bedpost, turned so he could reach the Colt from the bed. He placed his old Navy six-shooter under the pillow, on the other side of the bed. Sure he was as ready as could be for any more trouble that came his way, Nathan slipped into bed.

As he drifted off to much-needed sleep his last thought was of Grace Hopewell's arms wrapped around his body and her head on his chest. The smell of her hair, as if she was still there in his arms, followed him into sleep and filled his dreams with images of a beautiful red-haired lady whose green eyes gazed at him with a look of more than affection. They spoke of an even deeper love.

Chapter Seven

Nathan woke and quickly dressed in his denim pants and buckskin shirt. He strapped on his gunbelt and retrieved his Colt Navy from under the pillow. He grabbed his Bible from his saddlebag and headed to the lobby to find a quiet place to read.

Nathan entered the lobby and found a large leather wingback chair in the corner overlooking the lobby and the street. Nathan settled in, opened his Bible, and read from Micah, Chapter 6. As he was reading the chapter, two verses jumped off the page at him, almost as if the Lord was trying to tell him something. They said **"He hath showed you, O man, what is good, and what doth the LORD require with thee, but to do justly, and to love mercy, and to walk humbly with thy God? The LORD'S voice crieth unto the city, and the man of wisdom shall see thy name: hear ye the rod, and who hath appointed it."**

Nathan sat contemplating them and once more he heard the voice of his grandfather almost as if he was in the room with him. *"That be your calling, boy. To do justice and love mercy while bein' humble. You're the rod God is sending to the west. Bring 'em to Jesus boy. Show 'em how to live holy and punish those who stand against justice out here."*

Nathan sat contemplating what he had just read and what he thought God was trying to tell him; when suddenly there was a shadow blocking some of the natural light that came from the window. Nathan looked up and there in front of him stood a cowboy with two tied-down gunbelts.

"You the fella they're calling the Preacher?" Dark brown eyes bore into him with scorn and hate.

"I don't know if 'they're calling me the Preacher but I am a preacher. Name's Nathan Ryder. Can I help you with something, mister?" Nathan stood and held out his hand.

The cowboy looked at Nathan's outstretched hand and knocked it aside. "Yer the one I'm lookin' fer. They say yer the reason my little brother is in jail and three of my partners are headed to Boot Hill. My name is Black Bart Cody and I aim to set the scales straight."

"What exactly do you mean by 'set the scales straight', Mister Cody?" Nathan was sure he knew what Black Bart was going to say next but he was praying he was wrong.

"I didn't know that your brother was wanted. I thought he would have to sleep off his drunk then be released. As for your friends, they forced me to draw down on them. I tried to walk away, I even offered to buy them a drink and concede they were the experts at gunplay."

"That may be true, Preacher, but you're still responsible. We may be outlaws and your God may have turned his back on us but we still have a code. You broke it and I aim to fix it. Now you be out in that street at noon with your iron on or I'm gonna come looking for ya and then you and whoever you're with when I find ya will go to Boot Hill together."

Bart turned and started to walk away. Nathan felt a nudge from God so he called out. "Bart, wait a minute."

Bart turned to see what he wanted. "I know you want to get even for the wrongs you feel I did to your brother and friends, but that isn't going to happen 'til noon, right?"

"That's what I said, Preacher. You meet me in the street at noon and we are fine. If not, then you got problems."

"Okay, then if I agree to meet you in the street at noon, will you agree to have breakfast with me right now?"

Surprise registered on the outlaw's face. "What kinda trick is this, Preacher?"

"No trick, Bart. I just want a chance to talk with you about something you said that concerned me."

"Oh, I get it!" Bart shook a finger at Nathan. "You want a chance to preach at me about how I'm going to hell so I'll be thinking about that before our meeting at noon."

Nathan looked the big man in the eye and suddenly didn't see a killer standing in front of him. He didn't see an outlaw with murder in his heart. Instead, Nathan saw a man lost and afraid. Nathan recognized that all the bluster and bravado hid a heart that was scared. Bart was scared of what would come on the day he wasn't clever enough or fast enough to leave a fight on his own two feet.

"That was never even a thought in my head, Bart." Nathan looked down and realized he had the perfect way to prove his point. "I swear to you with my hand on the Bible, I never thought of that at all. Have breakfast with me and listen to what I have to say. I promise I won't even mention hell once."

Bart looked down at Nathan's hand on the Bible, then up into his eyes. "Preacher, you are about the strangest creature I've ever met. I sure can't figure you out, but since you swore on the Holy Book, and I know you believe in the sacredness of that, I'll take ya up on it. However, iffen you're gonna eat with me we're gonna do it at the saloon where no one will bother me. Take it or leave it."

Nathan never even hesitated. He knew the gunslinger would never turn his back on him, so Nathan said, "Fine with me." He headed straight for the swinging door. On the way he noticed James and Mark watching him closely. James looked at the counter and Nathan realized his hand was under it, holding a gun. With a slight shake of his head Nathan indicated that it was okay to let it go.

The two men moved into the saloon and without a word both headed for a table in the corner where both their backs could be against the wall and they could see the whole room. Nathan was again impressed by how much alike they were; just two men trying to live through the day. The only difference was, while Nathan didn't want to die, he wasn't afraid of it.

"Well, Preacher, what you want to talk about?" Bart asked as he motioned for the bartender to come to their table.

"Bart, you said something to me that just slapped me right in my face and I don't even think you knew it."

"Oh, I knew it, Preacher. Most men feel like that when I call 'em out."

Nathan shook his head. "That's not what hit me. You said something about God having turned his back on you already. That's what hit me, because that isn't true."

Bart laughed at him and started to answer when the bartender arrived at the table. Bart turned his attention to the nervous man, who was wringing his hands in his apron.

"Barkeep," he said, "bring me the Cowboy Breakfast and make it quick." Then he reached out, grabbed the man by the shirt front, and pulled him down close. "You tell that cook iffen he burns my bacon I'm gonna plant him boots up." Then he released him and turned to Nathan. "How 'bout you Preacher, whatcha eatin'?"

Nathan, with a smile at the bartender, said; "I'll have the same, and bring us a pot of coffee, please."

"And a bottle of whiskey," Bart added.

Nathan looked at Bart and shook his head. "Kinda early for that, ain't it?"

"Not iffen you're gonna insist on talking about God it ain't."

"Fair enough."

""Now you were saying something ridiculous about God not having turned his back on me?"

"It's not ridiculous. It's the truth."

Bart paused for a second as the bartender came back with a pot of coffee, a bottle of whiskey, two mugs, and two shot glasses.

Bart grabbed the glass bottle, filled both shot glasses, and swallowed one right down. He offered the second one to Nathan.

Nathan pushed it back toward the outlaw. "I don't drink that stuff but help yourself." He filled a mug with coffee and took a swig.

"Listen, Preacher, I might be on the hoot owl trail now but wasn't always the case. But even an ol' sinner like me knows that with all the men I done killed and the things I done went and done, God has already given me to the ol' devil. Even if it was possible for me to walk away from my reputation and live the straight and narrow, there is no way I would balance the scales, let alone tip them to God's side."

"See, that's what I'm talking about, Bart. You keep talking about balancing the scales like you think good people go to heaven and bad people go somewhere else. That's just not true."

"Oh, come on Preacher, everyone knows that's how it is. Why that book you swore on earlier says bad people can't go to heaven and you know it."

"You're right Bart, it certainly does, but I don't think you know who it says is good enough to go to heaven."

"What are ya talkin' 'bout, Preacher?"

"Let me show you." Nathan opened his Bible and turned to a passage in Romans. "Right here in the book of Romans, Chapter Three, I want you to see who God says is good enough for heaven. It starts right here in verse ten."

Nathan put his finger down on the verse and began to read,

"As it is written, There is none righteous, no, not one: There is none that understandeth, there is none that seeketh after God. They are all gone out of the way, they are together become unprofitable; there is none that doeth good, no, not one. Their throat is an open sepulchre; with their tongues they have used deceit; the poison of asps is under their lips: Whose mouth is full of cursing and bitterness: Their feet are swift to shed blood: Destruction and misery are in their ways: And the way of peace have they not known: There is no fear of God before their eyes.

Now we know that what things soever the law saith, it saith to them who are under the law: that every mouth may be stopped, and all the world may become guilty before God' According to this, the whole world is guilty before God."

Bart banged a fist down on the table just as the bartender returned. He began to set two large plates with scrambled eggs, half a rasher of bacon, and fried potatoes on the table, shaking the whole time. When he got done, Nathan reached into a pocket, pulled out two dollars, and asked, "Does that cover it or do you need more?"

Shaking so bad he could hardly take it, the bartender said, "Oh, that's too much, Preacher, sir, its only fifty cents for the breakfast and the same for the whiskey. Coffee comes with the cowboy special."

"Well, you and the cook split the other one then, under one condition."

"Wha-wh-what's that, sir?"

"Don't let anyone disturb us 'til we're done talking"

The bartender looked down at the open Bible between them and nodded his head, a look of wonder on his face. Then he turned and walked away.

Bart had been staring at the passage Nathan had read the whole time Nathan was dealing with the bartender. "I don't think I'm understandin' that-there piece right, Preacher."

"Why do you say that, Bart?"

"It seems to me that-there piece in the Bible just said God finds everyone guilty. That can't be what it's saying, can it?"

Nathan laughed, "That's exactly what it is saying, Bart. According to God, every single man, woman, boy, and girl on earth is guilty. You know what happens to guilty people don't ya?"

Bart looked up, shock still evident on his face, "'course I know what happens to guilty people. They's punished."

"That's exactly right, Bart. Listen, I'm gonna let you in on a secret here. I may be a preacher, but I am no better than you."

"Oh, come on, Preacher. I don't think you is as bad as me."

"Really? Then let me tell you something. Yesterday when I had your brother's gun in my hand and he was looking down the barrel, there was a part of me that for one split second wanted to pull the trigger. I don't mean to upset you, but I want you to understand. The same anger and murder that is in your heart is in mine. In spite of that, I know if I lose today, I'll be in heaven before my body hits the dirt."

Bart leaned back and stared hard at Nathan. His thoughts could be easily be read on his face. "How can you sit there and tell me we're the same inside but you know you'd go to heaven iffen you was killed?"

Nathan smiled, "It's easy. Look, the Bible tells us that too." Nathan flipped a few pages to Romans Six and he dropped his finger to verses twenty-two and twenty-three.

"But now being made free from sin, and become servants to God, ye have your fruit unto holiness, and the end everlasting life. For the wages of sin is death; but the gift of God is eternal life through Jesus Christ our Lord."

"Remember, I said for a *split second* I wanted to shoot your brother dead, but I didn't. He was unarmed and a knock on the head would make him harmless to anyone. I still could have pulled the trigger. You and I both know the code of the west. He went for that gun first. Nothing would have been said if I had shot him dead right there. So what made me different than you in that second?"

Bart looked at the verse and back up into Nathan's eyes. "I know you think these two verses will tell me the answer but I don't get it. What made you different?"

"Somehow I had been lifted above being guilty and made free from sin. I'd made a choice that made me free not to act on what was in my heart. Just thinking about wanting to kill your brother makes me guilty and worthy of the cost of sin. That cost is death, but God gave me a gift instead, eternal life.

"But where did that gift come from that we just read about?"

"Hey, I went to church as a kid. I know where it came from. It came from Jesus. That's what your gonna tell me, ain't it?'

Nathan tipped his head forward. "You're right. That was what I was gonna tell ya. But do you understand, Bart? All you need is to give your life to Jesus and then no matter what actions you've committed 'til now, they won't keep you out of heaven. Romans Ten tells you how to do that."

Nathan flipped there and put his hand on verses nine and ten, *"That if thou shalt confess with thy mouth the Lord Jesus, and shalt believe in thine heart that God hath raised him from the dead, thou shalt be saved. For with the heart man believeth unto righteousness; and with the mouth confession is made unto salvation.'* You can have a new start and God will accept you, Bart. Why don't you take my hand in friendship and right here come to Jesus?"

Bart looked at Nathan for a long time, then very deliberately looked down at his hand. Bart reached out and placed a fork in Nathan's hand. "You've had yer say so I expect ya to be in the street at noon. Now eat your eggs before they get completely cold."

Bart took up his fork, shoveled eggs and taters into his mouth, and refused to look at Nathan again until the last forkfull was gone, along with one more drink of whiskey. Without another word he got up and walked out of the saloon.

Nathan said a little prayer asking God to work quickly, then tucked into his food. When the last bite was done he stood, tipped his Stetson to the bartender and walked out of the saloon as well.

Over the backand-forth batting of the swinging saloon doors, Nathan heard the bartender's voice. "What kinda man is this Preacher? He just preached a sermon to Black Bart right here in my saloon, and Bart listened!

Chapter Eight

Nathan quickly returned to his room and put his Bible on the bed. He decided to check on Grace before he headed out to take care of business around town. He headed out of his room and turned left toward the door of Grace's room. He knocked but after a few minutes without any answer he figured she had already gone to breakfast. Deciding he would catch up with her at the café he headed for the lobby once more.

Reaching the lobby, Nathan saw a young boy start to hand James a telegram just as James noticed him. "Mister Ryder, this young man is Greg Logan. His grandfather runs the telegraph office. He was about to leave a telegram here for you."

Nathan looked at the boy and held out his hand as if greeting a business associate. "Hello, Greg. Nice to meet you."

Greg automatically took his hand and they shook. "You too, sir. My granddad asked me to get this to you first thing. He said you was expecting it." The boy held out the telegram towards the man everyone was calling the Preacher. As Nathan took the telegram Greg looked him over.

He knew he was young and had never been anywhere but Franklin, but this man looked nothing like Preacher Barnes over at the church. He was not as old first off. His hair, what could be seen stickin' out the front of his Stetson, was a brownish blonde. His eyes were friendly and a strange blue with yellow flecks in them. The strangest thing was this preacher wore a Colt Peacemaker tied down low just like all the gunfighters Greg had read about in the dime store novels his grandfather bought him.

Nathan reached into his shirt pocket and pulled out a dime which he flipped to the boy. "Thank your granddad for me, Greg. Hey, let me tell you a little secret that you probably already know." Nathan leaned down closer to the boy who responded by leaning in closer too. Nathan noticed that James also leaned in. Him wanting to hear the secret too made Nathan smile. "Granddads are the wisest men in the world. You must listen to every lesson he teaches you because it will turn you into a wise man too."

Greg's smile grew so wide you could see the tooth he had lost just a few days before. "Yes sir, I will, Mister Preacher sir."

Then he clutched his dime tight, turned, and ran out of the hotel, headed back to the telegraph office. He wanted to ask his granddad how come this out of town preacher wore a gun like a gunslinger.

Nathan unfolded the telegram knowing that it would be from his mother. Finally he would know what had happened to Nate.

To Nathan Ryder STOP

From Gloria Ryder STOP

Nate wouldn't let us contact you STOP

Caught influenza after you left NY STOP

Father says follow God Come home STOP

Love and miss you

END MESSAGE

Nathan folded the telegram and placed it in his pocket. At least now he knew Nate died of influenza, but he'd done it quick and hard, just like everything else in life. Nathan wished at the end of his life people would have the same kind of thoughts about him. That thought led him back to his destination and with a goodbye to James he headed out the door and up the street.

On the way to the sheriff's office he caught sight of a distinctive head of red hair over in the café. His heart jumped in his chest and, almost like they had a mind of their own, his boots turned and headed in that direction.

When he entered the café every eye turned his way and a hush fell over the room. From somewhere deep in the room he heard a voice. "That's him, *the Preacher*. They say he outdrew four men yesterday."

From someone else he caught the whisper, "That's the Preacher Black Bart was lookin for."

Sue saw him and called out, "Howdy there, Preacher, what can I getcha?"

Nathan tipped his hat, then pushed it up high on his forehead.

"Just some coffee, Sue. I had breakfast with Bart Cody this morning."

All noise ceased again as everyone strained to hear more. Sue dropped the coffee cup she had started to pick up and it shattered, breaking the silence. Nathan moved over to the table where Grace was sitting as Sue hurried toward them. "You did what? Preacher, you know that man is looking to kill you, don't ya?"

Nathan looked down at Grace's worried expression. "Nathan, is that true?"

Nathan pointed at the chair opposite her, indicating he wanted to sit. Grace nodded and he took off his hat and sat down. "I guess you could say he feels like he has to live up to the code of the west. I'm the reason his brother is in jail and three of his friends are in the grave."

"Why would you have breakfast with a man you knew wanted to kill ya, Preacher?" Sue asked.

Nathan, without looking, could tell everyone in the café wanted to hear that answer. "Sue, I had breakfast with him because God told me to. I wanted a chance to talk with him about God, salvation, mercy and forgiveness. No matter what he wants to do to me, I have to do what God wants me to. After all, He's my boss."

"You're really a preacher aren't you? Some people here were speculating that people just called you the Preacher because of the way you dressed. But you look like a cowboy today so that can't be it." Sue poured his coffee and walked away.

Nathan looked at Grace and knew she wanted to know what was going on. "Look, it isn't all that drastic. Kid Cody's brother wants to have a showdown at noon. I made him a deal. If he would have breakfast with me and listen to what I had to say I promised to meet him in the street at noon."

"You can't! Nathan you promised to take me to Redemption. If you meet that man in the street you might end up dead. I don't understand how you can keep killing these men, being a preacher. Doesn't it bother you to shoot them dead?" Grace was crying and gripping his hand. The confusion and heartache on her beautiful face was almost more than Nathan could bear.

"Grace, I'll try to explain this because you have to understand the place you've agreed to teach at. This is the west. It is nothing like New York or even the south where you grew up. The west has its own set of laws, and a code men live by. What might seem ridiculous and wrong to do in the east is the right way to go here. It is not considered murder or killing if both parties wear a gun. Then it is considered a fair fight, and an acceptable way to settle your differences."

Crying without shame, Grace said, "Then don't wear a gun. If you aren't armed no one can force you to shoot them or get shot."

Nathan knew what he had to tell her was going to be hard to understand but he had to try. "It's not that simple, Grace. A man who doesn't wear a gun out here is considered a coward, and is easy pickings for the outlaws. I can't be either of those things if I want people to take my preaching seriously.

"I have to be a man of the west. Nate understood that. It was why, when I told him that I felt like I was supposed to be a preacher in the west, he insisted on teaching me the code of the west. If you are going to live here you'll have to understand it too. Sometimes even the women of the west have to take up arms to protect themselves and those they love. If you can't do that then you need to go back to New York or back home down south."

Grace angrily wiped the tears from her face. She answered, "Thank you Nathan, for your lesson. I have much to think about. If I could, I would take your advice and return to New York. However, as you have already informed me, my benefactor there is dead, and since illness took my family and swindlers took my home down south from me as well, it seems I have no choice but to continue west. Now if you will excuse me, I will return to my room and pray that you don't die before you fulfill your obligation to your grandfather to see me to my new home."

Grace stood, walked over to Sue, and paid for her breakfast. Nathan got up, dropped a nickel on the table, and headed out the door toward the sheriff's office.

As he walked he prayed God would calm Grace's heart and show her the truth of what he'd said. He continued to pray and ask God to show him a way out of this mess he was in today.

He entered the sheriff's office and poured himself another cup of coffee from the pot on the stove in the corner. Then he walked over to the sheriff's desk and sat down facing the sheriff.

"Preacher, help yourself," The sheriff said with a half grin. "I hear you met Black Bart and are supposed to face him in the street at noon. I also heard you preached him a sermon in the saloon and broke fast with him."

Nathan nodded. "You're well-informed, aren't you?"

The sheriff shrugged. "It's my town. Kind of hard not to be informed about your doings. It seems you've gained a reputation overnight. All the people of my town can talk about is the preacher who wears an iron like a gunslinger and is fast as lightning. So, is it true? Did you really agree to meet Bart in the street at noon if he would listen to you talk about salvation?"

Nathan took a good hard look at the sheriff. "Let me ask you this first, Sheriff. Are you a Christian?"

"As a matter of fact I am. I gave my heart to Christ ten years ago."

"Then you'll understand when I say I felt the Lord urging me to make that deal, so I made it."

"Well how'd that work out for ya?"

"If by that you're asking me if Bart threw down his pistols and accepted Christ, then the answer is no. However, it wasn't as bad as you might think. He listened and he even learned some things that got him thinking."

Nathan paused, then asked what was really on his heart. "Let me ask you another question. How do you, as a Christian, justify this job you have? I mean, I'm sure you've had to shoot some men. I know you've had to send some to the noose. How do you justify sending sinners to hell and shedding blood with your faith in Jesus?"

The sheriff looked Nathan square in the eye. "Last night's botherin' ya, ain't it? Yeah, and the thought of today too. It's written all over your face. For me it's simple. I feel like God called me to protect people as a sheriff. Yes, sometimes I have to shoot someone or send them to stand before God to be judged.

"However, in doing so I save others in this town who get the chance to know God. I protect the ones who want to find God so that preachers like you can introduce them to Him. Now for those who have chosen to go the other way and break the law sometimes I get the job of introducing them to God face to face."

Nathan, with a thoughtful look on his face replied, "Thanks. I guess that helps me some. Listen; speaking of following that still small voice, will you check something for me?"

"Sure if I can, what is it?"

"Let's just say I'm curious. If I should come out on top today how much more money am I gonna make in bounties for Black Bart?"

"You know, I don't believe I have a warrant for Bart." The sheriff picked up a stack of wanted posters and flipped through them. "No, from what I can tell, Bart isn't wanted in Missouri."

"Is there a way to check and see if he is wanted anywhere?"

The sheriff stood and grabbed his hat. "Sure. I can send a warrant alert to all the telegraph stations. If he's wanted for something we'll know in a few minutes. Why?"

Nathan shook his head. "Not sure yet. Just something he said. He made a big deal about following the code. Not something you hear from outlaws much, is it?"

"No it isn't. Come on. Let's head over to the telegraph office."

Nathan and the sheriff headed across the street. As they entered the Western Union Office the agent looked up and smiled. "Preacher, Jack, how can I help you two gentlemen this fine morning?"

Sheriff Jack walked around the counter and shook the old man's hand. "Will, I need you to do an all stations warrant check, coast to coast, for me."

"Sure thing. Let me just clear the line." Will typed a *clear the line* signal three times. "Who we checking on?"

"Bartholomew Cody, alias Black Bart Cody."

The telegraph agent sent the dots and dashes into the wire, then turned to the two men waiting. "Should have an answer soon. If there's nothing in five minutes I'll send it one more time. If nothing after that, it means nothing was found."

Just as he finished talking the paddles started clicking and clacking and Will started writing. After a few seconds he called to the sheriff. "Jack, you better come here and read this."

The sheriff went over, read the message, and frowned. "Send the answer, Will."

Nathan couldn't contain himself. "What does it say?"

Jack looked back at him. "A police chief in Philadelphia, Pennsylvania asked who was asking for information on Bart Cody."

"Does he have a warrant in Philadelphia?"

Will handed a telegram to Jack. "You boys ain't gonna believe this."

Jack looked at it and pushed his hat up on his head. "Well, that changes everything." He handed the telegram over to Nathan. "Guess you got your answer, Preacher. Now what ya gonna do with it?"

Nathan read the telegram over twice, folded it, and put it in his pocket. "Pray, Jack, I'm gonna pray real hard."

Chapter Nine

Nathan spent the rest of the morning sending telegrams, making some arrangements, and running a couple of local errands. All the while he prayed for God to show him the answer to the dilemma he was in. At about five minutes 'til noon the sidewalks were filled and every window facing the street had a face or two in it.

Nathan entered the hotel, walked up to Grace's room, and knocked on the door. She answered and it was obvious from the redness of her eyes what she had spent all her morning doing. "What do you want Nathan? Don't you have to go get killed in a minute?"

Nathan took her in his arms and smoothed her hair like last night, which released the floodgates. Grace began to weep and sob into his shoulder. "Grace, I want you to stop and listen to me." He waited until she had gotten some control. "I made a promise to you, to see you to Redemption. I also made a vow to Bart, to meet him in the street at noon. I aim to keep both of those promises, but I intend to keep one more. I promise you right now no one is going to die in the street this time. Not by my hand and not by Bart's."

Grace stared, bewildered. "How can you make me that promise, Nathan? You don't know what that outlaw will do."

"You're right Grace. I don't know what Bart will do. I do know what I feel God's telling me. He urged me to make you this promise. Will you trust me and Him?"

Grace pulled away and stamped her foot on the floor. "David Nathan Ryder the Third, you don't fight fair! How is a girl supposed to stay mad at you when you keep bringing God into the fight?" She sighed. "Fine. I will trust God. You, however I'm still not sure about."

"Good enough," Nathan laughed "Now come on out to the street and watch what God is about to do. Believe me; you don't want to miss it."

Grace pulled her door shut reluctantly and began to follow Nathan.

"What have you got up your sleeve, Nathan? You're keeping something from me."

"Just watch and wait, and for heaven's sake, pray!"

Nathan left her standing on the sidewalk next to the sheriff and walked out into the middle of the street. Just as he arrived, the church bell started to peal out the stroke of twelve. The crowd to the east parted. Out into the street walked Black Bart, hat pulled low and both six-guns tied down low and tight. "I see you're a man of your word, Preacher. I kind of wish you'd left town so I didn't have to kill ya, though."

Nathan turned and looked at Black Bart. Suddenly peace filled him and all doubt was gone. He knew what he was about to do was going to work, and that a man's life was going to change in the next few minutes.

"Bart, I just want to be plain on something here. I swore to you I would be here at noon and I kept my word, did I not?"

"You did." Bart replied with bewilderment on his face. Bart watched the young preacher and saw something he had never seen before when he had faced a man in a showdown. The Preacher looked completely relaxed and at peace. Could it be that this kid knew something he didn't?

The Preacher continued to walk toward Bart. "I know you're a man who lives by the code of the west Bart, so I know that you will keep your word and not go after anyone else who has been my friend."

"You're here. I told you if you made me chase ya then I would take it out on you and whoever you were with. So yes, this finishes it between us."

"Just to be clear, what exactly did I swear to you on the Bible this morning?"

Bart sighed; maybe he was just misreading this Preacher. All this talking seemed like stalling. "You swore that if I had breakfast with you and listened to what you had to say you'd meet me here at noon."

Nathan pushed his hat up on his head and placed his hand on his gunbelt, right by the buckle. "Are you satisfied that I kept my oath to you?"

"Yes, I'm satisfied. Now quit stalling and prepare to draw, Preacher!" Bart got himself into his stance and set his hands to draw.

"That's all I needed to hear, Bart." With that, the Preacher's gunbelt fell to the dirt.

"What are you doing?" the gunslinger roared. "Put that gun back on and make your play."

"Not going to happen, Bart. See, God showed me a secret about you that everyone else has missed. You aren't an outlaw at all. You're a true man of the west. You actually believe in the code and you live by it. You have never actually killed anyone. I know you won't start now. As long as I don't draw on you, then we both get to leave here alive."

"Preacher, you don't know what you're talking about. I'm a wanted man. I'll kill you right here and now, one way or another." Bart was stunned. No one had ever called his bluff like this before.

"No, you won't, and you aren't wanted Bart. The sheriff and I checked. There is not a warrant for you anywhere in this country."

"Well, you boys better look again because you missed it. I'm wanted for murder back east." Bart all but screamed. This can't be happening, he thought, what is going on?

Nathan shook his head, slowly moved his left hand up to his shirt pocket, and pulled out a yellow Western Union Telegram. He held it out to Bart.

"If you're talking about Pennsylvania you need to read this. It's from your old police chief. It states that you ran off before allowing the investigation to end. Your service revolver was used to kill that man, but three separate witnesses identified the shooter as Kevin Cody, alias Kid Cody."

Bart was floored. He found himself walking walked up to the Preacher and snatching the telegram. As he read, all the blood drained from his face. He looked over at the sheriff. "Is this for real? This isn't a trick you two cooked up?"

Jack stepped forward. "No, it's no trick, Bart. I sent a request for warrants this morning and instead received this."

Bart looked back and forth from Nathan to Jack, twice. "This is real? I could go home? I never needed to run in the first place?"

"It's real Bart. You were cleared of any wrong doing."

Bart dropped to his knees right there in the middle of the street. "Preacher you win; you and God. This is nothing short of a miracle. I surrender. I confess Jesus is Lord. He died for me and rose again. He is Lord and I accept him."

There was a murmur of surprise through the crowd. Many of those who had come *to watch a showdown began to wonder to each other who is this Preacher? He can out draws gunslingers and break the hearts of the hardest of men!*

"Ok folks," Jack called out. "Show's over. Get back to your homes and businesses. There's nothing to see here." The crowd began to disperse but most of them watched as the Preacher knelt beside the gunslinger, placed an arm around his shoulder, and the two prayed together right there in the middle of Main Street.

Nathan thanked God and pulled Bart up to his feet. They walked over to the hotel together. "Bart, that's not all. I have another surprise for you. Maryanne never stopped loving you or waiting for you. However, she has decided not to wait any more."

"Well, she has every right to move on with her life," Bart muttered, fighting back tears.

"I don't think you understand me, Bart. She isn't waiting for you to come home. She took the morning train from Pennsylvania. She'll be here in two days' time. She said to tell you -- aw, here." Nathan pulled another telegram out of his pocket and gave it to Bart. As Bart unfolded it and began to read he wandered away toward the livery stable, leaving just two people standing on Main Street.

Nathan looked at Grace Hopewell standing there with her mouth hanging open. Before he could stop himself he laughed and yelled, *"Thank ya, Jesus!"* Just like a crazy drunk on a Saturday night he began to dance a jig right there in the middle of the sidewalk for all to see. Grace started to laugh. Both at the silliness of her benefactor's grandson, and from the release of fear and doubt in her heart.

She heard the still small voice that had called her to salvation whisper to her, *"Trust me my daughter I am always with you."* She turned and walked up to her room to spend time praising God herself. However, she was first and foremost a southern lady, so she would dance before God in the privacy of her boudoir.

Nathan stopped his dancing and watched Grace walk away. Once she was gone he picked up his gun-belt and strapped it back on. When he looked up toward her window, he saw a now very familiar silhouette, cutting a rug, just before the blind snapped down.

Chapter ten

Nathan turned and headed to the livery stable. He had heard a rumor that the owner might know of a wagon train heading toward Santa Fe. As Nathan walked down the street he couldn't help but see the looks people were giving him. The sooner his business in Franklin was complete the better. He was becoming known for all the wrong reasons in this town. He wished he could redeem his reputation as a preacher, not that gunslinging fellow 'The Preacher'.

Sunrise stuck his head out of his stall and snorted as Nathan entered the stable . Nathan rubbed the stallion on the neck and checked his feed and water. The stallion leaned into his rub and lifted his head as if to say, *Let's hit the trail.*

"Soon, ol' partner," Nathan told him. "We'll be back on the trail in a few days. Until then, you enjoy your rest. One of us should have a peaceful time while here in Franklin."

"Not having a good time here in town, Preacher?" Asked a voice from the stall beside him. The livery owner popped his head up.

"Not particularly. I can't seem to keep from being threatened by people."

The man walked out of the stall, carrying a feed sack. "So I've heard. Also heard you've had no trouble taking care of yourself. Somehow I don't think that you come down here just to talk to your horse. What can I do for ya?"

Nathan grinned." You're right, I didn't, but he don't need to know that, does he? There are a couple of things I need to discuss with you. First, I need to board Sunrise here for a few more days. I have some legal business to attend to before I can leave."

"No problem there. He's a good horse. I'll take good care of him. How long you reckon you'll be in town?'

"Just a couple of more days, I hope."

"All right, why don't I just run you a tab you can settle up with me when you're ready to leave town? That will keep you from having to worry about seeing me every day to make arrangements for him."

Nathan grasped the man's hand and gave it a shake. "Thank you, sir. That means a lot to me."

"Glad to do it, and just call me Hank. Everyone else does."

"Hank, good to meet you. I'm Nathan. Listen, word around town is there's a wagon train preparing to head to Santa Fe. I figured if it was true the livery owner might know where they're staging and if they still have room for more wagons."

Hank grinned. "Figured they'd be buying feed from me, did ya? Well the word for once is true. There is a train preparing to leave next Monday. They're staged over in the cattleyards on the south side of town. Just head over there and ask for Mister Thompson. He's the man putting the train together."

"Great, I'll do that." With a sheepish shrug, Nathan asked, "You wouldn't know where I could get a covered wagon 'round here, would ya?"

Hank shook out his hanky and, lifting his hat, wiped his forehead. "Might be I could find one out back there someplace ... iffen someone was looking to buy one."

"How much do you figure that would cost ... if someone were looking?'

"Nathan, you ain't planning to try and pull a wagon to Santa Fe with that beautiful horse of yours, are you?"

"Oh, absolutely not. If I was looking to wagon train, I would be looking for a complete rig -- live-stock and all.

Hank rubbed at his chin and clamped his tongue between his lips like he was thinking hard. "Seems to me for a pair of horses, a wagon with cover, and water barrels, I might could find a fella who would sell all that for ... three hundred dollars.'

Thank goodness, Nathan thought, *Nate taught me how to horse trade.* "Well I don't know. For three hundred those would have to be some mighty good horses. Since the best horse I see in this-here stable already belongs to me, and most wagons are pulled by oxen. I don't see how a fella could possibly pay more than ... one fifty for the whole set up."

Putting on a hurt look, Hank took his turn. "Young fella, you wound me to the quick. Let me show you the two horses I had in mind, and the wagon. Then you'll see why I couldn't possibly sell for less than two seventy-five."

Nathan followed him out to the corral behind the stable. Sitting under an old pole barn was a wagon with covered staves. It looked to be in fairly good condition, as Nathan looked it over. He could tell someone had taken good care of it. The wheel axles were well-greased. A spare wheel hung on the side. Right behind the driver's bench, on either side of the wagon, were water barrels, both empty, but in good condition.

Then Hank took him into the paddock. Two of the biggest work horses Nathan had ever seen stood there. "What in the world are those beasts?"

Hank laughed. "Those, my young preacher, are Belgian plow horses. They're the finest and strongest work horses in the world. This set's been raised together from colts and work like a fine-tuned machine."

Nathan realized they both stood over sixteen hands tall and were as wide as any bull he had ever seen. "Well, feeding these two brutes on a drive all the way to the New Mexico territory would likely break a fella. I would have to say two hundred would be about all that worn-out ol' wagon and these two monsters would be worth to me."

Hank took off his hat and tossed it on the ground in mock outrage. Nathan could see he was really enjoying this haggling and blessed Nate for teaching him right. "Broke down nothing! That's the finest rig you're likely ta come across, and you know it."

Nathan tried to hide the grin that was threatening to burst into an outright laugh. "I don't know ... I might could go as high as two twenty-five, but that would be paying more than it's worth."

"Mister, them two horses alone is worth more than that," Hank growled, "Two fifty, and that's my final offer. Take it or leave it."

Nathan spit in his hand and held it out. "Deal! Under one condition -- I actually get into the wagon train."

"Agreed." Hank spit into his hand and the two men shook, sealing their deal just like true men of the west.

"Hank, I'll be back in a few hours to settle up with you. I need to go see that Mister Thompson and go by the bank here. I'm gonna saddle up Sunrise. I figure you and he both will appreciate it if I give him a bit of exercise. He can get mighty restless just sitting in a stall."

"That's fine with me, Nathan. When you get back just put him out in the corral and I'll make sure he's rubbed down tonight. When you're ready to settle up on the wagon and Belgians come see me in my office. It's up on the second floor. Oh, and when you see Thompson, tell him I sent ya."

"Will do. Thanks for the information about the wagon train." Nathan walked back into Sunrise's stall. "Hey, partner, you ready to run a few errands around town and work out some of your kinks?"

The big palomino tossed his head up and down as if to say, *What are you waiting for?* Nathan led him out of the stall and threw his blanket and saddle over the big stallion. He tightened up the cinch, then slipped the bit and reins into his mouth. Once he was sure all was as it should be, he swung up into the saddle and headed out of the livery.

He fast trotted Sunrise towards the north side of town. They passed the train depot and crossed over the tracks. On the other side sat a series of cattle corrals. On the other side of the corrals sat eight or ten covered wagons. Nathan slowed Sunrise to a walk and circled to approach the wagons from the west. When he came up close to the first wagon, a man with sandy brown hair came out from under the wagon with a pail of axle grease and a brush in his hand. "Howdy. Can I help you?"

"Yes sir, I'm looking for a Mister Thompson. Can you direct me to him?"

"I'm Thompson. What can I do for you?"

Nathan swung down off of Sunrise and dropped the reins to let the big stallion know he could graze a little but to stay close. "Mister Thompson, my name is Nathan Ryder. Hank over at the livery told me you were putting together a wagon train to Santa Fe. I was wondering if you had room for one more wagon?'

"Nathan Ryder you said your name was?" Thompson inquired. "You that fella everyone is calling the Preacher?"

"Yes sir, I reckon I am."

"Well I don't know that I want a gunslinger in this train. Nothing against you personally, Preacher, but I have a responsibility to make sure these folks are safe and get to their destinations with the least amount of trouble."

"I understand that, sir. However, I think you've got the wrong impression about me. I'm not a gunslinger. I really am a preacher. I'm escorting a young lady to Redemption where she will start as the school teacher and I will take over part of an established circuit."

"I don't understand." Thompson put the brush back in the bucket and set them both on the side of the wagon. "I heard you out drew four men yesterday and was supposed to meet Black Bart in the street an hour ago. You're here and he isn't so you must have out drawn him too. How can you stand there and tell me you're a preacher and not a gunslinger?"

Nathan was beginning to get irritated. He took a deep breath and slowly let it out. He understood this man's responsibilities but he hated that a reputation he never wanted and hadn't asked for was starting to cause him problems.

"All those things are true, except I didn't shoot Black Bart in the street. I out drew the first man, who was drunk and accosting the school teacher I told you about. I had no clue he was an outlaw.

"Then on the way to my hotel room last night three of his gang accosted me and insisted that I draw against them. They were pretty drunk and I got lucky and beat them to the draw.

"This morning Black Bart, who was the brother of the drunk I had arrested last night, wanted to meet me at noon to fulfill his honor of the code of the west. I talked to him about salvation and met him at noon. Instead of us shooting each other, I lead him to Christ.

"Now, I don't expect you to take my word for all this, so go talk with the sheriff or any of the people who witnessed the event. I'll come back tomorrow and we can talk. I didn't ask for this reputation I'm earning, but I'm also not gonna roll over and be killed just to make people see me as a man of God. You check things out and we can talk tomorrow." Nathan grabbed his reins and swung back up in the saddle. He turned Sunrise around and started to head back to town.

Just as he was about to kick Sunrise into a walk Mister Thompson placed a hand on his leg.

"Son, I'm sorry for the assumption. You certainly talk like a man of God, so I'm gonna check out your story. If it is true, then I see no reason why you and the school teacher can't join the wagon train.

"Again if it weren't for my responsibility to keep these folks safe I would just take you at your word. However, I owe it to them to check you out. You come see me tomorrow and we'll get this thing settled. Okay?"

Nathan looked down at the man and nodded. "Sure, I'll be back sometime tomorrow. Thanks for your time, Mister Thompson."

"Just call me Frank, Preacher. If you ride with us it's gonna be a hard journey, so we ought to be on a first name basis with each other."

"I'll do so, Frank, if you'll call me Nathan. I'm sick to death of that Preacher fella." Nathan kicked Sunrise into a walk and then into a trot. As they crossed the tracks again Nathan slowed his horse back to a walk and headed to the bank to cash in his vouchers. Tomorrow Mister Smythe would arrive and Nathan could sign whatever he needed to sign. Monday, he could put this town behind him, and it would be none too soon, as far as he was concerned.

Chapter Eleven

Nathan, having cashed in his bounty vouchers at the bank, headed over to Gunderson's dry goods store. Nathan tied Sunrise to the hitching post out in front and entered the store. He stepped to the right, placing the outside wall behind his back, and waited for his eyes to adjust to the light. Inside he cringed. *Have I become so accustomed to someone trying to kill me that I'm now worried about getting shot in the back?*

"Howdy, Preacher, is there something we can help you with today?" The voice was deep and rich in contrast to the five foot tall man behind the counter. He had a shock of white hair forming a ring around his head, just over his ears, but what he lacked on the top of his head covered his face. Beside him was an equally small woman. Her hair was a long silver braid that lay over her right shoulder. Both of them gave him friendly, expectant smiles.

"Howdy yourself." Nathan walked toward the counter. "I am looking for some clothes first, shirts and pants for everyday."

The little old lady stepped from behind the counter and looked Nathan up and down. "You're a tall drink of water aren't you? I think we might have a few things in your size over on the last aisle. Won't be nothing fancy, like what you're wearing today. Not sure if we have anything in buckskin right now, but I'm sure there were some denim and flannel shirts close to your size. Pants will be denim. Not sure they'll be long enough, though."

Nathan smiled. "That's been the story of my life, ma'am. My mama almost always had to let the hem out of any store bought clothes she got me. As long as they cover the tops of my boots when I'm in the saddle, they'll be all right with me."

Nathan followed the woman to the appropriate place, where she proceeded to pick up various shirts and hold them up to him until she found six or seven that looked like they would fit him. Nathan had to kneel down for her to reach his shoulders. These she placed on top of his pile, then moved on to the pants.

When she was finished there was a goodly selection that should fit him. Nathan thanked her for her help and picked out five shirts and three pairs of pants. On the way to the front he grabbed several pairs of socks as well.

He placed his clothing on the counter and looked up. "Is that one of those new Winchester repeating rifles I've heard about?'

"Why, yes sir, it sure is. Would you like to take a look at it?" Without waiting for an answer the rotund little man climbed up on a small step stool and pulled the rifle off its hooks. "I just got these in last week. Haven't sold one yet, but they sure do look handsome, don't they?"

"They sure do." Nathan looked down the sights, noticing how much lighter than his Sharps long rifle it felt. "I have a Sharps, but I can certainly see how having more than a single shot could come in handy."

The merchant smiled with the look of an angler playing with a big catch. "It's much more convenient too. That-there rifle uses the same ammunition as your Peacemaker does. That'll keep you from having to carry more than one type of ammunition all the time."

"But are they as accurate as a Sharps? That'll be the key to them catching on big, won't it?"

The little man tilted his head, looking thoughtful for a minute. "I reckon they're as accurate, up to a point. After all, the smaller barrel and ammunition means the shot won't travel as far. I figure they wouldn't be as accurate at the four hundred yard and longer mark that the Sharps got. Then again, being able to fire twelve rounds without reloading would make them more deadly at ... say ... two hundred yards."

Nathan nodded his agreement, ran his hand over the stock, and opened the chamber, noticing how the shells would go in the bottom instead of the back like his Sharps as well. "I'll take it, and four boxes of shells, if you have them."

With a huge grin, the merchant reached back onto a shelf, brought out four boxes of 45 cartridges, and laid them on the counter next to the clothes. "You gonna want a saddle boot for that gun, youngster?"

"Probably should. Wouldn't do me any good if I couldn't use it from horseback."

The boot quickly joined the growing pile on the counter. "Anything else we can help you with today?'

"Actually there is. I am trying to outfit a wagon for the wagon train leaving Monday. There are going to be two of us traveling. Could you set me up with food stuff, cooking and sleeping gear, and anything else you think I might need? I'll pick them all up to-morrow."

Now the proprietress stepped up, smiling. "I think I can do that for you, Preacher. Is there anything in particular you want to eat or do you just want me to load you up with the basic staples?"

"The basics would be fine. Oh, but make sure there's coffee and a pot in that kit if you can."

"Be glad to. Now do you want your clothes and rifle today or do you want me to hold it all 'til tomor-row?"

Nathan chuckled at the slick way the lady of the business had maneuvered him into payment time. "Boy, you two've got this sales thing down to an art form. I bet you both saw me coming from a mile away. I'll take that pile there with me today, thank you."

While his wife started calculating Nathan's total, he could see that her husband wasn't about to let the town's most talked about visitor leave without an-swering a few questions. "Preacher, you mind if I ask you something?"

Here it comes, Nathan thought. "No, not at all. Go right ahead."

"The sheriff says you really are a preacher. Is that true?"

"Yes sir, it is. I know I've gained a reputation as something of a gunhand here in Franklin, but in reality I've just gotten lucky. I'm headed to the New Mexico Territory to ride a circuit there."

The man smiled even wider. "I understand about how things can just happen. You've kind of thrown everyone because our circuit rider doesn't wear a gun. He carries a scatter gun in his saddleboot, but that's it."

Nathan had a thoughtful expression. "Wish I could get away with that. But to be honest, I would be dead if that was all I had done. Those three last night would have caught me unarmed because I wasn't riding. I don't think they would have cared either."

"I figure you're right. I saw what you did for Black Bart out there today, and I heard from Joseph over at the Cattleman's Saloon that you even witnessed to Bart over breakfast this morning. That takes a man pretty sure of what God is doing to attempt those things."

Nathan now beamed with genuine pleasure.

"Thank you, Mister Gunderson. I appreciate that. Most people just see me as a gunslinger here, and think the Preacher is a name I got because of the way I was dressed that first day. But I really am ordained, and I try to follow the Lord's leading in everything I do."

Mister Gunderson nodded as he listened. "Well sir, I'm the head deacon over at the church, and our preacher is up on the other end of his circuit right now. That means I would be leading worship this Sunday. If you are leaving with the wagon train on Monday, maybe I can persuade you to fill the pulpit for us before you go. Might be an opportunity for you to let people see who you really are."

Nathan praised God for the mysterious way he worked sometimes. "Mister Gunderson, there is nothing I would like more than to preach at your church this Sunday. Thank you for asking."

"Great. That will be wonderful."

Just then Mrs. Gunderson put a wrapped bundle in front of Nathan and laid the new Winchester, already in its new boot on top. "That will be twenty-seven dollars so far, sir."

Nathan bent down to pull the money pouch out of his boot when one last thing caught his eye. "Add that guitar to my order, if you would please."

As Mister Gunderson pulled it off the shelf, Mrs. Gunderson made the addition to the tally. "Make that thirty dollars then, Preacher."

"Here's forty. You can put the rest toward what it will take to fill my standing order." Then he had a thought. "Mrs. Gunderson, I will be escorting my grandfather's ward to New Mexico. I don't know if she is set for the trip, but if she needs anything I'll send her to see you. Will you just add what she needs to my bill, please?"

"I'll be glad to my boy, but it might be easier to do if I knew her name? Otherwise I might give every female stranger things on your account."

"Oh, that's true. I'm sorry, her name is Grace Hopewell. I'll tell her if she needs anything for the trip to see you. Thanks again to you both. You know, I never ceased to be amazed at how God works. Anyway, you two have made my day." Nathan gathered up his purchases and headed out the door.

He tied his package to the back of Sunrise's saddle and attached the rifle boot. Pulling the Winchester from the boot, he loaded the rifle with 45 shells from his gunbelt . After returning the rifle to its saddle boot he climbed up on Sunrise and headed to the hotel.

Arriving back at the Cattleman's, he greeted Mark and James and went up to his room. Nathan unwrapped his purchases. He placed the clothes in his saddle bags and put the guitar in the corner by the bed. He took the four cases of shells and placed them in his bags, pushing them down under the clothing. Finally, he took the open box of shells on his dresser and refilled his gunbelt. Satisfied everything was as it should be, he exited to see if Grace was in her room.

Nathan knocked on Grace's door and waited. While doing so he marveled again at all God was doing for him and through him. Then, as if to emphasize the point, the door opened and Grace's beauty was once again revealed. "Nathan, what can I do for you this afternoon?"

"Grace, I was just checking to see if you would have dinner with me this evening?"

"I think that would be pleasant, as long as we don't eat at your breakfast establishment," Grace teased him.

Nathan blushed, then decided to have some fun of his own. "Well, the food was delicious, but for you I will try and resist the temptation of trying their dinners."

They both laughed. "Grace, I don't know if you need everyday western wear, or if you have enough things suitable, but I have made arrangements at the dry goods store for you to get anything you might need or want. Just go and see Mrs. Gunderson and she will set you up."

"Nathan, again, that's too much. I am starting to feel like I'm obligated to you, or some kind of charity case."

"Nonsense. I've already told you I am just fulfilling Nate's obligation to see you safely to Redemption and installed as the school teacher there. I also informed you that up to half of the reward money is yours to use, so please don't think twice about my offer."

"I will try to keep that in mind, Nathan, but it just feels so wrong taking all this from you. It would be different if it was Uncle Nate, because I knew him, and he was old enough to be my grandfather. You ... well ... to be honest ... you're more like husband material than benefactor material."

Nathan was stunned by Grace's observation. "I never thought of it like that. I guess I can see your point. Let's try this. You call my grandfather your uncle, so think of me as a long lost cousin who is just fulfilling his family obligation."

Grace was disappointed that Nathan seemed to miss her hint that she thought of him as more than family. "I guess I could accept your offer of travel clothing, though. I could use a couple of simple dresses and a pair of more sensible shoes."

Nathan smiled at the thought that women everywhere were the same when it came to shopping. Then he remembered she didn't know about Monday. "Oh, and I bought a covered wagon and team today. There is a wagon train leaving Monday that will head into New Mexico and past Redemption. I asked to join it because I wanted to preserve your reputation when we reached your new life."

Her eyebrows shot up. Nathan hurried on, but she was making him downright nervous with these puzzling looks. "I mean, I didn't want to have to marry you because we have to travel so far alone together. As you said, I may be fulfilling my Grandfather's obligations, but I am much younger than he was, and I wouldn't want gossip about either of us."

"Oh, a wagon train. That sounds interesting. Thank you for thinking of my reputation. However, I don't think having to marry me would be such a chore."

"I didn't say it would be a chore. I said I didn't want to have to marry you out of obligation. I don't want to marry anyone out of any reason other than that I love them, and God shows me they are my life-long partner."

Grace, a bit embarrassed that her true thought had slipped through, just looked away. "Well, I wasn't implying that I wanted to get married, either."

Nathan took a deep breath. "This conversation isn't going the way I meant at all. I'm just telling you that anything you might need for the trip, let Mister or Mrs. Gunderson know when you're at the dry goods store. If you want to see our rig and team you can go by the livery and ask Hank to show them to you. Or if you would prefer, I can take you by to see them before dinner. I will probably be busy all day tomorrow. Grandfather's attorney will be here tomorrow to settle his affairs."

Grace just wanted to end the conversation too, but she also desired to spend more time with this man who had truly become her knight in shining armor.

"I think a stroll before dinner would be lovely. Shall we say four-thirty? That will give me time to go to the dry goods store before dinner."

"Sounds good. I'll meet you in the lobby at four-thirty then." Nathan took his leave relieved that he hadn't made a worse mess of things.

After he let Sunrise loose in the corral and placed his riding gear on the back wall of the stall, Nathan headed up to Hank's office in the livery loft. He knocked on the door.

"Come in. It's open."

"I've come to settle up for my wagon and team, Hank.'

"So you got a spot then?"

"Well not exactly, but either way I'm gonna need that wagon and team. I have to get Miss Hopewell to Redemption some way. Sunrise is strong, but I doubt he could carry both of us plus all the supplies we'll need."

"Thompson didn't have a spot for you?" Hank seemed surprised.

Nathan shook his head. "He didn't say that exactly."

"What exactly did he say?"

"Said he didn't want the trouble having a gunslinger traveling with them would bring. I explained to him I am not a gunslinger, just a guy at the wrong place at the right time. He said he would check out my story, then let me know."

"Well, if that don't hang all. That man don't know a good thing when he sees it. It's obvious you know how to protect yourself and have the willingness to protect others. You'd think he'd be glad to have a talented gun along. Pay me the two-fifty so I can go and set that idiot straight."

Nathan counted out the two hundred fifty dollars and handed it to Hank. "Now, how much are you gonna charge me to feed and board those two brutes you just sold me?"

Hank laughed. "I told you, Preacher, those are two of the finest horses you'll ever find, and gentle enough that your young lady could drive them with no problem. However, seeing as how they've been here all this time, I can't charge you for a few more days. Least I can do for all you've already done for our town. Plus, I heard you're saving us all from having to listen to Gunderson's dry attempt at sermonizing this week. That alone is worth a few buckets of feed."

"Well thank you, Hank. I appreciate it."

"Now get going. I got a feather-headed wagon train master to go set straight," Hank rumbled with a smile.

Chapter Twelve

As Nathan walked back from the livery stable, he tried to get his head around how he felt about Grace Hopewell. It was funny. He had only met her the day before, but he felt like he was already halfway in love with her. He knew a large part of it came from being her rescuer and then finding out she was his grandfather's last unfinished business.

Still, there was something about her that just felt like a balm to his saddle-sore soul. She was beautiful. That was certain, but so had been most of the young ladies his mother had paraded through their house to catch his attention. He had known what his mother was up to. She was trying to get him married off before he left home. Though some of them had been very lovely to look at, and had personalities to match, not a one of them had made him feel like one day with Grace Hopewell had.

Nathan knew no matter how he felt he had to keep things from progressing while they were traveling together. He wanted no hint of impropriety to land on Grace when she arrived in Redemption. He knew there was no way he could avoid that himself. Reputations like his had a way of following you throughout the West.

However, if he could keep Grace from having to endure the same gossip about how she arrived in Redemption, he would. Even if it meant taking his joke from earlier seriously and marrying her here in Franklin before they left.

That thought took root in his head. But he spotted Bart Cody heading into the barbershop, which led to the thought of how one moment could change a life, one moment when Nathan had been listening to the Holy Spirit. It had changed not only his life but Bart's, and Bart's estranged wife Maryanne's too. He smiled as he thought of the reunion that would take place tomorrow at the train depot. He wasn't sure what the future held for the couple, but he said a prayer for them, asking God to reunite their hearts no matter what.

As he started past the barbershop Nathan noticed movement in the shadows across the street. In the alleyway beside the drygoods store was a man, trying to appear invisible. Had it not been for the slight glint of sunlight off his rifle barrel, Nathan would never have noticed him.

Nathan sat himself in one of the chairs out in front of the barbershop and pulled his boot off like he had gotten something in it. As he shook it out he cautiously began checking for more signs of trouble.

Two more glints from across the street caught his eye as he started to put the boot back on. One came from the roof of the bank. Just to the left of the bank sign stood another rifleman. Still another seemed to signal someone on this side of the street from the far corner of the dry goods store roof..

Bart noticed him as Nathan slowly entered the barbershop. He began to smile until he saw Nathan's face. "What's wrong, Nathan?"

Nathan slowly drew Bart and the barber with him deeper into the barber shop. "I don't know if it's me or you, but one of us has a lot of company waiting for a clear shot out on the street. There are at least four shooters, maybe more. I know I saw three with rifles across the street; one in the alley, two on the rooftops. I think there is at least one more on the rooftop on this side of the street."

Bart took the barber's cloth off and turned to look at the barber. "You got a back door out of this place?"

"Yes, sir."

"Ok, you and I are gonna go out it. I want you to go up to the sheriff's and let him know what the Preacher just said. I'll deal with the guy on the roof over here."

He turned to Nathan. "Do you think you could arrange a surprise for those fellows on the other side?"

Nathan smiled. "I might just be able to do that. Give me about five minutes."

"That should give the sheriff time to get in position too. Where are the fellows on the roofs?"

"There's one on the bank and one on the dry goods store."

"All right Barber, you make sure you tell the sheriff what you just heard. Tell him the Preacher and Black Bart are asking for his help."

"Yes, sir, I'll do it." Off he went toward the back with Bart right behind him.

Nathan loosened his Colt and exited the barbershop. He saw that the sun was shining off the windows, making it impossible for those across the street to see inside. "Okay, well, I'll be back in about twenty minutes when you're done with Bart there," he proclaimed.

He slowly crossed the street and entered the dry goods store. The Gundersons and Grace all turned to look at him. Nathan motioned for them to be quiet and shut the door.

"I need another one of those Winchesters and some shells right now. There's a bunch of bushwhackers set to cause trouble."

Gunderson didn't say a thing, but tossed first the rifle, then a box of shells, to Nathan. As Nathan loaded the rifle Mister Gunderson reached under the counter and pulled out a Greener. Nathan shook his head. "I appreciate the thought, but me, Bart, and the sheriff got this covered. It'd be better if you stayed here in case the women are put in danger."

Nathan moved around behind the counter, through the stockroom, and silently sneaked out the back door.

Sure enough, there at the corner of the alley stood a man with a rifle. It was aimed at the door of the barbershop across the street.

Nathan looked around and saw the ladder the other man had used to get on the roof of the dry goods store. He remembered one of ol' Nate's stories about getting the drop on some bushwhackers and decided to implement Nate's plan.

He leaned down, placed his rifle on the ground, then took off his boots and put them on the ground too. He picked up the rifle and snuck up on the bushwhacker in his stocking feet, quiet as an Indian. When he was directly behind him he laid the barrel of the Winchester on the man's shoulder. The bushwhacker jumped and Nathan spoke low and slow. "Smartest move you can make, partner, is to ease the rifle back to me nice and slow."

The man did, handing it over his right shoulder.

"Now slowly, and I mean slowly, drop your gunbelt to the ground. I don't want to hear it make a noise."

The gunbelt slowly lowered to the ground.

"Okay, turn around nice and slow now. Any sudden move may be your last."

The gunhand turned to face him and just as they got face to face, Nathan reversed the rifle and struck the outlaw on the top of his head, knocking him cold. "Sorry about that, son, but I can't have you warning your partners."

Nathan stuck his head back in the dry goods store and motioned for Mister Gunderson. Whispering, Nathan told him, "I knocked one of them out. Get some rope, tie him up, and stuff something in his mouth to keep him quiet."

Gunderson smiled, reached over to the counter, grabbed a pair of long johns, and shoved them in the outlaw's mouth, tying the legs around the back of his head. Then he proceeded to tie up the killer's hands and feet with some lengths of rope.

Nathan stifled a chuckle and began, still in stocking feet, to climb up on the roof of the dry goods store. He repeated the process with the outlaw up there and sent the shopkeeper to tie him up. Then he rounded the back of the alley, looking for a way up on the bank roof.

He found a ladder and climbed to the roof of the bank. He started toward the man crouched behind the bank sign. Somehow the outlaw became aware of the Preacher sneaking up behind him and spun to face him. Nathan calmly raised the rifle and sighted it on the outlaw's forehead. "Stand very still, varmint. I already got your two pals on this side of the street. If you will look across the way there you'll see Bart got your buddy."

"It don't matter, Preacher. You may keep us from killing Bart but you'll be getting yours soon enough." Then he raised his rifle above his head, surrendering without a fight.

The sheriff came up onto the roof. "I got this one, Nathan. Thanks for your help, again."

"No problem, Jack." Nathan grinned. "I enjoyed playing Indian. You might want to rescue the two over at the dry goods store. Last I saw, Mister Gunderson had them trussed up like a cow at brandin' time with a pair of long johns in their mouths."

Jack laughed, "Yeah, ol' Abner can get a bit carried away in these situations. But he's one to ride the river with for sure. Listen, Preacher, in all seriousness, don't head back to the hotel just yet. Let's check both sides of the street first. I heard this snake threaten you and it wouldn't surprise me if there's another team of bushwhackers up the street."

Nathan agreed and went down the ladder first, then stood at the bottom. He kept the Winchester trained on the prisoner as he came down the ladder, followed by the sheriff. They retrieved the two hogtied outlaws from Abner Gunderson. Then they led the whole group to the jail.

As they arrived Bart came up toting a semi-conscience outlaw of his own. "Nathan, this feller told me there's four more set up by the hotel waiting for you to return. They were gonna take us both out, then all come for the sheriff here and spring my brother."

Jack looked at the two of them. "Well, let's go get them." He went back to his desk and opened the top drawer. "Guess I should save the state of Missouri some money. Hold up your right hands, you two."

Bewildered, Bart and Nathan held up their hands.

"Say *I do.*"

"I do."

Jack pulled his hand out of the drawer and tossed a deputy's badge to each of them. "Good. You're both sworn deputies of the town of Franklin, effective ten minutes ago. Now I don't have to pay you any bounties, so let's go finish this."

With a shrug Bart and Nathan followed their boss out the door and down to the dry goods store. Jack entered the store and shut the door, spinning the sign around to *closed.*

"Abner, you've been deputized for the day, so get your Greener and come around here. We got four more men on rooftops down around the hotel. No sense in playing Indian this time. They have to know by now something went wrong with their plan. So here's what I want us to do.

"Nathan I want you to go right down the center of the street. I hate to use you as bait, but when they see you they'll all want a shot at you. They'll expose themselves trying to get it.

"Abner, you take the right side of the street and keep your eyes peeled for movement on the roof on the left.

"Bart, you trail along with Nathan and each of you keep your eyes open for movement up on top of the buildings. I'll take the left side looking right.

"Gentlemen, these outlaws mean to harm people in our town. Their target may be Nathan, but we all know they'll shoot everyone who goes for a gun. Don't try to capture or wound these…" Jack stopped and composed himself. "Sorry, ladies, almost slipped there and called them what they was. Just make sure the only four people who go to Boot Hill today are the outlaws. Got it?"

Nathan and Bart nodded and Abner Gunderson went behind the counter, took a third Winchester off the wall and loaded it. When all the men looked at him he grinned. "Been looking for a reason to test one of these out. Figure it'll be safer than that scattergun out there in the street."

They turned and started for the door. Grace, face white with fear, grabbed hold of Nathan. He looked her in those soft emerald eyes and said, "It's all right. Nothing's going to happen to me."

Grace looked at him a second more and whispered, "You promise?"

Nathan, not sure what came over him, leaned down and kissed her on the lips. Grace responded and clung to his neck like it was a lifeline. When Nathan broke the kiss, he winked. Turning to the door he said, "I promise I'll be back and we'll go to dinner. I think we have a lot to discuss."

Without waiting for the others, he set off down the street knowing that no matter what, these three men, who were quickly becoming friends, would have his back. They'd make certain he lived to keep his promise.

As he went out the door Grace whispered once more, so that only Wilhelmina Gunderson heard her. "He's going to marry me someday." Then she started to cry. "If he doesn't get killed first."

Wilhelmina came and took her in her arms. "Honey don't you worry none, my Abner may be old but he's a dead eye. Won't nothing happen to your man with those three at his back."

Then she held her like a mother would and wished once more she and Abner had been able to have kids.

Nathan slowed for Bart to catch up to him. Abner and Jack hung back just a hair on either side, eyes trained on the rooftops. As they got right in front of the hotel, four men stood up on rooftops on either side of the street, forming a deadly crossfire pattern to kill their target. Before any of them could draw a bead on the Preacher, four rifles fired as one and four outlaws tumbled dead into the street.

As one synchronized unit, the sheriff and his recently appointed deputies met in the street. They turned and walked back to the dry goods store, leaving the undertaker to his work.

Abner chuckled to himself, thinking it was just a typical day in the west. He wouldn't want to live anywhere else. When he saw Nathan he thought he needed to talk to Wilhelmina about those two. He couldn't see nothing good come of them traveling together right now. He secretly hoped she'd have a wise idea, because he couldn't think of nothing short of a wedding that would make that work out right.

Chapter Thirteen

Nathan collected Grace from the dry goods store. He suggested they go and look at the wagon and team he had purchased for their trip west. Neither Nathan nor Grace talked about the kiss before the shootout, but the tension between them was more real than it ever had been before.

They both knew something had changed in their relationship, and knew they would have to talk about it soon. However, they weren't ready to tackle the subject yet. Instead, Nathan started talking about the wagon and the two horses to pull it and how good a deal they had gotten . Grace hung on every word he said, but it was clear her mind wasn't on the outfit when she said, "I'm sorry. What did you just ask me?"

"I wanted to know if you had ever driven a team before?"

Grace stopped walking and placed her hands on her hips. "I, sir, am a southern born lady. Of course I can drive a team. How do you think I got to New York to begin with?"

"So if I were to need you to drive our team at times you'd be ok doing that?"

"Nathan, I just told you I drove a team all the way to New York. Why are you making such a big deal of this?

Nathan, trying to hide the smile that was threatening to consume his face, took her by the arm and led her out to the corral where the Belgians were exercising. "I'm not making a big deal; I just wanted to be sure you were fine with the idea. Now that I know, I won't bring it up again."

He walked up to the corral fence and placed a foot on the lowest rail. With a flourish, he waved at the two huge Draft horses. "Miss Hopewell, meet your team of horses."

Grace took one look in the corral and turned pink. "Those aren't horses, Nathan, they're monsters. What in the world are they?"

From behind her came the voice of Hank the livery man. "Oh, no, ma'am, they aren't monsters. Those are Belgian Draft Horses and they're the most gentle creatures in the world."

Nathan began to laugh. "I guess they're not like the team you drove all the way to New York, huh?"

"Oh, you men!!" Grace stomped her right foot. "Stop joking and show me our team."

Nathan dropped to the ground laughing hard as Hank walked up beside Grace. "Little lady, them there are Tiny and Mouse, and Nathan here bought them this very afternoon."

"You mean you want me to drive *them?"*

"There may be times you may need to, yes," Nathan managed to say.

"But they're the size of trees."

Hank laughed. "Miss, Tiny and Mouse are the gentlest horses y'all is ever gonna meet and they're easy to drive. Why, they practically drive themselves. They've been taught to haul and to follow. They've never been anything but docile. Why, they wouldn't harm a fly."

Just then one of the monster sized horses snapped at a fly, as if to call Hank a liar.

"Okay, so they would hurt a fly, but nothing else."

Hank entered the corral, caught one of the brutes by the halter, and led it up to Grace. "Tiny, meet Miss Hopewell. She is one of your new owners. Miss Grace, reach out and rub his nose. Let him get to know ya."

Grace, with a hand that was shaky, reached up to the horse's muzzle and timidly stroked it.

The giant animal responded like an overgrown puppy and leaned his head into Grace's hand, begging for more love and attention. His contented snort drew Mouse over to the fence, demanding her turn at a rub.

Grace laughed at the antics of the two big babies and quickly settled into rubbing both their huge heads. After a few minutes she clearly couldn't even remember why she had been so apprehensive.

Nathan smiled, watching her pet the two beasts. Her enjoyment was like a balm to his still disquieted soul. The moment stretched and soothed him after the action of the afternoon. Now he was ready to get cleaned up, take this beautiful lady to dinner, and discuss their future. That was a conversation he wasn't particularly looking forward to, especially since he wasn't sure how he truly felt toward her.

Was this feeling love or just infatuation? Was it only because she was a link to his recently departed grandfather or was it a real connection between them? Why had he kissed her? Just as importantly, why had she responded? This was all new territory for him and one that was made even more complicated by the uncertainty of his own future.

Nathan turned to Grace. "Are you ready to go to the hotel and get dressed for dinner?"

Grace, grinning from ear to ear, gazed at him. "Yes, I think that may be a wise idea. We do need to have a little talk, don't we?"

"I believe that may be the understatement of the day, Miss Hopewell."

Laughing, Grace took his arm as they headed back to the Cattleman's Hotel.

As Grace cleaned up and prepared to meet Nathan for dinner she tried to sort out her feelings for the young preacher. He was certainly one of the most confusing men she had ever met. Part eastern preacher and part just like his grandfather. She wondered if her attraction for him was because he had rescued her from Kid Cody, or if it had more to do with him being a younger version of her "Uncle" Nate.

She admitted to herself that she was attracted to him. She had even declared to Mrs. Gunderson that she wanted to marry him some day. The depth of that desire surprised and frightened her at the same time.

Here she was starting a new life and out of nowhere came the desire to be a wife. Grace wondered if it was just the stress making that old childhood dream rise to the surface, or did she really want to be Mrs. David Nathan Ryder the Third?

More importantly, *how would he react if she told him the truth about her past in New York? Would he be like his grandfather and believe the past was covered by the grace of God, or would he react like a typical preacher and condemn her for what was beyond her control? Did she dare tell him or hope that he never finds out?*

Grace put her pondering aside and decided to just enjoy dinner and let Nathan lead the conversation. Maybe all this was for nothing. For all she knew he kissed her to make her feel better and there was nothing more to it. She finished dressing just as her dinner companion knocked on her door.

Chapter fourteen

Nathan and Grace walked contemplatively to the café. The tension between them was so thick even Mrs. Sue could tell something was up. "I declare you two are wound as tight as a couple of cats with their tails caught in the butter churn."

The phrase brought a smile to Nathan's face, relieving a bit of the nervous tension he had been feeling. "You're right as rain Mrs. Sue, but it's nothing your good home cooking won't cure."

"Preacher, you's old enough to know that home cooking don't cure everything. But some good southern soul food just might help. How about tonight's special- chicken fried steak and mashed taters, both covered in a good serving of pan gravy. I even got some apple pie for dessert."

Nathan looked at Grace, who smiled as big as he did. "Sounds great, and some coffee to go with it all?"

"Bring ya'll a pot right over." With that Sue turned and practically waltzed to the kitchen.

Nathan grew more sober as he looked at Grace, his thoughts still not settled in his mind. "I guess we need to talk about what happened this afternoon."

"Yes, I guess we do."

"Grace, I want to start by saying that I am sorry. I shouldn't have taken liberties like that with a lady no matter what the circumstances. I apologize profusely. I know it is no excuse, but the only explanation I have for you is that the tension of the situation caused me to forget myself."

Nathan knew this was going badly by the look of sorrow, then anger, which flashed across Grace's countenance. "Your ONLY explanation is the tension of the situation? David Nathaniel Ryder the Third, are you telling me you only kissed me because you thought you might die?"

"No, of course not! I admit there's obviously some attraction between us. Still, it was unseemly of me to overstep my bounds and play so forward with your emotions."

Sweat began to run down the back of Nathan's neck. It seemed the more he tried to explain the worse a mess he was making of this whole thing.

"You admit there is some attraction between us. Nathan, you swept me in your arms and kissed me like you had every right to. Now, I'm not saying that I didn't make matters worse by responding to your attention. Are you seriously gonna set there and tell me all you feel is a slight attraction to me?"

Nathan squirmed like a schoolboy caught dipping a girl's pig tail in the ink well. "Grace, honestly, I am unsure how much to trust my emotions right now. With the death of Nate and all the danger I've been in since arriving in the west, not to mention taking on the responsibility of getting you to Redemption. I am a veritable train wreck of emotions right now.

"Don't get me wrong. I'm certainly attracted to you and find myself thinking about you constantly. However, I know my life in Redemption is going to be a busy one. I've never even contemplated the thought of a romantic entanglement in my life. After all, I'm going to be riding a circuit and only be in one place for a few days at most. Just long enough to preach a monthly sermon."

"I see, and of course, I came west to find a husband and settle down. I can't believe you have the nerve to sit here and tell me that I'm a complication in your life. If you truly feel that way, I'm not sure I need you to escort me to Redemption. I will just find a young family to travel with to the New Mexico territory."

Nathan was truly distressed that Grace thought him so insensitive. "That isn't what I meant, Grace. I know you came west at my grandfather's request to take on teaching at the school in Redemption. I was just trying to explain that I don't know what to make of my feelings for you.

"Honestly, I've never felt this way about anyone before. I've just been trying to say I don't know if what I feel toward you is love or just a passing affection. However, you do bring up another thing we have to talk about; our traveling together to the Territory."

Nathan and Grace had been so intent on their conversation that they had failed to even notice when Sue had brought their food. Nathan was so intent on explaining his concerns that he had also failed to notice the group of hard cases that had entered the café and were beginning to harass some of the other patrons.

The sound of a woman's distressed voice finally penetrated Nathan's senses. He looked toward the front of the restaurant and saw four men surrounding a table with a young eastern couple. "I said you're setting in my seat, Greenhorn. Now get up and let a real man get to know the little lady."

The cowboy talking was wearing two guns tied low. His hat was pushed forward, practically covering his eyes. The look on his face was one of mischief. His three buddies looked just as cantankerous and capable of trouble. Nathan slowly reached into his shirt pocket and pulled out the deputy's badge he had been given earlier and pinned it to his chest.

Grace reacted to Nathan's change in demeanor by reaching across the table and touching his hand. "Go. I know you can't help but get involved. Please be careful, though."

Nathan, with a half-grin, stood and settled his Stetson on his head, pushed back all friendly like. As he started toward the commotion the hard cases noticed him for the first time. The leader, who was egging the young man to get up, saw his partners tense and looked toward this new challenge.

Nathan stepped up to the table and addressed the young man. "Evening, sir. Are these gentlemen part of your dinner party?"

The man visibly relaxed as he noticed the tin star attached to Nathan's chest. "They most certainly aren't, Deputy. They seem to think they have the right to harass my wife and I because we aren't from around here."

Nathan hooked his thumbs into his gunbelt. "Well, I'm sure it was just a misunderstanding. The citizens of Franklin are a friendly group."

He glanced at the five men, then focused on the big cowboy who had been shoving on the easterner. "Isn't that right, boys?"

"Shove off, Deputy," the leader snarled. "The boys and I are tired of all these Yankee's coming out here and acting like they own the place. We plan to introduce this Yankee to the true west, and this filly to real men."

Nathan's eyes changed in a blink from friendly to cold, hard steel. "No, I don't think you are. You're welcome to find a table and get some dinner, but if I even think you're about to cut loose in Mrs. Sue's place you're gonna have more trouble than you can handle."

"Tin horn, you just bought yourself a trip to Boot Hill. Once we've planted you we'll come back, plant this greener and claim both his and your fillies."

Nathan saw the tightening of muscles in each of the cowboys. He sighed and shook his head. "Last chance, fellas. If you keep pushing this ya'll either end up in the ground or in the jail. Why don't you boys just walk on out of here and hit the trail?"

One of the others looked at their leader and smirked. "You hear that, Lefty? The tin star here just told us to leave town."

"Yeah Rusty, I heard 'im. Lookie here, Deputy, we are gonna be staying. Seems a friend of ours has been wrongly imprisoned here and we ain't leaving 'til we find the Yankee who bushwhacked him. Now either get out of our way and let us finish with our fun here, or you'll become a part of our business."

Nathan shook his head sadly. "Can't let that happen, boys. We only got three guys in our jail and since I was responsible for each one of them being arrested I can guarantee you they each belong there."

Shock registered on Lefty's face. "You arrested them? Story we heard was some eastern dandy calling hisself the Preacher tricked our pals. So unless you're that lowdown, yeller-bellied fella called the Preacher you better just back off before I loose my temper."

Nathan stepped back so that he had a clear line of sight to each of the hard cases. "Well, that just happens to be what people are calling me here, so I reckon we've got ourselves a bit of a problem."

Lefty drew himself up straight and turned to fully face Nathan. "All right, Preacher, I think you got my attention now. Let's step outside and finish this. 'Cause one way or another, you and me are gonna have it out tonight."

Nathan stepped back and motioned toward the door. "After you, gentlemen."

The hard cases headed to the door, followed by Nathan. As the last of the cowboys exited the door Nathan pulled both his sixguns and cocked back the hammers as he exited. The sound of the hammers turned the four cowboys towards Nathan. "Ok, boys, nice and easy now, drop them gunbelts in the dust."

Lefty swore as he slowly moved his hand toward his belt buckle. Nathan kept his eyes locked on the cowpoke and saw the motion of his left hand streak toward his left hand gun just as his right loosed the buckle. Nathan's right hand gun bucked and belched fire. Lefty dropped his gun, grabbing his hand where the deputy's bullet had caught him. "Get im, boys!"

Chapter Fifteen

As Nathan was diving for cover behind the watering trough he heard his grandfather admonishing him. "Never shoot to wound, boy. If it is worth shooting at a man, it's worth killin' 'im. If you wound 'em they can still end your life or someone else's."

Thanks, Nate, I sure wish you had piped up a little earlier and saved me a fight. Nathan peeked over the edge of the trough to see the four men spreading out, trying to catch him in a crossfire. As they moved around they were keeping up a steady stream of gunfire in the general direction of Nathan's hidey hole. Nathan ducked to avoid being hit and pondered his situation. If he didn't think of something quick he was going to be pinned down and facing his Maker.

Quickly, he popped up and fired a couple of shots in the direction of the most directly lined up gunny. He was satisfied to hear a grunt and see the cowpoke slump to the ground. He ducked back just as two rounds punched through the glass window of the café. He heard a woman's scream and turned just in time to see Grace slip to the floor with a spreading red stain covering her neck and chest.

Nathan lost all fear as rage took over. He jumped up and sent lead flying from both his sixguns. The men he faced didn't stand a chance. Before they even had time to aim three of them were down, shot clean dead. Lefty was hiding behind his horse, cradling his wounded left hand. Seeing that he was alone, he tossed his right hand gun out at Nathan's feet. "I give up, Deputy. Go ahead and arrest me."

Nathan, with the cold rage of murder on his face, picked up the gun and tossed it back at the outlaw. "You ain't going to jail, Lefty. I believe your own words were *one way or another we were gonna have trouble tonight.* Well, you got it, bucko. Pick up that gun and make your play. One way or another, you're going to Boot Hill with your partners before this fight is done."

Nathan holstered his irons and moved clear of the café.

Lefty looked into the face of the Preacher and realized he was seeing death staring straight into his soul. Slowly he started to back away from the gun lying at his feet. He got about two steps away when Nathan's hand streaked to his pistol and a slug tore up dirt right between Lefty's feet.

"I said pick it up, you yella bellied son of a bitch. You done shot the woman I love, and there ain't no way out of this for you but to put a slug in me. I promise you this, if you don't pick up that shooter and face me, I'll put the next one right between your eyes." He cocked back the hammer and raised the barrel about six inches so the outlaw was staring straight down the barrel of death.

Lefty, shaking with fear, knelt, picked up the gun, and shoved it into his holster. "Preacher, you don't want to do this. I'm sorry about your girl, but if you keep pushing you're gonna be on the other side of that badge."

"Shut up, you skunk, and prepare to meet God face to face," Nathan snarled and, dropping his Colt into the holster, set himself. Just as he was getting ready to fill his hand the loud boom of a scattergun sounded from behind him. Spinning, Nathan prepared to face this new threat. Mrs. Sue stood beside the sheriff, who was pointing a shotgun straight at him.

"Don't do it, Nathan. That owl hoot is right. If you keep pushing this, it will be your neck I'll be stretching. Why don't you calm down and think whether this is what your granddad would want you to do? Is this the way you're gonna honor his memory and legacy?"

Nathan stared at his friend and temporary boss. Jack took a step back as he saw the anger and anguish in Nathan's eyes. Experience told him that the Preacher was holding on to sanity by a thread and one wrong word or motion would drop him over the edge. As good as Nathan was, blood would run in the streets if they didn't get him under control soon.

"Jack, he or his pals killed Grace. I've already dishonored Nate's memory and legacy. Now either leave or pull that trigger, but this slime is gonna meet Jesus tonight right alongside my Grace."

Mrs. Sue walked up and smacked the young man right across the face. "Preacher, you should be ashamed of yourself. That girl ain't dead, and even if-fen she were, this isn't the way she'd want you to be-have. Now step aside and let yer boss do his job."

She turned and headed back to her café. "I declare you men are more dramatic than a hundred women."

She looked back over her shoulder at Nathan. "Well, boy, are you gonna come and check on that girl or stand there looking like a bigger fool than you already do?"

Nathan looked back and forth from Lefty to Mrs. Sue, then turned to follow the older woman back into the café, slipping the hammer thong onto his Colt as he went.

As he entered the café he saw the young easterner tying a cloth around Grace's shoulder. "That should hold you until I can get you over to the doctor's office. You'll need a couple of stitches to close that wound but it should heal fairly easy. You were lucky, miss. A few inches over and you might have shattered your collarbone."

Seeing Grace alive and sitting up, Nathan sank to his knees and began to weep like a baby. *My God, what did I almost do? Where did that rage come from? Was I really willing to break every rule of conflict Nate taught me and one of God's commands for this woman?*

He thought about it for a minute, and as she came over to kneel down beside him, he realized that he knew exactly what his feelings for her were. He was totally, madly in love with her. He couldn't see himself living without her.

With that thought he stood, swept her up in his arms like a small child, and headed towards the doctor's office to have her patched up. The last thing the people in the cafe heard as he headed out the door was: "Grace, I was wrong. I know exactly how I feel about you. If you will let me, I will take care of you for the rest of our lives. I love you."

No one caught her reply but the set of the Preacher's shoulders made the answer obvious as all tension left him and a new purpose seemed to settle over him.

Chapter Sixteen

Nathan woke the next morning and had two thoughts almost simultaneously. The first was *I have to meet the train today. Mister Smythe will be arriving.* The second was the harder of the two. *What have I done? I almost killed a man last night, not to mention I came close to drawing down on the sheriff.* While not looking forward to the first duty, meeting Smythe and settling his grandfather's estate was the easier of the two.

He went into the washroom, dumped last night's basin into the tub, and pulled the lever to drain it into the street. He quickly washed, dressed, cleaned his six shooters, and reloaded his guns and cartridge belt.

Having completed his dressing routine, Nathan grabbed his Bible and headed to that chair in the lobby he had procured for his time with God. He sat down and opened God's Word.

His Bible had fallen open to Matthew Chapter Five. What he saw there caught his attention and kept him from turning to his daily passage.

"For I say unto you, That except your right-eousness shall exceed the righteousness of the scribes and Pharisees, ye shall in no case enter into the kingdom of heaven. Ye have heard that it was said by them of old time, Thou shalt not kill; and whosoever shall kill shall be in danger of the judgment: But I say unto you, That whosoever is angry with his brother without a cause shall be in danger of the judgment: and whosoever shall say to his brother, Raca, shall be in danger of the council: but whosoever shall say, Thou fool, shall be in danger of hell fire. Therefore if thou bring thy gift to the altar, and there rememberest that thy brother hath ought against thee; Leave there thy gift before the altar, and go thy way; first be reconciled to thy brother, and then come and offer thy gift. Agree with thine adversary quickly, whiles thou art in the way with him; lest at any time the adversary deliver thee to the judge, and the judge deliver thee to the officer, and thou be cast into prison. Verily I say unto thee, Thou shalt by no means come out thence, till thou hast paid the uttermost farthing."

Nathan thought about that and knew what God was trying to tell him, he hadn't been very righteous last night. He was supposed to offer up a sermon to the people of this town in a few days, but Nathan always thought of his sermons as part of his offering to God.

His sermon would not be accepted by God unless he went first and made things right. He really needed to see Jack Cole this morning. As he continued to read he knew God wasn't through with him today.

"Ye have heard that it was said by them of old time, Thou shalt not commit adultery But I say unto you, That whosoever looketh on a woman to lust after her hath committed adultery with her already in his heart. And if thy right eye offend thee, pluck it out, and cast it from thee: for it is profitable for thee that one of thy members should perish , and not that thy whole body should be cast into hell. And if thy right hand offend thee, cut it off, and cast it from thee: for it is profitable for thee that one of thy members should perish, and not that thy whole body should be cast into hell. It hath been said Whosoever shall put away his wife, let him give her a writing of divorcement: But I say unto you, That whosoever shall put away his wife, saving for the cause of fornication, causeth her to commit adultery: and whosoever shall marry her that is divorced committeth adultery."

Again God pricked his heart. Though his relationship with Grace had grown into something real and deep, his initial kiss and even earlier reaction of showering attention on her, was born out of a more primal emotion, lustful attraction.

So not only did he need to make things right with Jack, he needed to make them right with Grace too. How could he do that and not damage the relationship that was blossoming between them? He didn't know, but he knew what he had to do.

"Again, ye have heard that it hath been said by them of old time, Thou shalt not forswear thyself , but shalt perform unto the Lord thine oaths: But I say unto you, Swear not at all; neither by heaven; for it is God's throne: Nor by the earth; for it is his footstool: neither by Jerusalem; for it is the city of the great King. Neither shalt thou swear by thy head, because thou canst not make one hair white or black. But let your communication be, Yea, yea; Nay, nay: for whatsoever is more than these cometh of evil. Ye have heard that it hath been said An eye for an eye, and a tooth for a tooth: But I say unto you, That ye resist not evil: but whosoever shall smite thee on thy right cheek, turn to him the other also. And if any man will sue thee at the law, and take away thy coat, let him have thy cloak also. And whosoever shall compel thee to go a mile, go with him twain. Give to him that asketh thee, and from him that would borrow of thee turn not thou away.

Ye have heard that it hath been said, Thou shalt love thy neighbour, and hate thine enemy. But I say unto you, Love your enemies, bless them that curse you, do good to them that hate you, and pray for them which despitefully use you, and persecute you; That ye may be the children of your Father which is in heaven: for he maketh his sun to rise on the evil and on the good, and sendeth rain on the just and on the unjust."

Nathan sat back, shocked at what he had just read. *Surely God wasn't saying what it looked like he was saying. He couldn't do it! NO! This was too much. He wouldn't go and apologize to Lefty. God didn't expect that of him did He?* Then his eyes and heart were drawn to the rest of the chapter.

"For if ye love them which love you, what reward have ye? Do not even the publicans the same? And if ye salute your brethren only, what do ye more than others? do not even the publicans so? Be ye therefore perfect, even as your Father which is in heaven is perfect."

Without even realizing it, Nathan's head had bowed and his eyes had closed. *Oh, God, what a hard thing You are asking of me. I want to be like You. I want to please You and follow your calling in my life. I am trying to act justly, to love mercy and to walk humbly with You.*

I am trying to reconcile the two gifts You have placed on my life, but this is a hard thing You are asking of me. I confess that my actions have not been what You expect of me. I have no problem confessing that to You, Jack or even to Grace. However, confessing to that Lefty that I acted wrongly towards him is a hard pill to swallow. Right now I don't want to do it. God, I know that my heart has to be right for my confession and apology to be accepted by You, so all I can say at this point is, change my heart toward this man. Give me Your desire and Your heart for him. Take away my selfish pride, Father. Amen.

Nathan looked up from his prayer and was startled to see Bart leaning up against the post beside the chair. "Is this going to become a daily habit, Bart? Because if it is, you should just join me for Bible study time and breakfast instead of sneaking up on me."

Bart chuckled, "I may take you up on that, Nathan. I didn't mean to startle you, but I heard about your little meltdown last night and wanted to check on you and see if you were ok. You are ok, aren't ya?"

Nathan was touched to see the true concern on the face of this man who just the day before had been ready to take his life to honor his brother.

"Bart, to be honest, I'm not sure. Don't get me wrong. I don't want to kill the varmint today, and I am glad that Jack and Sue stopped me from making the biggest mistake of my life yesterday. But what God just told me to do is a hard bronc to break."

Bart sank into the chair beside Nathan. "What do you mean? What is God asking you to do that's so difficult?"

Nathan turned the Bible around and handed it to Bart, "Read verses forty-six through forty-eight. That is the part that is relevant to the man from last night."

Bart took the Bible and sat reading for a few minutes. Nathan knew when God revealed the same thought to Bart as He had Nathan. Bart looked up with surprise and doubt on his face.

"If I'm reading this right, you're telling me God is asking you to apologize to that low down dirty woman shooting snake because you pushed him to draw on ya?"

"That's exactly what God is doing, Bart."

"Why? Iffen you'd shot him he would have gotten exactly what he deserved."

"No, Bart, he wouldn't. He'd surrendered to me and I was going to kill him, if he picked up his gun or didn't. I would have done it, too, if Jack and Mrs. Sue hadn't arrived when they did."

"Still, you didn't kill him, so why do you need to apologize to him?"

"Because in my heart I had. Go ahead and back up and read from verse twenty to twenty-two."

When Bart had finished reading and looked up, Nathan continued. "See, to God, what I wanted to do and planned to do is no different than having done it. I pushed Lefty to pick up his gun so that I would appear innocent in the eyes of the law, but in God's sight, he saw my heart. He knew I was going to end Lefty's life if he picked up the gun or not."

"Nathan, you are the most honest and righteous man I know. I can't see God holding it against you just because you slipped up a little."

"But he does, Bart, because my heart actions are just as important to my walk with HIM as my actual actions. When you came up, I was confessing to God that my heart doesn't want to apologize and that I needed Him to change my heart. I asked Him to let me see Lefty like God sees him, to let me love Lefty the way God loves him, so that my heart will change and I will want to apologize."

Bart looked from Nathan to the Bible and back. He handed Nathan back the Bible with a sigh. "I reckon I still got a lot to learn about this following God stuff. Thanks for explaining it to me. If you weren't kidding earlier, I think I will take you up on that Bible study and breakfast thing."

Nathan smiled and pushed the Bible back towards Bart. "I was kidding, but only partly. You are more than welcome to have breakfast with me any time and we can talk about the things you are reading in the Bible. I don't figure you've had time to get yourself one, so keep mine. I'll get another one later today."

"I couldn't do that, Nathan. You've done so much for me already. Helped clear my name, introduced me to Christ and helped give me the chance to make things right with Maryanne."

"Seriously, Bart, keep it. I want you to have it. Read some of it before breakfast tomorrow and we can talk about any questions you might have."

"I'll do that, Nathan, but only 'til I can get one of my own."

Together the two gunslingers turned brothers walked into the saloon and took what was becoming their normal seat. Bart laid the Bible on the table just as the bartender scrambled over to them.

"Black Bart, Preacher, same as yesterday?"

Bart looked at the man and saw the nervousness that the reputation he and the Preacher had put on people's faces.

"No, my good man, relax. We aren't gonna bite you. Bring us two cowboy plates, but don't bring the whiskey. Just coffee with two cups."

The bartender's shock showed as he turned and walked away to fill the order. Both Bart and Nathan heard him muttering as he walked away. "What kind of man is that Preacher?"

They both threw back their heads and laughed.

Chapter Seventeen

After his breakfast with Bart was over Nathan decided to start with the one that was most important to him. He went looking for Grace. *God help me know what to say to her and how to say it.* He went up to her room and knocked on the door. After a few minutes the maid opened the door and let him know that Miss Hopewell was not there.

Next he tried the café, and as he entered he realized there was someone else he needed to make things right with. Mrs. Sue came up to him and gave him a hug. "If you are looking for Grace, she is with the Gundersons. When Wilhelmina heard Grace would need help with her arm for a few days, she offered to let her stay with them'til your wagon train leaves."

"Well, that will save me from running all over town looking for her. But I actually need to talk with you." Nathan looked around at the breakfast crowd. "Is there someplace a little more private we could talk?"

"Well, Honey Chil', I can't leave all these people without someone to check on them. If you want to come back to the kitchen I can keep an eye on everyone and we will only have Harold to overhear."

"Thank you, Mrs. Sue. I really appreciate it."

As Sue and Nathan entered the kitchen, she pointed to the cook. "Preacher, that's my husband Harold. Harold, this is Nathan, the preacher I was telling you about."

"Hello, sir." Nathan shook Harold's hand. "I have been enjoying your good home style cooking."

Harold smiled. "Thank you, son, now go speak to Sue. I know that's why you came back here."

Nathan walked over to where Sue was waiting. "Sue, I want to thank you for your wisdom last night. In addition, I want to ask your forgiveness for acting so unchrist like and putting you in that situation. I honestly would have killed that man if you hadn't shown up when you did."

"Oh, Nathan, child, there is no need to apologize. I think anyone with your training in gunplay would have reacted the same way."

"That may be true, Sue, but as a Christian and pastor I'm supposed to live according to a higher calling."

"Oh, hawgwash, boy. Pastors and Christians are people too, with real feelings and real failings. In the end you made the right decision, so I don't want to hear anymore about it."

Nathan, realizing the older woman was trying in her own way to accept his apology, nodded, reached out, and hugged her. "Thank you, Sue. I appreciate your understanding."

He reached into his pocket, pulled out a double eagle, and put it in her hand. "This will cover the cost of the window that got shot out last night. Now, don't be stubborn and try to refuse. It was my actions that caused the window to be broken, so I will not take no for an answer."

"Well I will say this for you, Nathaniel David Ryder the Third, you are as stubborn as your ole grand pappy, and just as charming. That ol' wrangler has got to be smiling down from heaven at you right now, for sure."

Nathan watched as the coin disappeared into her apron pocket. "Now, shoo. Go find that girl and check on her. Tell Wilhelmina I'll bring over some lunch for them before the noon rush hits."

Nathan left, feeling a bit lighter in his spirit, but he knew he had a ways to go before he was completely right with God and man. The next two would be hard but he still had no idea how he was going to face the third man he needed to make things right with.

Nathan went around to the side of the dry goods store. There he climbed the stairs to the second story apartment Abner and Wilhelmina called home. He said a quick prayer for strength to do what he came to do, then knocked on the door. It was Abner who answered. "I wondered when you would show up, young fella. I figured that ole southern jabber box would tell you where your young lady got off to."

"Yes, sir, she just did. If it is convenient I really need to speak to Grace."

"Well, I reckon you do at that, boy. Let me go get her for ya. Have a seat, take a load off, and I'll be right back."

Abner left the kitchen and went down the hallway. Nathan had just gotten seated when Abner came back in, holding Grace by the arm to steady her. Nathan jumped up and pulled out a chair for her. She gingerly sat down in it, careful to avoid bumping her left shoulder.

Nathan must have looked extremely concerned because Abner chuckled and pointed at the chair Nathan had just vacated. "Sit back down, Nathan. She's ok, just a little unsteady because of the dose of laudanum the doc gave her just before you got here."

He helped her get situated, then turned back to Nathan. "Don't take too long, son. She needs to rest and that medicine is gonna make her sleepy in a few minutes. Wilhelmina is in the girl's bedroom. Just help her back there when you're done. Then come downstairs. I need to have a few words with you before you leave."

"Yes sir, Mister Gunderson. This won't take long, I promise. I'll see you down stairs in a few minutes. I want to thank you and Mrs. Gunderson for doing this."

"Nothing to it youngster. We just follow the Lord's leading like we're supposed to. I'll see you in a while. Grace, you don't let him talk too long, and get some rest, young lady." Abner left and went to open his store.

Nathan moved over closer to Grace and took her good hand in his. "I am so sorry you were hurt last night, Grace. My pride blinded me to the danger to everyone in the café."

"Oh, Nathan, you had no way of knowing what would happen, so it wasn't your fault."

"That may be true, but that isn't the reason I came to see you this morning. I want to start by telling you I meant every word I said to you last night. Nothing would make me happier than to take care of you the rest of our lives. However, God revealed to me this morning that I owe you an apology."

Nathan stopped to suck in a breath and swallow the lump in his throat.

"Whatever are you talking about, darling?" Grace looked deep into his eyes, confusion on her lovely face.

"I was reading the Scriptures this morning and I realized that I have not treated you the way a young Christian woman should be treated. I took liberties with you and have taken even bigger ones in my head and heart. God reminded me today that such thinking is the same as the actions in his eyes. Therefore, I've come to ask your forgiveness. I further pledge to treat you with the respect and honor you deserve until our wedding day, if you'll still have me."

Grace, with tears in her eyes, pulled her hand from his and laid it against his cheek. "Oh, my love, of course I forgive you, and of course I'll still have you. What a precious man of God the Lord has blessed me with."

Nathan could see she wanted to go on but the laudanum was starting to take over. He stood, picked her up just like he had last night and, quieting her, carried her to the bedroom where Mrs. Gunderson waited and laid her on the bed. "Rest now, my love. We will talk more later."

"Anything you need for her, ma'am, put it on my tab." Nodding to Wilhelmina, he turned and left to go speak with Mr. Gunderson downstairs. In doing so, he failed to hear her say, "Wait there's something I need to tell you too."

Wilhelmina pulled the quilt up around her and tucked her in. "Rest now child you'll have plenty of time to talk to him. That boy ain't going to be far away if I'm any judge of character."

As she drifted off to drug induced sleep Grace struggled to speak. "But it's important, and could change everything." Then her eyes closed and she said nothing more for a while.

Wilhelmina sat at the foot of the bed wondering what could be so important that Grace would fight sleep to try and tell Nathan. She had no clue, but she prayed for the young girl anyway. "God heal her body and give her peace."

Chapter Eighteen

Nathan knocked on the back door of the dry goods store, knowing Abner Gunderson was inside waiting for him. In the short time he had known Abler Nathan had come to respect him as a Christian and a dear old saint of God.

Abner opened the door and ushered him in. "Thanks for meeting with me, Preacher. I have about an hour 'til I have to open to the public, so let's just get right to it, shall we?"

"That's fine with me, Mister Gunderson. I have a couple of things I need to accomplish this morning as well. First off, let me thank you again for all you and Mrs. Gunderson are doing for Miss Hopewell. I greatly appreciate it. I told your wife anything ya'll might need for her, don't hesitate to let me know."

Abner looked hard at the young man before him. "Young feller, we are just helping our neighbor like the good book says, as you know. This here store provides very well for us, so we can afford to take care of the young lady for a few days. Besides, my Wilhelmina has kind of half adopted her already, after all that went down yesterday.

"What I need you to understand is, Miss Grace isn't gonna be in any condition to travel on Monday. According to the doc, it will be at least two weeks before she can travel without risking tearing her wound open."

"Two weeks? But that means the wagon train will have left by then. Abner, I don't know what to do. We can't travel alone together, and we can't wait 'til another wagon train decides to head west."

Abner sat himself on the stool behind the counter and rubbed the top of his balding head. "Well, I kinda have an idea about that. I am going to put together my own wagon train. Wilhelmina and I are going to sell the store to a young feller who's been asking to buy it, and head west to start a supply depot out on the trail. I figure we should ride the trail once before we set up in the wilderness."

"Why would you want to leave all this behind?" Nathan indicated the store and their surroundings.

"We opened this store when the town was part of the wild frontier. It and we grew old and comfortable together. I thought I was content until the sheriff deputized me.

"Wilhelmina and I talked all last night and came to a decision. We are heading for the frontier again. We already have another couple who'll be going with us, plus if you and Grace go, then Grace can drive your rig and sleep in ours. It answers your problem, unless you plan to get married this week?"

"No, I don't think that would be wise. I want her to understand what she is agreeing too before she agrees to be my wife. I'll be riding a circuit in the territory. She needs to understand exactly what that means."

Abner stared deep into Nathan's eyes. "But you do plan on making her your wife eventually?"

"Yes, I love her."

"Just making sure, youngster. You've already pushed what some would say were the boundaries of decency."

Nathan hung his head in shame. "I know, sir. It was one reason I was looking for her this morning, to ask her forgiveness for the way I've treated her. Also to promise her I'd act in righteousness and holiness toward her from now on."

Abner stood and headed toward the front door. He flipped the sign to 'Open' and unlocked the door. "Good. Well, after lunch I'll have the Missus watch the store long enough for me and young Henderson go see the solicitor and have a bill of sale drawn up for a week from now. Preacher, looks like we're a-traveling west together."

Nathan shook Mr. Gunderson's hand. "I reckon we are, Abner. I'll talk with you later. I have a couple more people I need to see before the train gets here. I'm meeting my own solicitor to conclude my grand-father's estate today."

"Yeah, I heard about Nate's passing. The world will be a might less interesting with that ol' trapper gone."

"You knew my grandfather?"

"Sure enough did. That ol' rascal stopped here for supplies many a-time when he was heading down to his ranch in the territories."

Nathan walked out, shaking his head. *Just how big a legacy had Nugget Nate left him to follow, and how he was supposed to fill those boots?*

Don't walk my path boy, he heard his grandfather say. *Find your own way and walk it.*

"I'm trying Nate. I'm trying."

Chapter Nineteen

Sheriff Cole looked up as Nathan entered the jail. He held up a coffee mug. Nathan nodded and Jack poured two cups. He walked to his desk and took a seat, sliding one cup across to Nathan. "Well, Nathan, how is Miss Grace doing this morning?"

Nathan took a sip and set the mug back on the desk. "She's all right. The Gunderson's have laid claim to her 'til she's mended. When I left there this morning she was sleeping. Doc says about two weeks before she can travel, though, so I guess you're stuck with me until then."

"Well, just make sure you keep that badge on where everyone can see it. Maybe it'll deter some of the gunhands from bracing you."

Nathan took a long draw on his mug, then faced Jack square on. "That's part of why I'm here, Jack. I came to ask your forgiveness for my conduct last night. It was neither Christian nor law-abiding. You'd trusted me to help uphold the laws of this community and I was ready to kill a man in cold blood."

Jack leaned back and kicked his boots up on the desk. "Not sure if there is anything to forgive, Nathan. From what I've pieced together you stood up for the laws of our community.

"As to what happened with Lefty, well let's just say all's well that ends well. However, since I know you mean it, your apology is accepted and forgiveness was given before you asked."

Nathan physically relaxed at those words, but only for a second. "Well then, I need to ask another favor of you."

"What's that?"

"Let me start with a question. What are you charging Lefty with?"

"Drunk and disorderly, resisting arrest, and attempted murder."

Nathan nodded. "Can I get you to drop the last one? After all, striking Grace was an accident and if I'd handled the situation differently they wouldn't have had a chance to throw lead."

"Nathan, if I don't charge him with attempted murder, then all I can do is hold him 'til he is sober, charge him a few dollars, and release him. There'll be no jail time."

"Jack, I understand, and I want to pay his fine myself and have a chance to speak to him before you release him."

Placing his feet back on the floor, Jack leaned forward and stared at his temporary deputy. "Preacher, what are you up to now?"

Nathan pushing his hat back on his head as he tried to look innocent. "I'm not up to anything, Jack. I realized that I'm as much to blame as Lefty is for last night's situations. I have made restitution to Mrs. Sue for the damages to the café already. I know God wants me to ask Lefty for forgiveness as well and show him that I'm truly repentant. I don't know of any better way to do so."

Sheriff Cole had been thumbing through wanted notices while Nathan talked. He put the notices back on his desk and shook his head. "I keep forgetting you're really a preacher until you go and say or do something like this, Nathan. Well, I don't see any wanted notices on Lefty so I'm willing to drop the attempted murder charge. The fines for the rest will come to around five dollars. If you want to pay them I can't stop ya. Are you sure about this?"

"Yeah, I'm sure. Can you keep him locked up 'til I get back? I have to go meet the train. My grandfather's lawyer is arriving to settle the estate. I need to get him settled in and make arrangements to finish my business with him."

Jack got up and walked back to the door leading to the cells. He opened the window and peered through at the prisoners.

Turning to Nathan, he nodded. "It looks like he is still sleeping off the effects of his liquid courage. I reckon he won't wake for a couple more hours."

"That should be all the time I need. I'll be back before then and pay his fines." Nathan stood and shook Jack's hand and headed for the door.

"Nathan, one more thing before you leave." Nathan turned toward the sheriff. Jack pointed at Nathan's chest. "Like I told you already, put your badge back on and leave it on 'til you're ready to leave my town. Maybe it will dissuade some of the owl hoots from gunplay against ya."

Nathan reached into his pocket, pulled out the tin star Jack had given him the day before, and attached it to his shirt. "From your lips to God's ears, boss."

Nathan left in a hurry, heading to the train depot. He was halfway down the block when he heard the first whistle, signaling that the train from the east was running on time. He picked up his pace, almost running. He didn't want Mister Smythe to be left standing on the platform looking for him.

Chapter Twenty

Nathan arrived at the train depot and stood waiting on the platform for Mister Smythe to disembark. He watched as the various railroad workers loaded and unloaded the various stock and baggage. He caught sight of two things that fought for his attention. The first was Lightning, his grandfather's mustang stallion. The second was a cedar chest that looked suspiciously like the one that had always sat at the end of Nate's bed.

Before Nathan could get close enough to determine if indeed the chest was Nate's, there was a whiney and yell as Lightning broke free. Rearing on his hindquarters and jerking the reins from the man trying to corral him into the stockyard, Lightning took off. The stallion thundered down the platform, headed straight for Nathan. Passengers and railroad workers alike dove to the side as the horse flew by. Nathan wondered if he should move as well, but he had seen Lightning do this with his grandfather before. He never did it with anyone but Nate. Maybe Lightning realized that Nate was gone.

The stallion slid to a stop right in front of Nathan and his head lightly bumped the man on the left shoulder. Nathan realized then his grandfather was truly gone. Wrapping his arm around the mustang's neck and burying his face in the stallion's mane, his sorrow broke over him for the first time since hearing Nate was dead. Nathan held on to his grandfather's steed and wept out his loss.

After what seemed like an eternity Nathan became aware of a hand gripping his shoulder. A voice from his past resonated behind him.

"I see you found Nate's horse."

Wiping the tears from his face, Nathan turned toward Mister Smythe. "So it'd seem; but I think it's more Nate's horse found me."

The two men shook hands just as the rail worker arrived to take control of Lightning.

"Sorry, Mister Smythe, I don't know what got into him. I'll get him corralled right away."

Nathan took hold of the lead rope. "Don't worry about it. Mister Smythe and I will take him over to the livery."

Smythe nodded to the worker and handed him a dollar. "For your trouble, my good man. This was the person I was delivering the horse and trunk to, so if you will just fetch that trunk we'll be on our way."

The railroad worker ran over to the baggage area and wrestled Nate's chest off to the side. Grabbing a two-wheel cart he wheeled the chest over to Mister Smythe. Nathan, anticipating the need to get the chest over to the hotel, pulled another dollar out of his pocket. "I'll add a dollar to what Mister Smythe has already given you if you'll deliver that chest to the Cattleman's Hotel and tell the bellhop it goes up to Mister Ryder's room."

"Be glad to do that for you, sir," came the reply, accompanied by an upturned palm.

Nathan, with a chuckle, placed the coin in the man's hand. The rail worker placed the coin in his pocket and hurried down the street toward the hotel. Nathan turned to Smythe, catching the lawyer giving him the once over.

"Well my boy, life in the West seems to agree with you, just like it did your grandfather."

"It's certainly been as adventurous as the tales Nate used to tell me, that's for sure." Nathan indicated the direction of the livery. "Do you need to get your baggage?"

Smythe indicated the large attaché case at his feet. "No, everything I need is right in here. Your grandfather's will and one change of clothes. If we can have a few hours today I would like to catch the eastern-bound train tomorrow afternoon."

As they talked about the plans for the day they headed over to the livery stable. Lightning followed along behind them, occasionally head-butting Nathan. Each time the horse did so, Nathan chuckled, remembering Nate pretending to get angry at the mustang when he would do that.

After getting Lightning into a stall, Nathan arranged with Henry to get his growing string of horses taken care of for two more weeks. Then Nathan and Mister Smythe headed to the hotel.

Entering the hotel, James caught Nathan's attention. "Mister Ryder, how is Miss Grace doing today? No one here has seen her since last night's unfortunate incident."

"She is resting well, James. The Gundersons are taking care of her for the time being. So if you would have Mark move her stuff over to their place I'd appreciate it."

"Certainly sir. I'll get it taken care of right away. Will there be anything else, sir?"

"Actually, James, there are two more things I could use your help with. Have Miss Hopewell's room linens changed, as Mister Smythe here will be staying the night. Also, if you have a room that we can use for a few hours to take care of some pressing private business, I'll make it well worth your trouble."

"Oh, Nathan, it's no trouble at all. We do have an accounting office that may be suitable for your business. Follow me." James came around the end of the counter and headed down the hall between the saloon and the hotel. He showed them a small office with a desk and three chairs.

"It is a bit small, but I think, if it is just the two of you, it should fit your needs."

Mister Smythe looked it over. "It will do just fine, James, and please allow us to pay you for its use, as this is official estate business. Will five dollars suffice?"

"Oh that's more than sufficient, sir."

Smythe placed five dollars in the hotel manager's hand. "I'll need a receipt for that, and if you have a few minutes later, I could use you as an official witness to some legal documents of transfer."

"Just let me know when you need me. Can I get you gentlemen something to drink before you begin?"

Nathan nodded. "Could you send someone over to Mrs. Sue's for some of her sweet tea for us?"

James smiled. "Of course, Preacher. I'll run over and get a pitcher myself."

Nathan and Mister Smythe entered the office as James hurried down the hall toward the café. Mister Smythe took one of the seats in front of the desk and turned it slightly toward the other. Nathan followed suit and the two settled in. Mister Smythe reached into his breast pocket and pulled out an envelope. "Before we get started on reading your grandfather's will, your mother asked me to give you this letter. She said to tell you she apologized for the shortness of her telegram, but your father insisted on keeping it short and inexpensive."

Nathan accepted the envelope and opened it. "Do you mind if I read this before we get started?"

"No, that's fine. That way when we get started we'll be able to get our business concluded."

Nathan pulled the sheet of his mother's stationary out of the envelope. Her neat handwriting brought a twinge of homesickness to his heart.

My Dearest Son,

I am so sorry about the way you had to learn of your grandfather's passing. As I said in my telegram he contracted influenza the day after you left to visit your friend in Chicago. His plan had been to catch the train, meet you there and ride to Franklin with you. Instead he just got worse and worse. I think he knew the last couple of days that he wasn't going to make it. He called Mister Smythe and made some last minute changes to his will. They were all about you.

He also seemed concerned about the daughter of an old friend of his from his travels. Kept talking about having Nathan take care of little Grace, whoever that is. If you run into a young lady who is named Grace and looking for your grandfather please honor his wish and look after her.

Your Father said to tell you; 'if you have come to your senses and want to return home' he still has that position at the Dorchester Cathedral open for you. He said to inform you that 'with Nate gone this foolishness can end. You have no reason to continue to carry out this ridiculous dream the two of you cooked up'. He says 'let the less educated carry the gospel to the unwashed heathens in that God forsaken wilderness.'

Personally, I say that you should do exactly what you feel God has called you to do, regardless of both your father and grandfather's influence. Come home if you feel called to, or continue west, just so long as you are obeying your Heavenly Father.

Know that I am proud of the man of God you have become. However, if you continue west, keep your eye open for a suitable wife. I may not be able to see and hold them but I still want to know that I have grandchildren to carry on the Ryder name.

If you have time, please let me and your father know your decision. If you are coming back I want to get your room ready. If you are continuing on I want to know how to pray for you. Write as often as you can.

Oh, one final thing. Your sister Elizabeth and her husband are expecting their first child in about six months. I know you will find out what your grandfather did for her, so know they will be well set. I will try and send letters to you if I don't see you soon.

Your loving Mother.

Nathan folded the letter, put it back into the envelope, and slid it into his pocket. "I'll have to compose an answer for her before you leave tomorrow. Will you see that she gets it for me?"

"Of course, Nathan. I will be honored as I was to carry her letter to you."

"Thank you, Mister Smythe. I know you were my grandfather's lawyer, but you have also been a good friend to him and my family. For that I thank you."

"No thanks are necessary, young man. Nate probably never told you how I came to be his lawyer, did he?"

Nathan could see the tears just behind the attorney's eyelids threatening to fall. "No, sir, he didn't. I always assumed he found you through some of his business contacts."

Smythe laughed. "Hardly, young man. I had just finished college and thought I would hang my shingle down by the wharf and do legal work for the shipping companies. Instead, I wasn't getting any clients and about to go under.

"I actually was considering going to work as a sailor when a young lady walked in and hired me to do a simple divorce settlement for her. She had proof that her husband, the captain of a cargo ship, had been cheating on her.

"I drew up the papers and presented them to the court, which granted her request. To save myself some money I decided to deliver the papers to her husband myself when his ship arrived in port.

"I got up the next morning and went down to the harbor. As soon as the gangplank was lowered I demanded to see the captain. I was ushered into the captain's mess, where the captain was having breakfast with his only passenger, your grandfather.

"Little did I know that the scraggly man in buckskins and wearing an old beat up coonskin cap was the wealthy owner of the entire cargo of that ship. I just took him for an old mountain man who had booked passage on the cheapest vessel he could find.

"I walked up to the captain and officially handed him the divorce papers. He looked them over, then asked me where he could find this Jefferson Smythe, attorney at law. I informed him I was Jefferson Smythe, and suddenly I was looking down the barrel of an old cap-and-ball pistol.

"That seaman marched me up on deck and called out to his first mate to bring him some rope and a ballast rock. I found myself tied hand and foot to the rock and about to be cast off into the harbor.

"Just as the captain and first mate were about to host me overboard I heard this voice come from behind me. It said, 'Captain, I ain't got much use fer attorneys myself, but if'n you think I'm gonna let you pollute my harbor with one, you got another think a-comin'. Now put that young feller down and cut him lose; or I ain't gonna pay you one red cent for this-here cargo.'

"The captain ranted and raved, but your grandfather never backed down. Finally, after what seemed like forever to me, they cut me lose and your grandfather escorted me off the ship himself.

"When we got to the dock your grandfather said to me; 'Son you is either the bravest lawyer I have ever met, or the stupidest. But either way, ya gave me a good laugh today. Plus, the situation helped me get a better price on the cargo. So, I reckon I owe ya.' He handed me a card with an address on it, and told me to meet him there that afternoon.

"When I got there he showed me his books and asked me to become his lawyer. We became fast friends and I, as much as any man, will miss the old scallywag. Even if he did yank my chain about my name every chance he got."

Nathan laughed as he saw in his mind's eye his grandfather doing just what the old lawyer had said he did.

"Mother said that he made some last-minute additions to his will just for me. Can you tell me about them?"

"I can do better than that, Nathan." Smythe reached into his pocket again and pulled out another envelope. "I'll let your grandfather tell you about them. He gave me this envelope the day before he died and informed me of what it said. He knew he wasn't going to make it, but said God had showed him some things you would need to have and to know about. This letter will explain better than I could."

Nathan took the letter with trembling hands. As he tore it open, Mister Smythe stood. "I'll leave you alone to read this and have his chest sent in, since the letter pertains mostly to what is in it. Read the letter and go through the chest. I'll wait in the lobby 'til you're ready to conclude our business." Placing a hand on Nathan's shoulder for a minute, Jefferson Smythe exited the room and shut the door.

A few minutes later James and Mark carried in the chest. They set it in between the two chairs facing Nathan and quietly exited as well.

Nathan pulled out the pages of his grandfather's last words to him. Taking a shaky breath, he unfolded the letter and started to read.

Nathan,

If you're reading this, then you know I've entered the eternal roundup. I ain't sorry to be going, as I've lived a full and interesting life. To be honest, I ain't as spry as I once was and I miss your grandmother a heap. So I figure God done decided I was finished here on this shadow world.

There are two things I regret. One is not getting the chance to see what God is gonna do in you out west. The other is not having the time to make things right with your pa. I sent a letter to him telling him the same thing, so maybe it'll be enough. I pray so.

Boy, I don't know why, but God has laid it on my heart to send ya some things. I told that no account fancy pants lawyer to make sure you get my chest and Lightning. I know you got a fine horse in that palomino   of yers, but Lightning is a cowboy horse and belongs out west. All I ask is that you exercise him and take him back to the Dueling Ns Ranch. Find 'im a cowboy or use him yerself but don't let him go to waste. He was a fine horse and a finer friend.

Everything else God laid on my heart to send ya fit in my chest, so use it as you can to further his plan fer ya. Oh, and I don't understand it, but I felt like I was supposed to include my ol' Bible.

I know yer Father gave you that fancy preacher's Bible at yer ordination, so use mine for what ever God lays on yer heart.

Also, this is a big request, but I sent the only living child of one of my ol' mountaineer buddies to Franklin to await us arriving. Her name is Grace Hopewell. I got her the position of schoolteacher in Redemption. Please find her and explain my situation to her. I need you to see to it she gets to the Territory safely. I would count it a personal favor to me iffen you would.

Finally, son, remember that God has placed a call on yer life. I feel impressed that by now you realize it ain't exactly what you thought it would be. However, I want to encourage you to use all the gifts and talents He gave you. The ones you inherited from yer father, in preaching the Word and the ones ya learned from me, about justice and mercy. Stay true to your calling and heritage, son, and you can't go wrong.

Oh, and when you get to the Dueling N's you tell that rascal Cookie to fix me one last plate of beans, and iffen he burns em, I'll come back through those pearly gates and haunt his fat butt.

Till we meet again, keep yer powder dry and yer sixgun loaded.

Nate.

Nathan opened the chest and there, right on top, laid lay the old, well worn Bible. It was the most precious gift Nate left him, because it had been his grandmother's before it was Nate's. Nathan swiped at the tears rolling down his face. He realized that before he had even met Bart, God was replacing the Bible he had given up with one that was even more precious to him.

Under that was Lightning's saddle and bridle. Of course, that was just like Nate. He wouldn't give Nathan his horse without giving him the tools to use it. Next was Nate's rawhide gut line. Finally, across the bottom of the chest, was every weapon Nate had carried when he was out west. His six-gun and rig, the bowie knife given to him, if you believed Nate, by Jim Bowie himself. Finally, a small metal hatchet, the very one, if the tale was to be believed, which saved Davey Crockett's life and won Nate his nomenclature of *Nugget Nate*.

Nathan carefully packed everything back in the chest and placed the letter in the front of the Bible. He placed the Bible on top and went to flip the lid closed, when out of the top dropped Nate's old coonskin cap. Nathan had no idea why Nate had included it, but was sure there was a reason, so he placed it lovingly in the chest and shut the lid. Then he exited the office to get James and Mark to carry it back up to his room and find Mister Smythe.

Chapter Twenty-One

Mr. Smythe, after returning to the accounting office with Nathan, got straight down to business. "Now that the personal things are out of the way, we need to take care of your grandfather's estate as laid out in his will."

"You mean that Lightning and his chest weren't the part of his estate you came to discuss with me?"

"Certainly not! Nathan, the delivery of those two items was a personal request from my friend and client. They had nothing to do with my legal reason for needing to see you."

Nathan looked at Mr. Smythe with confusion written all over his face. "I don't understand. Nate knew I was heading west to preach. What more could his will have to do with me?"

"How about you just let me read the will? I believe it answers all your questions."

"I am sorry. Certainly."

Mr. Smythe smiled at Nathan and cleared his throat.

"In the name of our Lord and Savior Jesus Christ, Amen. I, David Nathaniel Ryder, Sr., known as Nugget Nate Ryder of New York County, New York, being in perfect health, body and mind, yet knowing that it is appointed unto man once to die. I make and ordain this last will and testament in the following manner.

First, to my son, David Nathaniel Ryder Jr. I leave all the holdings that were originally his mother's, including her share of the stocks in all my business ventures. I further leave to him the house and grounds that he has been living in. It is my hope that these items will once and for all show him how precious he is to me.

Second, to my granddaughter, Elizabeth Margret Bryne, I leave all my New York business, including Ryder Shipping Company and docks, the Ryder First Bank of New York and my shares in the New York railroad. I also leave to her my New York residence and all the grounds that belong to it. May they provide a happy place to raise your family.

Finally, to my grandson, David Nathaniel Ryder the Third, I leave all my holdings and stocks outside of New York, including the Dueling Ns Ranch, Ryder Mining, the Bank of Redemption, and various other stocks, the details of which will be in the hands of Smythe and Jones, Attorneys at Law.

Signed, Nathaniel David Ryder, Sr.

Witnessed this 16th Day of June 1886 by Randolph J Smythe, Attorney at Law.

Nathan sat in stunned silence for a minute. "Are you telling me that everything my grandfather owned outside of New York is now mine?"

"That is exactly what I am telling you. We need to sign some papers, transferring deeds and stocks to you. However, after that is done, you will be worth close to four million dollars."

Nathan's mouth dropped open in shock "Four million dollars! What in the world am I going to do with four million dollars?"

Smythe laughed. "I imagine anything you want. I know that was your grandfather's plan. When he made this will last year I asked him why he would leave the majority of his estate to you. His answer was that if you had this kind of freedom he prayed you would follow whatever plan God had for you without fear of how it would be paid for."

"But four million dollars?"

"Nathan, I don't think you understand, as of yesterday you were worth four million dollars. Your holdings will continue to grow."

"You mean I'm gonna make more money without even trying?"

"Your grandfather hasn't taken on a new investment since the war, Nathan. Yet his net worth increased by several hundred thousand a year, every year, since then. Yours will be a little less because you won't have the New York accounts. However, just the ranch and mining operations bring in a couple hundred thousand every year. So, yes, your money will likely continue to increase."

"What if I refuse to accept this generous gift my grandfather left me?"

Randolph Smythe looked shocked. "I don't think you understand, Nathan. This isn't a gift. This is what your Grandfather made legal before he died. If you don't except the money, stocks, bank, mine and ranch they are still yours. If you don't do anything with them, then they will just sit, and go unsupervised. Your Grandfather's legacy will eventually fall apart and disappear. Are you going to sit there and tell me you want that to happen?"

Nathan lowered his head into his hands. "No, I don't want that to happen. What do you need me to do?"

Smythe began to lay out stock certificates, land deeds, and mining claims. Then he stepped out into the hall and called for James to join them if.

James entered the room and Smythe asked Nathan to sign each of the papers in front of him, acknowledging his receipt of the transfer. After each signature, Smythe signed them and asked James to sign them as witness to the transfers.

Smythe then pulled out copies of each paper already in Nathan's name and handed them to Nathan. "Congratulations, Mister Ryder, you just became one of the richest men in the west. I'm sure you just became the richest preacher in all of these United States and the territories. You want to hang on to those papers. They prove your ownership. Lastly, here's a letter for the manager of the Bank of Redemption explaining that you are now authorized to handle all of your grandfather's business accounts."

Nathan looked at the ever- growing stack of documents in front of him. "Mr. Smythe, how am I supposed to oversee all these businesses and do what God has called me to do also?"

"Well if you will allow, we have always overseen these things for your grandfather so that he could concentrate on whatever he wanted to do. Seeing as how you plan to live out west here, why don't I send one of our younger associates to handle things as your business manager? His job would be to oversee your business and liaise between you and us as needed."

Nathan was flabbergasted. "Do you have an associate who would be willing to move out to the territories?"

Smythe smiled. "Actually, I believe I have just the young man for you. My son has been talking about moving west for years. I think you remember Justin?"

Now it was Nathan's turn to smile. Justin had traveled west a few times with him and Nate when the boys were younger. They had learned to shoot and ride together. "Of course, I just didn't know he worked for you."

"Not for me, with me. He made junior partner last year. However, he keeps talking about leaving the firm and heading west. Maybe this will be a happy medium for him. He'll still be part of the firm but handling our largest account while out west in the territories."

Nathan chuckled, remembering the summer they had tried to outdo each other on every task Nate had given them. "Well, if you think he'll accept the arrangement, then it's acceptable with me. Tell him I said I can still out shoot, out ride, and out rope him. If he doesn't believe it, he can come find out for himself."

Reuniting with his old friend might be just the thing to take his mind off how his calling had gotten sidetracked by this reputation he was developing. Justin wouldn't care about the Preacher, just about his friend, Nathan.

Randolph nodded. "Well, if you will excuse me, I believe our business is concluded. I'll go and wire my son with your job offer. If he's as accepting as I think he'll be, I'll suggest he catch the next train west, so as to not hold up your party."

Nathan shook hands with the man who had always been his grandfather's lawyer, and now, as Nathan knew, had also been his friend. "Tell Justin to take his time and get prepared, like Nate taught us. Anything he needs equipment wise, have him pick up at my expense. We'll be here at least two more weeks while I put together a wagon train to head to the New Mexico Territory. Come see me before you leave in the morning, so I can see you to the depot."

With those words the two men parted ways. Smythe went to contact his office; Nathan to go finish doing what God had convicted him to do that morning.

Chapter Twenty-two

Nathan stood in the hotel office looking at the stack of paperwork in his hands. He still couldn't fathom the idea that these papers made him one of the richest men in America. He knew Nate had been rich, but not this rich. *How does one cope with having more money than you could ever use?* He guessed that would be something for him and Justin to sit down and talk about.

One thing was right that he had heard. With that kind of money he could do anything God told him to do, without worrying about how to pay for it.

Just as he was getting ready to head out of the office and up to his room, he heard the faint sounds of gunfire drift in through the open window. As he turned to head for the door, it burst open as James came barreling through. "Preacher, there's trouble up at the jail. They say the last of Kid Cody's gang has come to get him out. The sheriff, Black Bart and Mr. Gunderson are pinned down inside."

Nathan thrust his paperwork at the hotel manager. "Put these in the hotel safe for me 'til I get back."

He grabbed his hat of the back of the chair and ran out of the office. Instead of exiting the hotel he ran up to his room and grabbed both his Winchester and Sharps.

Just as he was about to leave, Nate's chest grabbed his attention. He threw open the lid, and grabbed Nate's hatchet and Bowie knife, and slid them into place. The knife went into the back waistband of his pants. The hatchet he slipped under his belt, on the left hand side. He rushed out of the hotel and down the street, ready to do battle for the lives of his friends. In that moment his thought was: *"The more some things change, the more others stay the same."*

Nathan caught sight of a shadowy figure heading his way from between two buildings. Without hesitation, he dropped the Sharps, levered a round into the Winchester, dropped to one knee and took aim, all in the same motion. Just as he was about to squeeze the trigger, both arms on the figure went straight up in the air. "Don't shoot, Preacher." The young doctor from the night before emerged from the shadow, looking quite pale.

"Doctor, you just about got yourself shot. What were you thinking?"

"I was thinking that I owed you for risking your life for mine last night and it was time to pay up."

Nathan was irritated as he listened to the continuing gunfire coming from down by the jail. "Doc, no offense, but you aren't carrying and I doubt you could shoot your way out of a gunny sack, let alone do well in a firefight."

"You're right, I am not carrying a pistol. I don't know how to use one, but during the war I had plenty of experience with that Sharps you dropped in the dirt."

Nathan tossed the Sharps to the northerner, reached in his pocket, and pulled out half a box of paper shells. "Here you go, doc. I really could use the help. You just slip into the alley on this side, and climb up on the roof of the dress shop. From there, shoot anything that's pointing a gun and doesn't have a tin badge on its chest. Oh, and don't shoot to wound. Shoot just like you were back in the war."

The young man nodded and headed in that direction. Nathan got up and continued toward the jail at a slower more cautious speed. As he got within shooting distance he moved to the boardwalk and crouched lower to make himself less of a target. Kneeling behind a horse trough, he took stock of the situation.

There appeared to be about ten men on the ground spread out across from the jail, plus a few more on the roof. Nathan left his Winchester behind the trough and snuck around the side of the building to where he could see the back of the jail. Sure enough, there were a few more attempting to raise a ladder and get on the roof.

Just as he drew a bead on them with his Colt there was a boom from behind him. One of the men fell to the ground. The doctor had arrived, and was as good a shot as he had claimed. Nathan fired, taking down two more as the young northerner reloaded. The doctor took down the last one. Without breaking stride he reloaded again, headed for the back of the dress shop, and up the ladder he went. Nathan slithered back around front, took up his Winchester, and began to help thin out the numbers across the street.

As he and the doctor took out outlaw after outlaw, the return fire from inside the jail became more even and purposeful. Nathan knew the men in there were aware they were receiving help and were gaining hope of surviving the confrontation with every second. Then as the last gang member fell, Bart ran out the door, yelling for someone to get the doctor and hurry.

The young doctor dropped onto the porch roof of the dress shop and then into the street. "I don't have my med kit with me but I may be able to help while they fetch Doctor Simms."

"It's the sheriff, doc. He took one in the leg and I can't seem to get the bleeding to stop."

The young man quickly entered the door, leaving Nathan's Sharps on the ground at his feet. Nathan laid the Winchester beside it and went to check on the fallen outlaw gang. He collected guns while checking to see if any men were still alive. He watched as one lone gunman slipped up behind Bart and drew a bead on him.

Nathan's right hand Colt flew from its holster. He pulled the trigger and the hammer fell, landing on an empty cylinder. He had forgotten to reload before walking out into the street. He dropped it as his hand flew to Nate's hatchet. Just like Nate had taught him, he let it hurl. End over end it spun. Whizzing past Bart's shoulder, the hatchet buried itself in the chest of the gunman.

Bart spun as he heard the *thunk* of the hatchet hitting flesh. He watched the outlaw drop where he stood. All color drained from his face as he realized just how close to death he had come.

Here was still another debt he owed the Preacher. How would he ever repay the man he had been so set on killing just the day before?

Bart retrieved Nathan's hatchet and walked over to his friend. "Thank you Nathan. I would have hated you having to tell my wife she had become a widow one day before our reunion. To be honest, this gun-slinger reputation is gonna be an issue for me now. I wish there was a way I could start over with a clean slate."

Nathan felt the gentle nudge of the Holy Spirit. "Now it's interesting that you would say that, Bart. I may have a solution for you. How about we get a bite to eat after all this is cleaned up and talk about it some?"

The two deputies went inside the jail to check on their boss. They found him lying flat on the ground with his leg propped up on his desk chair. The young doctor held a piece of shirt to both sides of the wound while Abner tightened his belt around the leg.

The doctor looked up at them. "He's gonna be ok as far as I can tell. The bullet missed anything vital and just went clean through. When Doctor Simms gets here he should be able to sew up both sides and it'll heal nicely. However, the sheriff is gonna have to stay off of his feet for a while."

Sheriff Cole looked at Nathan. "I heard you were stuck here for a couple of weeks. I may need you to take over until I can get someone from the county sheriff's office in to watch over things."

Nathan nodded. "That's fine, as long as I can keep the two deputies on 'til then. I do need to put together a wagon train in that time."

"Sure. Keep them both. They've proven themselves extremely capable."

About that time the seamstress from the dress shop came in followed by the young doctor's wife. The wife had her husband's doctor bag in her hands.

"Doctor Simms is out on a delivery call. Miss Shinn saw me and thought you might need your bag to patch up the wounded."

The young doctor nodded, went over to the stove, and poured some hot water over his hands. "Mr. Gunderson, if you will slide the front of your belt off the wound I'll start to stitch it up." Out of his bag he pulled a spool of gut and a needle in a small jar of whiskey. He threaded the needle and sewed up the wound from the inside out. He repeated the process on the backside, and put a clean dressing around the wound.

"Gentlemen, if someone would see the sheriff home in a wagon or buggy, I'd appreciate it. I'll administer a shot of morphine to ease his pain. Tell his wife to give him a small spoonful of laudanum every four hours but nothing more. I'll give him a two day supply and check on him, or have Doctor Simms check on him before then."

Abner went next door to arrange a buggy. As soon as he was gone the doctor turned to Nathan.

"Mr. Ryder, did I hear that you were putting together a wagon train to leave in a few weeks?"

"Yes, doctor, I have to get myself and Miss Hopewell to the New Mexico territory. We both have positions waiting on us there. Why?"

"It seems that being involved in a shootout at the local café is reason enough for the wagonmaster to ask us to not travel with the current wagon train. I just thought, if you were open to it, maybe my wife and I could travel with your train."

"I don't see why not. We're planning to leave in two weeks. Can you be ready to go by then?"

The doctor looked at his wife, who was smiling through her tears. She then looked at Nathan. "Mr. Ryder, you're an answer to our prayers. Not only can we be ready, but we will provide any medical services needed along the way."

"Then I guess that settles it. We'll leave from the staging area two weeks from Monday."

Chapter Twenty-three

As the doctor and Abner got Jack into the buggy for the ride home, Jack removed the star from his shirt and handed it to Nathan. "I'll expect that back before you leave. Take good care of my town. Oh, and the prison cart will be here on Monday to take the Kid and his two friends to the capitol to stand trial."

Nathan realized, unless he put a stop to it, the drugged up sheriff would keep talking 'til the medicine wore off. "Jack, I got this. you go home and let Mrs. Cole take care of you. I think you're gonna want to make that trip *on* the morphine instead of after it wears off."

Abner took hold of the reins. "I let Wilhelmina know where I'd be. She is gonna try and find someone to take care of Miss Grace so we can keep the store open."

The doctor's wife stepped forward. "Is Miss Grace the lady caught in the shootout last night?"

"Yes, ma'am"

"I could sit with her for a while. I've been trained as a nurse and have sat with several of Luke's patients."

"Ma'am, I am sure my Wilhelmina would be glad for your help. We run the dry goods store. We live above it. If she isn't down in the store, she will be up in the apartment with Miss Grace. Just let her know that I sent you, and who you are. Thank you, young lady. You're a God sent answer to prayer."

The doctor's wife smiled. "You're the second man to ever tell me that Mr. Gunderson. I married the first one."

The doctor laughed and placed an arm around his wife. "I just realized we've never properly introduced ourselves. It seems every time I meet someone new in this town it's in the middle of a crisis. I'm Luke Sonaman and this is my beautiful bride and nurse, Kate."

Nathan, Bart, Abner and Jack shook the man's hand. Abner looked at Jack, then back at the men and woman standing beside the buggy. "I'd better get our good sheriff home while he's still medicated. I'll be back soon, and I'll send a telegram to the county sheriff." He snapped the reins and away they went.

Nathan and Bart headed back into the sheriff's office. As they were leaving, Nathan turned and stopped Kate. "Mrs. Sonaman, please let me know how much you normally get paid to sit with a patient. I'll take care of your payment, as well as anything else Grace needs.

Kate looked at the young preacher and recognized the tone in his voice and look on his face; it was one of total soul consuming love. "Oh, Preacher, you've got it bad. I'd never think of charging you. After all, my normal payment is a kiss and foot rub, but that comes from the only man I work for." She took her husband's arm and allowed him to lead the way to the dry goods store.

Nathan looked at Bart. "Now what do you think she meant by that?"

Bart laughed. "Well, I think you're wearing your heart on your sleeve for Miss Grace. As to the second part, I think she was telling you that you can't afford to pay her what the good doctor does." Bart laughed even harder as Nathan's face got red with understanding. "You crack me up Preacher, that's for sure."

Nathan, still kind of overwhelmed by everything that had happened during the day, didn't even hear his friend's last sentence. His mind was torn between what he needed to do about Lefty, and his own new status in life. One he could do something about right now. The other, he decided he would just wait, do some thinking, and pray about it later that night.

"Bart, I have a few things I have to take care of here before I can meet you for lunch. How about I meet you at the café in an hour?"

"You sure you don't need me to hang around? I figure you're planning to release Lefty and have that talk with him you mentioned at breakfast."

Nathan sighed. "You're right, I am gonna have that talk, and then release him. However, it's something I need to do alone. Plus, one of us needs to be out walking the streets. We need to reassure the town folks things are okay. They need to see law and order are still operating, even though Jack got wounded."

Bart polished up the deputy badge on his chest. "Sure is strange to be wearing one of these things again. Reckon I can remember how to patrol a city. See ya at the café in an hour."

Bart left the jail with a swagger in his step Nathan had never seen him use before. It wasn't the fearless walk of a gunslinger, but the walk of a man confident in his place in the world. *I sure hope Bart figures out that he is called to uphold the law like I'm called to preach the Gospel. Well, enough of that, time to finish getting right with others so I will be right with God.*

Nathan took the keys to the cells and entered the jail section of the sheriff's office.

"Well, lookie here, boys. It's that eastern dandy who tricks real gunslingers into jail."

The men in the cell with Cody laughed like it was the funniest thing they had ever heard. Nathan stopped and smiled at Kid Cody. "Lookie here, it's the big bad gun slinging bandit who has to force women to accompany him for a drink."

Kid Cody cursed the Preacher. "If you hadn't pistol whipped me when I was drunk we'd see who was the better gunslinger, ya fraud."

"Kid, you seem to forget that I outdrew you with your own gun. Drunk or not, the outcome would be the same. Now, if you want to talk about making things right with God before the prison wagon comes, I'll stay and talk with you. If not, then I pray God will send someone you will listen to."

Again the Kid cursed; this time both the Preacher and his God. "I ain't had no need for him before now and I ain't got no need for him now either. Why don't you be a real man, let me out, and face me in the street?"

Nathan just shook his head and unlocked the cell Lefty was in. "Come on, Lefty, we need to settle your fines, and I need to talk to you someplace where we won't be interrupted."

As Lefty headed out of the cell block he and Nathan heard the Kid railing once more. "Be careful, Lefty. That Preacher's gonna try ta save your soul and put you on the straight and narrow. Don't fall for it. You got great promise as a gunfighter."

Nathan shut the door to the cell block behind them and walked over to the desk, indicating that Lefty should take a seat. "I'm going to give it to you straight, Lefty. I talked the sheriff into only charging you with drunk and disorderly, plus resisting arrest. He wanted to charge you with attempted murder as well."

Shock registered on the face of the young outlaw. "Why would you stand up for me, Preacher? Last night you wanted to kill me for shooting your girl? That don't make no sense."

"You were right, Lefty. Last night I was headed away from the path God had set me on. This morning God showed me that Grace's injury was as much my fault as yours. I should have handled the whole situation differently.

"I want you to know that I paid your fine to the city and you are free to leave at anytime. Also, I need you to know I'm sorry for trying to force you into a fight last night. Once you surrendered I should've dropped things and arrested you. I'm asking you to forgive me for my actions."

The look on the gunfighter's face was beyond shock. "You're asking me for forgiveness? I don't understand. Why would you do that?"

Nathan leaned forward in the chair, "Because I was wrong. I pushed you and almost shot you in cold blood anyway. The Bible tells me that God wants me to act justly, but to also love mercy. By arresting you for harassing the doctor and his wife I was acting justly, but I forgot the mercy part when I tried to force you into a fight. How can I expect God to have mercy on me if I don't have mercy on you?"

Lefty sat staring for a few minutes at this man before him. "You think you owe me an apology even though I shot your woman? Even though I pushed 'til you had no choice but to arrest me, because you went too far and tried to force a gunfight on me?

"Preacher, I don't understand you, but I'll tell ya I forgive ya. To be honest, I kinda wish I'd took you up on the draw last night. Would have found out if I was as good as the Kid keeps telling me I am."

Nathan shook his head, opened the bottom desk drawer and pulled out Lefty's gun rig. "Lefty, take it from me. You aren't cut out to be a gun hand. The Kid doesn't care about you. He is just trying to build up his gang.

I know you haven't been riding with him long because there aren't any warrants out for you yet. Why don't you give it up and go back to whatever you were doing before you joined Kid Cody?'

As Nathan had been talking Lefty had stood and put his guns back on, tying them down low like a gun slinger. "Preacher, I know you mean well, but I ain't gonna go back to farming. I wanted adventure and gun slinging is that. I may not be the best yet, but I will be. Count on it."

Nathan shook his head. "Lefty, do me a favor. Take out your fastest gun and remove your bullets."

"What? Why?"

Nathan pulled his right hand gun and started unloading it. "Just do it."

When both men had their guns unloaded, Nathan said, "Now holster it. You want to know if you have what it takes to be a gunhand? Then draw your empty gun on me. See if you can beat me to the draw. After all, I've only been in the west a few days, and I'm just a preacher. If you can outdraw me then you might make it, but if not, I want you to consider something else."

"Fine, Preacher, you want me to draw empty on ya? Let's do it, and you'll see I can be a gunslinger." Lefty's hand headed toward his pistol. Before he touched iron he was looking down the barrel of Nathan's empty Colt. He jumped when the hammer fell on the empty chamber, making a snap.

Nathan dropped his Colt Peacemaker back into his holster. "Lefty, don't try and make your living by your gun. If you don't want to farm, try something else. If you want adventure, cowboy and learn to break broncs, but don't follow the path of the gun-hand. You'll be dead in no time."

Nathan handed him his bullets and replaced the ones in the Colt. "Your fines are paid and you're free to go. Think about what I said, and if you want to learn to cowboy come see me. I may be able to help ya with that. It seems I own a ranch now."

Without a word, the young western man loaded his six gun, turned, and walked to the door. Once there he stopped and looked back at the man who could have killed him twice now and didn't.

Lefty didn't know what he was gonna do but he decided right then he was going to make something of himself. Something that would make the Preacher proud of the fact that he had spared Lefty's life. Then he exited to figure out just what he was going to do.

Chapter Twenty-four

Nathan entered the café and scanned the room before finding Bart sitting in the back corner with his back against a wall. There was an empty chair in the other part of the corner so Nathan wouldn't have to have his back exposed either. Nathan strode over, flopped down in the chair, and poured himself a cup of coffee from the pot that was already at the table.

"So, Bart, I don't know about you but this has been a most peculiar day for me so far."

"Well it ain't been boring, that's for sure, Nathan." The smile that cracked the deputy's face didn't last long before worry of his situation settled back over him. "I still don't know how to face tomorrow, though."

Nathan sat staring at his friend for a moment. Just as he was about to offer what was buzzing around in his head Mrs. Sue walked up to the pair. "Well boys, you sure keep things active around here, don'tcha? Word is that Jack got shot this morning. Looking at your chest, Preacher, it must be true. I don't remember the last time that man gave his badge to someone, even temporarily. How bad is it?"

Nathan could see the worry for her friend and the town in the lines on the dear southerner's face. "Mrs. Sue, there's nothing to worry about. It was a clean shot, through and through. That young doctor patched him up and told him to keep off the leg for a couple of weeks. So, Bart and I promised to keep an eye on things 'til Jack was well enough to take back over."

"Well, good. You two boys have certainly livened things up here in Franklin. Now, I bet you both got a huge hunger going. We got a special treat today. Somehow that man of mine got his hands on a mess of crawdads and made a good, hearty, Louisiana gumbo. Let me get ya both a bowl full."

With those words the old southern bell was on the go again. From across the café patrons could hear her bellowing. "Hank, fix two big ol' bowls of your crawdad special," as she sliced several thick hunks of fresh bread, which she slathered with butter and arranged on a plate.

Bart snorted with humor before turning back to Nathan. "Well, Preacher, you said you might have an idea how I could leave my reputation behind and make a new life with my Maryanne. I'm mighty interested in hearing your thoughts."

Nathan took a few sips of his coffee as he tried to organize his half baked idea into a real plan. "Bart, seems to me that your biggest problem is that your name and look instantly make you recognizable for every two bit gunslinger wanna be here in Missouri."

"We both know how true that statement is, Preacher. What are you getting at here?"

"In scripture there are several tales of men who had their names changed after coming to follow the Lord. There is Simon, whom Jesus himself called Peter. Not only did his name change but so did his livelihood. Then there is the Apostle Paul, who before coming to salvation was a killer called Saul. So what if Black Bart became someone else?"

"Interesting idea, but I don't think just changing my name will help."

Before Nathan could say anything Mrs. Sue plopped a platter on the table with six slices of buttered bread and a large bowl filled with an aromatic stew and two smaller empty bowls on it. "Here's ya'll's gumbo, boys. Eat up now."

As she turned to go she looked straight at Bart. "Bart, you is about as thick as a side of beef, ain't ya? All them men the Preacher been telling you about did more than just change their names. They changed everything. Their looks, their careers, everything. 'Bout the only thing you changed is yer a riding on the side of law and order. You still dress like Black Bart, you still tote them two irons like Black Bart. Shoot you still *is* Black Bart. You just think on that a minute."

With those words she was off again in a whirl of skirts and apron to oversee feeding more of Franklin's town people.

Nathan ladled the thick red stew into his bowl and grabbed a hunk of bread. "Sue hit the nail right on the head, Bart. It'll take more than a name change. You'll have to change your whole life: your look, your attitude, everything."

"I guess I can see that, but even a clean shave and a change of clothes ain't gonna be enough to keep me from being challenged by every fast gun looking to make a name off my reputation."

"No, but maybe a change of name and look, going down to carrying one gun in a cowboy rig instead of a gunslingers rig would be a start. Then when Jack is back, come with me to the territory. Seems I now own several different businesses. Maybe one of them could use a man of your talents. I know we could use your help on our little wagon train. It would be a new start for you and your wife."

"That's an interesting idea. Let me think about it, and talk to Maryanne tomorrow. Speaking of which, will you come with me to the train station in the morning? I find that when it comes to facing a feller with a gun I'm fearless, but the thought of having to face that gal alone tomorrow scares me to death."

Nathan let out a big laugh. "I'd be honored to stand beside you, my friend. So let's think about a new name for Black Bart. What is your middle name, Bart?"

"Bartholomew is my middle name. I was named after my grandpa, so to keep confusion down I was called by my middle name. My first name is Levi."

"Well, why don't we just start calling you Levi then, and get you some new duds. Something not all black?"

"Good idea."

Levi shoveled gumbo in his mouth. "But not 'til after we finish off this chow. This is the best stuff I've ever put in my mouth."

Nathan, his own mouth stuffed with bread and gumbo, just nodded as the two tucked in with gusto to the treat Hank and Sue had placed before them.

****

Later that night as Nathan prepared to turn in, his thoughts returned to the astronomical changes in his life since morning. The words of his grandfather's lawyer ran through his head again. "Your grandfather felt this would allow you to follow God's calling without having to worry about how to pay for it."

That was true; he could do anything God wanted him to do now. He could help anyone and everyone God laid on his heart. He wouldn't have to worry about money for anything. "Lord, thank you for a grandfather who thought of how I could be of use to your kingdom with this blessing he left. Help me to be a wise steward of this great gift given into my care. Let me know how you want me to use it to further your kingdom. In Jesus' name, Amen."

The prayer still echoing in his head, Nathan slipped into a deep and peaceful sleep; the most peaceful he had since arriving in the west.

Chapter Twenty-five

The sun breaking through the window woke Nathan the next morning. As his feet hit the ground the reality of the day sank in again. He was one of the richest men in the west, thanks to Nate. *God, let me live up to his legacy with the same honor and compassion Nate had.*

After getting dressed and pinning the sheriff's badge to his shirt, Nathan headed over to the jail. He needed to make sure his prisoners got breakfast and were ready for the trip on the prison wagon that afternoon. As he arrived at the jail he saw Mrs. Sue entering with five plates of food. "'Morning, Preacher. I got breakfast for you and Bart, as well as them good fer nutin' skunks in the back. I reckon yer gonna be mighty happy to see them gone this afternoon."

With a smile like the dawn, Nathan nodded at her. "A good morning to you as well, Mrs. Sue. I am sure Levi and I will enjoy your fine breakfast. I agree the prison wagon can't get here soon enough for me. Hopefully, after the Kid is gone things will quite down around here again."

Nathan helped Mrs. Sue unload her tray onto the sheriff's desk. "Levi, is it? Well, I think that's a good new name for our deputy. I hope I get a chance to get to know this 'new man' and his wife before y'all head for the territories."

A sleepy, clean cut Bart came around the corner just then. "Mrs. Sue, I guarantee you'll get to meet my Maryanne this very day. I plan to show her off the moment she arrives."

"Well, Levi, you are not a bad lookin' catch yer-self. Them new duds and clean cut looks make you just like a cool drink on a dry summer day."

Mrs. Sue carried three plates to the jail cells with a loud, "Wake up boys, here's your vittles. Better eat 'em before they get cold. Ain't met a feller yet who liked cold grits."

From the cells Nathan and Levi heard the Kid's grumbling reply. "Grits, woman? Every day I tell you I hate grits. Why do you keep bringing them?"

"Oh, fiddle-dee! Everyone likes grits. You're just being ornery for orneriness' sake. You'll be wishing you got fed this good when you get to the capital city. I guarantee, ain't no good southern cooking in that there prison you're a headed to."

"Good then I won't have to choke down this sand you call food."

"Kid, you're gonna be wishing for that sand be-fore too long. Don't figure they's gonna waste a lot of food on some no account murdering outlaws whose necks they's gonna stretch. You just think about that as you is eating them fine vittles my Hank done fixed ya."

Nathan looked at Levi and both men tucked into breakfast to keep from laughing out loud. Mrs. Sue came out of the cell and looked at the two digging in. "Well, at least you two is grateful for what God gives ya."

"Yes, ma'am," was all the reply she got.

"Levi, you bring that woman of yours over to the café for lunch. I'm a lookin' forward to meeting her. Ya hear?"

"Yes, ma'am." Was again the only reply she got.

"All right, then, bring them dishes over when everyone is finished. I gotta go see to my real customers this morning." With a swish of skirts she was out the door and headed down the street.

"Well, Nathan, you never did tell me how your business with your granddad's lawyer went yesterday."

Nathan looked at his friend, "Let's just say I was seriously shocked."

"Why is that?"

"Levi, in less time than it takes me to tell you about it I went from a poor western preacher to one of the richest men in the country."

"What? Are you telling me Old Nugget Nate was more than just a legend of the West?"

"According to my lawyer, just the part of his estate he left me is worth four million dollars and climbing."

Levi sat staring at his young friend. "Did I hear ya right, Preacher?"

"Yep, four million. On top of which I own several mines, a bank, and a 160,000 acre ranch in the territories. I am not sure what all else, but Smythe is sending me a business manager to help me figure out what to do with it all."

"Did you have any idea Nate was worth that much?"

"No. I mean, I knew he was well off, but I never knew he was *that* well off. I couldn't spend all that money even if I tried. The four million is just his holdings outside of New York. He left all his New York holdings to my sister. I figure both of us are financially set forever."

"Guess you weren't kidding when you said you had some ideas on what I could do for work out in the territories, were ya?"

"Nope, I figure no matter what you want to do, I ought to be able to help ya get started for sure. Want to cowboy? You and Maryanne can stay at the Dueling Ns and cowboy for me. If you want to try your hand at banking, I can put you to work there. Want to try mining? Got that covered too. Anything else, I am sure we can work out some kind of arrangement to help get ya started."

"Well, let me spend the day getting reacquainted, and see what the wife wants to do. Cowboying I know, or law enforcement, but to be honest, I really want to live by my sweat and labor, not my gun. I've had enough of living by the gun to last me a lifetime."

"Well, I am sure the foreman at the Dueling Ns could always use another good hand. I got to go pick up Mister Smythe. I'll meet ya over at the train depot in about half an hour. Don't forget to get the dishes and return them all over to Mrs. Sue."

"Yeah, wouldn't want her to get upset with us, that's for sure. Hey are we gonna talk Bible later?"

"Yeah, let's do that at lunch today."

"Sounds good. I gotta couple of questions for ya about what I was reading this morning."

"All right, sounds good. See ya at the depot in a few minutes." Nathan grabbed his hat and started back to the hotel.

Chapter Twenty-six

As Nathan drew near to the hotel he saw Smythe surrounded by five cowpunchers who seemed to be giving the lawyer a hard time. Nathan heaved a deep sigh and slipped the hammer thong off his Peacemaker. Just once he wished he could get through a day without having to kill someone.

Smythe saw him over the head of one of the cowboys and relief flooded his face. "Nathaniel, thank goodness you're here. I was just explaining to these gentlemen how I needed to get to the depot to catch my train. Seems they think I owe them some kind of easterner tax?"

The cowhand not facing him laughed, and without turning, mocked Smythe's eastern speak. "Yes, Nathaniel, it is good you got here when you did. Now we can collect from both of ya and save ourselves some time."

His partners were trying to get his attention and quiet him up.

"Let me get this straight," Nathan responded. "It's the job of you gentlemen to collect this Eastern tax? That's funny. I've been here for almost a week now and this is the first I've heard of it."

The first guy spun around. "Well, see that's not…." His voice trailed off as he saw the tin star on Nathan's chest.

"Why don't you boys just walk away and we'll call this a misunderstanding."

The spokesman squared himself and set his jaw. "Look here, Sheriff; there are five of us, and only you with a gun standing here. Even if you was the Preacher hisself, you couldn't take us all."

One of his companions leaned forward and whispered, "Chester, that is the Preacher hisself. I saw him take out four guys night before last. Let's just go."

Chester's face went white.

"Chester, is it? You're right; I might not be able to outdraw all of you. I make you this promise, though. I will start with you. Even if I take lead, you won't live to see it. Take your buddy's suggestion and just walk away."

"Can't do it, Preacher. Done made the challenge, so it has to follow through to its conclusion. I can't back down."

Nathan shook his head. "Boys, I'm gonna tell ya again, just walk away. No one has to die over this misunderstanding."

Chester's partners turned, one by one, and walked away, until only Chester and his buddy were left. The friend was again pulling on his partner's arm. "Come on, Chester, let it go. Ain't no need for us to die here, or him either."

Chester shrugged off the hand. "Clem, you can leave iffen you want, but I can't back down. Not now, not ever."

Nathan turned to Clem. "Walk away, Clem. Your partner's got his mind made up."

"Wish I could, Preacher, but he's stood by me more than once. Code says I can't forsake him now. So I guess it's a good day to die."

"Ain't no day a good day to die, boys. Last time. Walk away. Let it go. I don't want to shoot either of you."

Chester and Clem moved toward the street, facing the Preacher. Chester got himself set. "Too late, Preacher. We can't back down and you won't pay, so this is the only option. Fill your hand."

In a flash all three men reached for pistols. Before Chester or Clem even touched metal there were two reports and both men hit the ground with bullet holes in their gun arm shoulders. Nathan walked over to each of them and removed their guns from their holsters. "Get yourselves over to the doctor and have him patch you up. Then you come find me at the jail. Remember, fellas, I could have killed ya both but didn't. Don't make me come find you today."

Nathan turned back to Mister Smythe, who was looking at the younger man with wonder on his face. "Nathaniel, not even your grandfather was that fast with a gun. How in the world do you move like that?"

"Honestly, Mister Smythe, I don't have an answer for you. I just draw and shoot like Nate taught me. Let's get you to the train, shall we?"

The two men strolled toward the train depot. Nathan saw Randolph Smythe to his car. "My son will be here in about a week. Let us know if there is anything you need from the firm before then. Oh, I almost forgot." Smythe took out a letter and gave it to Nathan. "This is a letter of credit for the bank here in town. They have been authorized to advance you up to fifty thousand dollars should you need it before you leave town."

Nathan took that, and in return handed Smythe a letter to give to his mother. He was letting her know he had decided to continue west and fulfill the call God had laid on his heart. After a final goodbye Nathan turned to find Levi and stand with him as he faced the love of his life for the first time in five years.

As he headed toward Levi, a family that was disembarking the train caught his attention. They were dressed in a style that bespoke eastern upper crust society. The man was in a full three-piece suit complete with top hat and white gloves. He held a gentleman's gold-tipped cane in his left hand. Directly behind him stood a raven-haired woman in a blue silk dress and hat. A string of pearls was around her neck, and a matching bracelet and hat pin adorned her. She held a lace handkerchief over her mouth and nose.

"Reginald, why have you brought us to this place? It smells and there is no refinement at all."

"I told you there is opportunity out west. You must get used to this new life. The children will follow your lead. Besides, we can help bring refinement to the place we settle."

The gentleman looked around. "Now where are those good for nothing servants? They should have found us by now."

Nathan tore his gaze away from the easterner and his wife. He had to focus on finding his friend before Levi caught up with his wife. He saw him standing just a few feet away searching the people getting off the train. Nathan walked up to him and placed his hand on his shoulder. Levi looked at him. "I'm as nervous as a cat on a tin roof, Nathan. What if she doesn't like the man I've become?"

"Levi, she just traveled two days by train nonstop to be with you again. I don't think you have anything to worry about."

"I hope you're right. There she is. Maryanne! Maryanne!"

Levi waved at a petite blond-haired, blue-eyed woman in a floral print dress. She was just stepping off the last car of the train. She looked toward the commotion and her eyes locked with those of Levi. She raced down the boardwalk and threw herself straight into Levi's arms. "Oh, my darling, thank God you're safe and sound." Their lips met and Nathan knew he had been completely forgotten.

As their kisses continued, Nathan's eyes turned to the small boy walking up to the couple and tugging on the woman's skirt. "Mama? Do you want me to go get our bags?"

Levi took a step back and looked at the youngster standing beside his wife. "Bartholomew, let me introduce you to your son, Levi. Levi, this is your father, whom I've told you so much about."

The young blond boy with dark eyes stuck out his hand toward the shocked cowboy. "Hello."

Levi looked from his wife to the boy and back several times trying to understand the situation. "I have a son?"

"Yes, Bartholomew, that was what I was trying to tell you the night you left with your brother. You have a son, Levi Bartholomew Cody Jr. He's almost five years old."

Levi dropped down to the boy's level, took his hand, and shook it. "A son! Well, young Levi, it's a pleasure to meet you"

Levi stood, turned to Nathan, and let out the loudest cowboy whoop anyone had ever heard. "Nathan, I'm a father. WHAAHOOO!"

He swooped the boy up in one arm and wrapped the other around his wife. He headed straight for the luggage area to claim their bags. Nathan stood to the side, thanking God for his love, forgiveness, and the power of his reconciliation.

Chapter Twenty-seven

Nathan entered the sheriff's office with a light heart. What a joy it had been to watch as his friend was reconciled with the family he thought he had lost forever; to learn that not only did his wife still loved him, but that he had a son who was anxious to meet him as well. Nathan took a moment to say a quick prayer for the newly-reconnected family.

He had just an hour or so to try one last time to share the gospel with Levi's brother Kevin before he was transferred to the prison wagon. From there he would be taken to trial for the numerous crimes he had committed throughout Missouri. Nathan grabbed his Bible from the desk. He said a quick prayer for wisdom and guidance as he headed into the cells.

"Well, if it ain't the eastern dandy. You may have all these people fooled but I know the truth. You ain't western and you ain't no gunhand.

"I never claimed to be, Kevin. All I've ever claimed to be is a pastor and a gentleman."

"DON'T CALL ME THAT. MY NAME IS KID CODY. KEVIN WAS A LOSER WHO DIED BACK EAST."

"Ok, Kid, take it easy. I didn't mean to upset you. I was just trying to connect with you as a person. Why would you say you aren't the person your parents named?"

"Listen, when Bart and I came west, I left Kevin dead in the east. He was a loser who couldn't control himself or his money. Kid Cody is always in control and always a winner, right up 'til you tricked me into this cell over a good fer nothing whore."

"Kid, the lady you accosted is a school teacher. You're mistaken."

"I ain't mistaken, Preacher, and you're a fool if you believe what she told you."

"Ain't just her. I'm believing my grandfather, Nugget Nate. He sent me a letter asking me to look after her. She is a school teacher, nothing more nothing less."

"Reckon she fooled you all then, but you'll learn one day. Then you'll remember that Kid Cody told ya straight."

"Kid, I didn't come back here to fight over the past with you. I wanted to talk to you about your future."

"You mean you want to talk about how they're gonna hang me and it's your fault?"

Nathan shook his head. "No, I was thinking more about how you could turn you life around with the help of God. Yes, you'd still have to pay for the crimes you've committed, but at least your soul would escape eternal punishment."

The Kid threw his head back and laughed. "Preacher, you are one funny fella. I ain't had no need for God before now and I ain't gonna go running to him now. You can just take your sermon over to the church tomorrow where it belongs."

"Kid, this isn't a sermon. It's genuine concern for you. Your brother's my friend, and I want to help you see how God could change you. He wants to give you real meaning in your life, just like he did Bart."

"My brother's weak. It's just like him to run to God for comfort. No thanks. Now leave me alone."

Nathan stood looking at the outlaw with anguish in his heart. Here stood a man who knew he was going to die soon and yet refused to even listen to how to have peace and eternal life.

The Kid looked back at Nathan with a look of hatred. "Don't count me as dead yet, Preacher. I promise you, I ain't gonna die at the end of a rope."

"Kid, the prison wagon will be here in less than an hour. You and your buddies will be dead by this time next week."

"Just watch, Preacher. You and me, we got unfinished business. I won't die 'til our account is settled. So until you hear I'm dead and buried you better keep one eye on the lookout for me."

Nathan turned. He walked back through the front and out into the street, leaving the prisoner screaming threats and curses behind him. He sat down on the bench in front of the sheriff's office to await the prison transport. No sooner had he gotten settled than two cowpokes with their gun arms in slings walked up in front of Nathan and stopped.

"Okay, Preacher, we did what you said. We went and had the doctor treat us, and now here we are."

"Well if it isn't the town's eastern tax collectors." Nathan stood, trying to hide the smile on his face. "Come on in and let's get this over with."

Both cowboys sauntered into the sheriff's office with heads hung low. Nathan followed them and sat himself behind the desk. He waved his hand at the two chairs on the opposite side. "Have a seat, fellas."

As the two sank into the chairs, Chester tried to appeal to Nathan. "I know you have to arrest us, Preacher, but I was hoping you would let Clem go. After all he was just backing my play according to the code."

"Well, Chester, the truth is Clem drew on an officer of the law. That makes him just as guilty as you. I appreciate that you're willing to own up to the blame in this situation, but, truth of the matter is, you both broke the law."

Nathan looked from one to the other and then reached into the bottom desk drawer. "Here's what's gonna happen."

He pulled out both men's guns and set them on the desk. "You're gonna take your guns and horses, go find your other buddies, and ride out of town. If I see y'all back here I'll throw your sorry butts in the hoosegow. Got it?"

Both men grabbed their weapons and holstered them. They turned without a word and cleared out of the jail as if the devil himself was chasing them. A few minutes later Nathan heard the sound of several horses heading down the street. He walked outside just in time to see Clem, Chester, and their pals heading out of town in a cloud of dust.

No sooner had the cowboys cleared town than the prison wagon pulled into town. Nathan watched as the wagon slowed to a stop in front of the jail. The guard riding shotgun saw Nathan and his eyes stopped on the sheriff's badge on Nathan's chest.

He stood and pointed his rifle at Nathan. Eyes filled with suspicion and determination, the man gave Nathan the once over. "Who are you, and where is Jack Cole?"

Nathan, careful not to startle the man, took a step closer and held out his hand. "My name's Nathan Ryder, and Sheriff Cole took a bullet to the leg. He asked me to fill in for a few weeks."

Not relaxing a bit, the guard kept his rifle trained on Nathan. "We didn't get any notification of that."

Nathan was getting a bit irritated. "Well, I know for a fact that a wire was sent out notifying the prison of the situation. I don't take kindly to having my word questioned, or having a gun pointed at me either. Why don't you have someone go check at the telegraph office across the street there?"

The guard nodded to the driver, who slipped down from the seat, walked around the back of the wagon, and headed for the telegraph office. In just a few minutes he came back carrying two telegrams. "The man's telling ya the truth, Jed. I got a copy of the original telegram sent to the prison and one for us from the warden telling us of the situation."

Jed lowered the rifle, hopped down from the seat, and extended his hand to Nathan. "Sorry 'bout that. Just don't like surprises when I'm picking up outlaws as famous as your prisoners."

"No problem. I reckon that's understandable." Nathan shook the man's hand, then turned toward the jail. "I figure you're ready to take these fellas off of our hands. I have to admit, it's been a might touchy 'round here since they was jailed."

Jed reached into a box on the side of the wagon and pulled out several sets of shackles. "Yep. Sooner we get 'em in the wagon, the sooner we can get 'em to their date with the hangman."

Nathan led them into the jail and back to the cell where Kid Cody and his partners were locked up. "On your feet, boys, and stand back against the wall. These fellas are here to take you to the capitol for your trial." The driver stood to the left of the door and trained his shotgun on the outlaws.

Nathan unlocked the cell and moved out of the way to the right. Jed entered the cell, spun Cody around and slapped the shackles on his wrists. "Kid Cody, as I live and breathe."

Taking a step back, he punched the prisoner right in the kidney, dropping Cody to his knees. "You probably don't remember me, Kid, but you shot my younger brother in the back when you were robbing the Capital City Bank. Iffen I had my way you'd be strung up right now."

Nathan moved to stop the guard from striking the prisoner again, only to find himself facing the driver's shotgun. "Just stand still, youngster. He ain't gonna hurt him too bad, and it would be a shame for you to get shot over a no good skunk like this."

Nathan moved to the right, grabbed the barrel of the shotgun, and shoved it up. At the same time he drew his Colt and pointed it at the driver. Then, before the guard could strike the prisoner again, Nathan's other hand drew his left hand gun and fired a warning shot into the ceiling. "That's enough, Jed. You aren't gonna beat this man in my jail, even if he did kill your brother. Your job is to take him to the prison for trial, and to stand for justice. If you want vengeance, then do it somewhere else."

Jed stared at Nathan with hatred in his eyes. "Look here, he deserves worse than what I'm gonna give him. Why would you side with this outlaw anyway?"

Nathan shook his head. "I'm not siding with him, but I won't stand for anyone taking the law into their own hands and neither would Sheriff Cole. You two get these men in the wagon and get on your way. And don't think about beating them on the way. Soon as you leave I'll be wiring the warden, telling him what condition the prisoners were in when they left my care."

Jed swore at Nathan and pulled Cody to his feet. He and the driver escorted the prisoners out to the wagon and placed them inside, locking their shackles to the side of the wagon. Jed locked the wagon and climbed up in the seat beside the driver. He took one last look at Nathan. "Well, Mister Ryder, don't think I'll forget this. You'd better hope our paths never cross when you ain't wearing that badge."

With a nudge from the driver, they took off, leaving Franklin in a cloud of dust. Nathan slowly holstered his weapons. He took one last look at the wagon disappearing into the horizon, then walked across the street to send a telegram to the prison warden about what just happened.

Chapter Twenty-eight

After sending his telegram, Nathan headed towards the café to meet up with Cody and his family. Before he got there, Mark came running down the sidewalk straight to Nathan. "Preacher, Mister James asked me to find you. He needs your help over at the hotel. There's some rich guy over there making trouble."

"Okay, let's go help Mister James with his trouble- making rich guy."

Nathan wondered what kind of trouble a "rich guy" could cause. He had a bit of an idea as they got closer to the open door of the hotel. Nathan stopped and listened to shouting coming out the door. "I DON'T CARE IF THE ROOMS ARE ALREADY GIVEN TO ANOTHER PATRON. I AM REGINALD PRESTON RICHMOND. WHEN I WANT SOMETHING I GET IT. MY WIFE WANTS THE ENTIRE FLOOR, SO JUST MOVE THE OTHER GENTLEMAN. NOW!"

Nathan heard James answer as calmly as he could, but the tension of the situation was obvious in his voice. "Sir, as I have told you already, I do not have a whole floor to give you. I can give you the last four rooms on the top floor. If you want two more rooms on a lower floor, which is the best I can do. I cannot force the guest who has those two rooms to move. If you want, I can ask him if he will move. However, if he insists on retaining the rooms he has paid, for then there is nothing I can do."

"THAT IS UNACCEPTABLE!! I DEMAND TO SPEAK TO THE MANAGER OF THIS ESTABLISHMENT."

Nathan had heard enough. As he entered the door, he saw the family from the train station, still in their immaculate eastern travel clothes. James was standing behind the counter, facing the family as well as the door. It was obvious he saw Nathan enter. He pulled himself more upright. "Mister Richmond, you are speaking to the manager, and I'm telling you what the policy of the Cattleman's Hotel is; I can only let out rooms that are unoccupied. That is the final word on this matter."

Turning toward Nathan, James smiled, completely ignoring the easterners. "Sheriff, what can I do for you today?"

The easterner's face went almost purple with rage. "NOW SEE HERE, I REFUSE TO BE IGNORED THIS WAY SO THAT YOU CAN TALK TO SOMEONE WHO CAME IN AFTER MY FAMILY."

Nathan turned to the man. He hooked his hands in his gunbelt just above his weapons. "Mister, I don't know who you are, but it was your bellowing that drew me in here. I suggest you calm yourself down and act like the civilized man you're dressed up as."

Before Mister Richmond could recover from the shock of being spoken to like a irrelevant child, his wife rounded on him. "Reginald, don't let this man speak to you like that. Tell him who you are and demand the respect owed to you."

His lips tight against his teeth, Mister Richmond snarled at his wife. "Priscilla, now is not the time for your help. Take the children and find us a suitable restaurant for dinner. I will catch up with you as soon as I take care of this little misunderstanding."

Mrs. Richmond looked like she was going to explode. Instead, she turned to her children. "Preston, Lucinda, let us go find someplace to eat. I doubt there will be a suitable restaurant in this town, but I did see a café across the street. We will leave your father to teach these uncouth savages a lesson or two."

The lady and her two children exited the hotel. Nathan could follow their progress across the street just by listening to the litany of disgust about the town coming out of Mrs. Richmond's mouth.

Richmond turned and set his sights on Nathan. "Sheriff, I am Reginald Preston Richmond, president of the Virginia Railroad and a member of the founding family of Richmond, Virginia. No one, and I mean absolutely *no one,* talks to me the way you just did."

Turning his attention back to James, Mister Richmond continued. "Now, I will tell you again, find a way to give me the entire top floor or there will be repercussions for refusing me. If not, then I will be forced to see the owner and have you terminated from your position here!"

Nathan knew lots of wealthy and important men back in New York, but he had never seen one act like the Richmond family. James looked at him like he had never seen anyone act like this either.

"Mister Richmond, I don't know what else I can say to make you understand. All I have available is four rooms on the top floor and two on the second floor. Hotel policy will not allow me to move a guest just to accommodate another guest."

Richmond's anger was evident on his face so before he got a chance to start bellowing again Nathan addressed him. "Mister Richmond, I suggest that you keep your voice to a moderate level or I will be forced to arrest you for disturbing the peace. James here has told you what he can do more than once now. If you persist I, personally, will show you the door. Is that understood?"

Richmond, head turning to look at one man then the other, took a deep breath, "Fine, gentlemen, since I can't seem to get through to you, point me in the direction of the owner of this sorry excuse for a hotel. I am sure he will be more reasonable."

James pointed towards the saloon. "The owner is usually in the saloon at this time of day. However, I'm sure he'll tell you the same thing I just did."

Richmond smiled as he headed for the saloon. Over his shoulder he said, "I don't think so. You see, I intend to purchase this place from him, and fire you."

He pushed through the doors of the saloon. Nathan looked at James. "Who does own the hotel, James?"

James smiled at Nathan. "Joseph Cattleman. You might know him as Joe the bartender."

Nathan laughed and said, "I'll be right back."

Nathan entered to find Mister Richmond addressing Joe. "When you see the owner of the hotel will you tell him I am over in the café and wish to have words with him?" Without giving Joe the time to respond, he stormed out the front door into the street.

Nathan walked up to Joe. "Why didn't you tell him you were the owner, Joe?"

"Well, Preacher, I was going to, but I overheard what he said to James as he came in here. Decided I'd let him simmer down a bit first."

"Will you sell him the hotel?"

"Depends on how much he offers me. Why?"

"How much would it take to get you to sell?"

"Honestly, Preacher wouldn't be that much. Since my wife died, I just wish I could leave Franklin and start somewhere with no painful reminders of her."

"I can understand that, but how much money would it take for you to move elsewhere?"

"That's the problem. A person would have to buy the whole thing hotel and saloon. Then they'd have to find someone to run the saloon."

Nathan smiled. "I understand. How much?"

"Preacher, ya just curious, or is this a serious question?"

"Let me put it this way. If I offered you twenty thousand dollars would that be enough to get you to sell?"

"Now why would you be doing that? I mean what kinda preacher owns a saloon?"

"Oh, I'll sell the saloon, but I figure if I buy it now, James won't get fired for refusing to give that snob and his family my rooms."

"Well Preacher, yer a mighty interesting fella. Reckon you just bought yerself a hotel and saloon."

"Okay, you get me the deed and I'll go to the bank and get you your money."

Nathan turned and walked back into the hotel. He walked right up to Mark and motioned for him to follow him to the counter. Nathan smiled at the two men. "Well gentlemen, I just bought the hotel. Mark, do you think you could take over as desk clerk for James here?"

"Yes sir, I reckon I could do that. Why?"

"I need to talk to James for a minute, and then I'll answer all your questions."

Turning to James, Nathan indicated for him to follow. They set off down the hall to the office. Once there, Nathan indicated for James to take a seat. "Here's the deal, James. I am not staying in Franklin, but I wasn't about to let that blow hard have his way. So I have a few questions and a proposal for you."

A few minutes later James returned to the front desk and informed Mark he had been promoted to desk clerk and would be paid what James used to make. When Mark asked where James would be, he smiled even bigger. "Mark, I'll be right next door, running my saloon."

"What do you mean, your saloon?"

"The Preacher just bought the whole place, and sold me the saloon for ten dollars."

Nathan left the hotel and walked over to the bank. Upon meeting with the manager they arranged for twenty thousand dollars to be transferred from his New York bank to Franklin and then turned over to Joseph Cattleman. Afterwards he headed to the café to inform Mister Richmond that arrangements had been made for his family.

Chapter Twenty-nine

Nathan entered the café and instantly found the Richmonds. If he hadn't seen them he could have found them by the whining coming from Priscilla Richmond. "First, you bring us out to this godforsaken place. Then, as if that wasn't bad enough, you embarrass yourself and our family by not being able to handle one simple bumpkin and get us the rooms we need. Now I have to eat this slop that they call food. Mother was right. I should have married your brother."

"Priscilla, I told you the bumpkin will be dealt with as soon as I find the owner and purchase that dump from him. As to this food, it seems to me the cook is a good southerner. Even our cook couldn't make dumpling's this good. Now sit there, be silent, and let me enjoy my meal, or so help me woman, I'll cut off your line of credit and leave you without a penny to spend."

"Some threat that is, Reginald. There is no place out here I would even consider a reputable place to shop."

Turning to her son, Mrs. Richmond laid into him. "Preston, you must stop this eating like a ruffian. A gentleman takes his time and chews his food. If you don't stop shoveling this swill like you haven't eaten in a month, I'll have no choice but to have it taken away."

The boy looked up at his mother, then over at his father, who nodded at him. After that, he slowed his pace, but only a little. Nathan noticed the only one who didn't seem fazed by the outburst at all was the daughter.

She was taking dainty bites and sneaking glances all around her with wide eyed enthusiasm. Nathan recognized the signs of someone set on having an adventure. He had been the same way the first time Nate had brought him west. He figured she must be around twelve or thirteen, same as he had been. Well she was gonna get her wish, thanks to the plan Nathan and James had cooked up for her family.

Nathan approached the table. "Ah, Mister Richmond, here you are. I just wanted to let you know I spoke to the owner of the hotel about you. I'm sure you'll be glad to hear that James will no longer be manning the front desk. He has been replaced. Also, I believe a floor of rooms has been reserved for your family at the discounted price of two hundred dollars for a week."

Reginald stood and took Nathan's hand. "Thank you, Sheriff. Perhaps I have misjudged you. As soon as my family is finished eating I will go and settle with the hotel. I knew once the owner knew who we were he would understand that we are above such trivial things like policy. Those are for the masses, not society's upper crust."

"I don't know about that sir, but I do know that the owner wanted to make sure you were aware he personally arranged your rooms. If I can be of any help during your stay, please don't hesitate to come to the jail and let me know."

Priscilla had to jump in at that point. "There is one other thing, constable."

Nathan turned to her. "It's Sheriff, ma'am. What may I do for you?"

"You can apologize to my husband for treating him like a common traveler earlier. It is the least you should do. After all, we aren't like these people you normally have to deal with." She indicated with a backward wave of her hand everyone else in the café. Out of the corner of his eye he could see Mrs. Sue was about to come and lay into her. Nathan indicated it was *ok* with a slight shake of his head and Sue held her tongue. Nathan could actually see her biting it to keep from speaking.

"You are right, Madame. You and your husband are nothing like the people I normally have to deal with. I hope my actions have been apology enough. If not then I will say I am sorry for having dealt with you all."

"Thank you. It is big of you to admit it." Sue's smile got wider as she realized Nathan had not apologized but subtley insulted the uppity woman.

Nathan smiled at the Richmond family. "Well, let me finally say, welcome to Franklin. I hope your stay here is enlightening. Now, if you'll excuse me, there is someone else I need to speak with. Good day, folks, and I hope you enjoy your rooms."

Nathan turned and walked to the back of the restaurant, where he saw the Cody family was seated. He was tickled to see the look of love and enjoyment on all three faces. He realized that of all the people in the café, these three only had eyes for each other. Arriving at the table Nathan smiled down at them. "Howdy, Cody family. Mind if I join ya for a spell?"

Maryanne Cody beamed up at him. "Not at all, Sheriff. Please do."

"It's just Nathan, ma'am. I'm not really the sheriff; just filling in for a while 'til the real sheriff recovers from a work related wound."

Bart, looking at Maryanne, didn't seem to be able to take his eyes off of her. "This is the man I have been telling you about, darlin'. He's the one who's responsible for bringing us back together."

"Oh, then I owe you a very big thank you, Nathan. You don't know how often I've asked God to reconcile my family to each other. You're an answer to all those prayers."

Nathan blushed slightly. "Shucks, ma'am, I was just doing what I felt God wanted me to do. It really wasn't that big a deal."

Maryanne settled her gaze on Nathan. "My husband seemed to think different. He told me how you could have handled the situation. He even told me he isn't sure but what you would have won. Instead, you listened to the voice of the Holy Spirit. I personally think that is a very big deal. From what I understand of the west, that is a very unusual quality."

"Maybe so, ma'am, but I honestly just did what I thought was right. I know you folks are just getting reacquainted, but I need to speak to you in private for a minute. If you're done could we possible move across the street to the hotel?"

Levi looked at him. "Problem?"

"No, just something I don't want to discuss publicly yet. I will explain all in private."

"Sure. Let me just go pay Sue and we'll be right over."

"Okay, just ask Mark to show you where I am." Nathan stood and, with a quick wave to Sue, headed back to his new acquisition.

Chapter Thirty

Nathan walked into the hotel, to be greeted by Mark's enthusiastic "Evening, boss!"

Nathan hurried over to the counter. "Mark, let's try and keep the fact that I own the hotel quiet for now, please."

"Sure thing, Preacher. Anything you say. I just want to thank you for giving me the chance to move up."

"You're very welcome, but if you should thank anyone, it is James. He vouched for you. He told me that you filled in for him on occasion and were quite capable of running this place. That's why I'm giving you this shot. Now are you clear on what to do with the Richmonds?"

"Yes sir. I'm to tell them that the owner personally had a floor cleared out for them. Then after they pay me I give them the keys to the rooms that are over the saloon."

"Exactly, but escort them to the back stairs. Has their baggage been moved into the rooms yet?"

"Yes, James took it up personally. He said it was the least he could do for them."

Nathan couldn't help but laugh. "Okay. I need you to give me the key to Miss Grace's old room, and the one on the other side of it. When Bart and his family come in will you send them to the accounting office?"

Handing Nathan the keys, he asked, "What am I supposed to do if they ask to speak to the owner again?"

"Just tell them the truth. You aren't sure where he is at the moment."

"But you just said you'd be in the office."

"No I didn't. I said to send the Codys to the office. I never actually said I'd be in the office."

Mark thought about it for a minute, and then smiled. "You didn't, did you? So as far as I know you could be anywhere."

"Now you're catching on. Have a fun evening."

"You, too."

Nathan let himself into the accounting office and reflected on everything that had happened to him in the last few days. Less than a week ago he was heading west to meet his grandfather and ride to his new career.

Since then he had learned his grandfather had passed away, met the woman who was the love of his life, gained a reputation for being quick with a gun, made friends with a famous gunslinger, and helped reconcile the man to his family. If that wasn't enough, he had saved several lives and been asked to act as temporary lawman for another new friend. He had also become one of the richest men in America, and bought a hotel.

If someone had told him a month ago that this was the direction God was going to take his life, Nathan wouldn't have believed it. Yet, here he was, right in the middle of an adventure God had orchestrated for him. He was pretty sure it was just getting started, too. "God, I don't know your plan, but I've put my trust in you. I know you have something special in store for me. I accept your plan and will follow wherever you lead me. Show me how you want me to use these gifts you've given me. In Jesus name, Amen."

Just as Nathan finished praying, there was a knock on the door. "Come in."

The door opened and Levi ushered his wife and son in. "Alright, Nathan, what's going on? Where is James, and what in the world are you doing in the office of the hotel?"

"That's part of what I wanted to talk to you about, Levi. I bought the Cattleman Hotel today."

"Why in the world would you do that? Last I heard you were set on going to the Territory and becoming a circuit rider."

"I still am, but it was the only thing I could think of to keep that rich easterner from buying it and firing James for not giving the entitled blowhard my rooms. I beat him to the punch and bought it myself."

"Then where is James?"

"To buy the hotel, I had to buy the saloon too. Didn't think it was right for a pastor to own a saloon, so I sold it to James for ten dollars. I believe he's running his new business."

"You did all this to keep that eastern dandy from bullying his way into taking your rooms? Nathan, you are a marvel to behold, for certain."

"Listen, I'd rather that no one knows I own the hotel 'til after I've dealt with this Richmond family situation. However, I had to let you know because I have something for your family."

Nathan handed Maryanne the two keys. "These are the keys to a couple of the rooms on the top floor. I don't know where Levi's been staying before you got here, but I want you to take these rooms as a gift of friendship."

Maryanne, with tears in her eyes, looked at Nathan. "We'll accept under one condition. Bartholomew told me you are preaching at the local church tomorrow. We would like for you to marry us again. We want this to be a fresh start for our family and we want to do it with unbroken vows."

Nathan looked at Levi, who nodded his head. "Certainly. I'd be most honored to help you with that. Does this mean you're going to take me up on my offer to come to the territory with me?"

Levi nodded again. "We've talked about it. Once we arrive in Redemption, I am going to put up my guns for good. So, if you were serious about that job on the ranch, I'll take it."

Nathan reached out and shook his friend's hand. "Great. I'm glad you are gonna come along. We'll talk more about the job along the way. I was serious about the offer, and will make sure we get something for you. Now all we have to do is find another wagon and get you outfitted. Since you work for me now, on Monday I want you to go see Hank over at the livery and see what he can find for you. Tell him I'll come see him about the cost when he lets us know he found something. Now, get out of here and get the boy to bed. He looks like he is falling asleep on his feet."

The Cody family left and headed up the stairs to their rooms. As they exited the room Nathan could hear Mister Richmond bellowing at Mark. "What do you mean; you don't know exactly where he is? What kind of an owner is not around his own business?"

Nathan walked up beside Reginald. "Mister Richmond, why is it that every time I run in to you in this hotel, you are disturbing the peace?"

"Sheriff, do you know where the owner of this sorry excuse for a hotel is? I think it's about time I had a few words with him."

"As a matter of fact, I do know where he is. Is something the matter with the rooms he arranged for you?"

"That is between him and me. If you would be so kind as to show me where he is and make the introductions, I would appreciate it."

Nathan had to turn around to keep from laughing at the purple coloration of rage that was washing over Richmond's face. "Certainly, sir. Follow me and I'll see if he is available to speak to you."

Nathan headed back to the office with Reginald Richmond right on his heels. When they arrived Nathan indicated for the Virginian to wait. "I'll just let him know you need to speak with him."

Nathan entered the office and closed the door behind him. He took off his Stetson and smoothed his hair. Then he called out "Mister Richmond, he has time for you. Come on in."

The door opened and in came the wealthy easterner. He took in the office in a glance and realized that there were only two men in the office. "What sort of game are you playing at, Sheriff?"

"No game at all, Mister Richmond. You asked me to introduce you to the hotel's owner. So here he is. Mister Richmond, let me introduce you to David Nathaniel Ryder the Third, owner of the Cattleman's Hotel."

Nathan stuck out his hand and straightened up to his full height. When next he spoke he had dropped all of the western patterns from his speech and spoke like a New York High Society businessman. "Mister Richmond, let me be frank with you. I bought this hotel today after our earlier conversation. I did not appreciate the way you tried to get the manager of this establishment to evict me from the rooms I had procured for myself and my traveling companion."

Richmond's mouth worked for a few seconds before and sound came out of it, "Since when can a town sheriff have access to enough funds to purchase a hotel?"

Nathan smiled, "Again you are operating from a faulty premise. I am not the sheriff of Franklin."

"THEN WHY ARE YOU WEARING THAT BADGE, AND WHY DID EVERYONE TODAY CALL YOU SHERIFF?"

"I am only going to say this to you one more time, sir. You will keep your voice to a reasonable level or you won't have to worry about your rooms because you will be sleeping in the jail. To answer your question, I am the *acting* sheriff of Franklin. The official sheriff was wounded yesterday in an attempted jailbreak. The only people today who called me sheriff were your family and the manager of this hotel, when I was acting in that capacity because of your behavior. In reality, I am quite wealthy, and bought this hotel with a very small part of my vast fortune."

"So you did all of this to have a laugh at my expense?"

Nathan sighed. "No, Mister Richmond, I did this to help you. You have a lot to learn about living in the west. You need to know that you made it possible for me to purchase this hotel."

"I made it possible? How so, sir?"

"You made it possible by walking right up to the previous owner and insulting him, by treating him like a servant. Then, you stormed out of his place without giving him a chance to tell you who he was. You made it possible by acting like having money and a society position back east entitled you to special privileges. This is the west, Mister Richmond. The rules out here are very different. Here a man earns respect, either with his actions or his prowess with a gun."

"Oh, please, Ryder, we both know that money and standing are universal. I demand you put my family in the rooms we are entitled too."

"That is exactly what I did, Richmond. You and your wife insisted you needed an entire floor of rooms. The floor I gave you is the only entire floor that is available at the moment. So you can take them or not. The choice is yours."

"This is completely unacceptable. I demand you move us."

"Let me make this as plain as I can for you. You can take those rooms, or, as far as I am concerned, you can sleep out under the stars. Personally, I don't think Mrs. Richmond would tolerate that."

Richmond turned purple with rage again. "That's it, sir. You have insulted me for the last time. I demand satisfaction."

Nathan let the refinement of his society pedigree slip into the background again, picked up his Stetson, and placed it on his head. "Be very careful what you say next, Richmond. Out here satisfaction comes from strapping on a sixgun and meeting in the center of the street."

"What? I don't know how to use one of those things. I meant fisticuffs by Marquis of Queensbury Rules."

"You want to have a fistfight to satisfy your honor?"

"That's right."

"Well then, Mister Richmond, after you."

Reginald exited the office with Nathan right on his heels. He made a beeline straight for the front door, unbuttoning his suitcoat along the way. As he passed through the doors, Nathan hauled off and kicked him in the backside, knocking him across the boardwalk and into the watering trough out front.

Richmond came up sputtering and turning toward Nathan. "Foul! I call foul sir! You've broken the rules."

As the last word came out of his mouth, Nathan planted a right uppercut to the easterner's solar plexus. When he bent forward to suck in air Nathan delivered a strong left cross to his jaw, dropping him to the ground again. "I already told you Richmond, the rules are different out here. The only rule is do what it takes to survive. You're gonna learn it if I have ta beat it into ya."

Reginald, almost blind with rage, charged straight at Nathan. Just as he was about to wrap his arms around the man, Nathan grabbed his arms and dropped straight down on his back. He lifted his feet, planting them in the Virginian's ample gut, and flipped him head over heels onto the ground. Nathan continued to roll until he was sitting on Richmond's chest. Once there, he delivered a quick left, right combination, and two jabs to the nose. Everyone who was gathered watching the fight heard the crunch of Richmond's nose at is broke under the assault.

Reginald had finally had enough. He bucked the younger man off himself and climbed to his feet. He swung a wild haymaker at Nathan's head. Nathan leaned back just out of the line of fire, and as Richmond staggered forward, Nathan laid a right cross on his jaw. Reginald Richmond collapsed to the ground, knocked out cold.

Nathan looked down at the man and shook his head. He turned to Mark and Joseph, who were among those watching the show. "Wake him up and deliver him to his room. If he makes anymore trouble today, send someone to get me."

Mark, filling a bucket with trough water, glanced at Nathan, "Where you going, Preacher?"

"I've had my fill of these people today. I'm going over to Gunderson's to see Miss Grace."

Nathan knocked the dirt off his hat and settled it on his head. With slow, deliberate steps, he walked away.

Chapter Thirty-one

As Nathan got close to the dry goods store he saw Abner sitting in a rocker on the front porch. "Well, youngster, I was a wonderin' if you was headed this way. I was gonna come tell ya that your young lady was askin' bout ya when I saw you tear into that eastern dandy."

"AblerAbner, I didn't have much of a choice. He demanded satisfaction and I thought it best to teach him the harsh truth about the west quick, before he gets himself or his family killed."

"Yep, guess he might at that. Been making a big splash ever since they got offa the train. Hope you didn't scramble his brains so much he forgets what ya was tryin' to teach him."

Nathan broke into a big old grin. "Well, if he does, guess I'll just have to suffer through teachin' him again."

Abner threw back his head and roared with laughter. "I swear, boy, yous got yer grandaddy's per-sonality. Maybe even a double portion of it."

"Abner, I came to see Grace, if she's up to it."

"Yep. Figured that. Didn't think you came to spark on my purty face. I need a moment of yer time first, son."

"Sure thing. Everything's okay with Grace, isn't it? Do I need to go get Doc Simms or Sonaman?"

"Whoa, boy, simmer down. Both docs were by this morning and Kate Sonaman is with her every wakin' moment. I need you to listen to me now for a minute."

"Okay."

"Nathan, that girl is plumb crazy in love with ya.'

"I know that, Abner, I feel the same about her."

Abner nodded and then rubbed his face. "I know you are, and I want ya to remember that when you see her this evening. She, Wilhelmina and I been conversatin', and Grace's got something she needs to tell ya. I ain't gonna say anything more about it than this: *Remember* yer plumb crazy about her. Listen to her, and then listen to God about her, before ya open yer mouth."

"Abner, I can't think of anything that she would have to tell me that would be that serious."

"Just remember what I said, son. Once words are said, ya can't take em back no matter how hard ya wish to. I know yer the Preacher, but remember the good book says to be slow to speak. I would heed it in the next little bit."

Nathan was puzzled. "Okay, I don't know if I want to see her now or not."

"Best to go see her and listen now. What she needs to tell ya you don't want to find out any other way. Just follow God's leading like ya been doing, and y'all be fine."

Abner locked up the store and the two men went up the back stairs to the Gundersons' living quarters.

On the way, Abner told Nathan the sale of the store would take place next week, giving him and his wife a week to pack what they wanted into their covered wagon and get settled over at the staging area. When they arrived at the door, Abner opened it and shouted in, "Hey, ladies, look who came draggin' his sorry tail up to our door."

Nathan entered the room and immediately Grace's face lit up like the sun had just risen over the horizon. "Nathan, I was wondering if you would visit me today."

"Well, wonder no more. Here I am, and I must say you are like a drink of cool water on this dry and thirsty heart."

Grace looked at Kate and they both started giggling like schoolgirls. Grace, laying her Georgian accent on thick, replied, "Why I do declare, Mister Ryder. With such a forward statement one would think you've a come a courtin'."

Nathan, his eye twinkling with mirth leaned down and took her hand placing a kiss on her palm, "Miss Hopewell, I wouldn't dream of trying to court you until you have the use of both your arms for a proper response."

Kate, still chuckling, stood. "Well the air is getting thick in here. I would love to stay and watch you two lovebirds banter some more, but I must get going. I'm sure my own man will be looking for his dinner soon. One thing I have learned being married to a doctor is this: never keep him waiting for his food. His patients don't like it when he is cranky."

She leaned over and hugged Grace. "Now take it easy tonight and make sure you take that dosage of pain medicine Luke left for you when you go to bed. It will help you rest so you'll heal faster."

Once she was gone, Nathan turned his attention back to Grace. "How are you doing today, really?"

"I'm all right. Still in some pain, but Mama and Papa Gunderson are taking good care of me. Kate has been helping nurse me during the day. How have you been? I haven't seen you since yesterday morning. I thought maybe you had forgotten about me."

Nathan sat down beside, her still holding her hand. "Oh, Grace, I could never forget about you. The last two days have been crazy, but I swear I was thinking about you constantly. I just couldn't break away until now." Nathan began to catch her up on everything; his inheritance, the shoot out, Bart's surprise family, and even the Richmonds and buying the hotel."

"Oh my, you have been busy. I'm glad you decided to make time for me, because I really need to talk to you. Can you stay a while?"

"Grace, there is nowhere I would rather be than right here with you. What do you need to talk about?"

Grace took a deep, shaky breath, and Nathan watched as tears began to pool in her emerald green eyes. "Hey don't do that. It can't be as bad as all that. I'm right here. I love you, and nothing you can say will change that."

Her tears broke into sobs. "Oh, Nathan, don't say that. You don't know what I have to tell you."

Abner walked around behind her and laid a hand on her shoulder. "Grace girl, do you need Wilhelmina and I to leave you two alone?"

Grace released Nathan's hand and clutched at Abner. "Oh, please don't. This is hard enough with your support. I'm not sure I could get through it without you two here."

"Ok, girl. We'll just sit here and be quiet."

Grace smiled at the older couple and took another deep, shaky breath. "I'm not sure how to begin."

Wilhelmina patted her hand. "Just start where you need to, dear."

Grace nodded and turned to look squarely at Nathan. "You remember how I told you that I had run into your grandfather in New York?"

"Yes, you said he had helped you get through school then arranged a teaching job in Redemption."

"No, Nathan, that isn't what I said. I said I had run into him and he had arranged this teaching job for me. He didn't help me through school. I didn't even run into him 'til after I was done with school."

"Okay, I guess I just assumed he had helped you with school."

"He wasn't the only person I ran into in New York. You see, after I got there and got enrolled in school, I was informed that my parents were dead and all my family's holdings and wealth were taken by swindlers. I didn't have any money to continue school, or pay for my room, or my servants. I lost everything."

"Oh Grace how terrible. How did you survive?"

"That's what I'm trying to tell you. See, I wasn't completely honest the night we met. I had met that Kid Cody before. He was a regular at the place I was working and living."

"But you said you had never met him before. I don't understand." Deep down something clicked in Nathan's mind and the Kid's words came back to him. *"Reckon she fooled you all then, but you'll learn one day. Then you'll remember that Kid Cody told ya straight."*

"Cody, he was telling the truth. You're Emerald. You really were the soiled dove he was talking about."

As those words tumbled out of Nathan's mouth, Abner's fat hand slammed onto the table. "Boy, what did I tell you about listenin'?"

Grace had her head down and was sobbing again. "I was Emerald, but I was not one of those girls. All I did was play piano and sing for the gentlemen's club. They wanted me to do more, but I refused. They had told me I was going to have to if I wanted to stay there, and that was when I ran into Nate."

"Are you telling me that Nate knew you were a... a... a... *saloon girl,* and he still arranged for you to become the school teacher in Redemption?"

"Yes, when we talked he told me that I had what it took to live in the west, because I had done whatever it took to survive. He told me God would forgive me and place it under the blood of Christ if I just asked him to. That's what I did. Coming west was supposed to be a new start; a way to put that all behind me, and now it's caught up with me again."

Nathan sat stunned as he watched the woman he thought he knew, the woman he thought he loved, weep into her hands. Without a word, Nathan stood and walked toward the door. Abner was right behind him.

"Where you going, son?"

"I don't know, Abner. I need to get away and think."

"Boy, what you need to do is get back in there and tell that girl it don't matter."

But it does matter, Abner. She lied to me from day one. How can I believe her now?"

Abner hauled back and struck Nathan right up side his head. "Boy, I'm ashamed of ya. Nate would be too if he was alive. I know you was raised better. If'n it don't matter to God, why should it matter to you?"

"I don't know why it does, but it does, Abner. I need to think. Tell her I'll talk with her later, ok?" Nathan walked out the door and into the quickly darkening night.

Abner returned to the kitchen and his heart near broke in two as he saw his dear Wilhelmina holding and rocking Grace, as the girl sobbed out her heart ache. "Oh I knew it. I've lost him. What am I gonna do?" Abner grabbed his hat and headed out too. He needed to burn off some anger or he might just find that Preacher and beat some sense into him.

Chapter Thirty-two

Nathan wandered, not knowing where he was going or what he was doing. He just kept hearing Kid Cody's voice in his head *"I ain't mistaken Preacher, and you're a fool if you believe what she told you."*

Was he a fool? Well, one thing he knew, he was a hypocrite. Less than an hour ago he was telling Reginald Richmond that out west one did what one must to survive. Then he gets upset because his girl had done exactly that. Why did he react that way? Abner had been right. His grandfather hadn't seen a problem. He had seen a damsel in distress and had provided a way of escape. Nathan was turning to go back and beg Grace's forgiveness when he heard someone shouting after him.

"Sheriff! Sheriff, I have been looking all over for you. Where have you been? Why haven't you been doing your job?"

Nathan turned to see Mrs. Richmond walking towards him with purpose, her shrill voice cutting the night air. Nathan stopped and waited for the infuriating woman to catch up with him. "Mrs. Richmond, what can I do for you?"

"You can do your job and arrest that man!"

Nathan looked around but saw no one but himself and Pricilla on the street. "I'm sorry, ma'am, what man are you talkin' about?"

"That hotel owner. Apparently, he accosted my husband in the street tonight. I want you to find him and arrest him. His name is Nathaniel David Ryder the Third."

"I see. You want me to arrest the man you are renting rooms from, because he attacked your husband in the street. Did your husband tell you this, ma'am?'

"No, the desk clerk and another man brought my husband to our room. It was obvious he had been beaten. When I asked who had done this terrible thing, the desk clerk said the owner. The other man said Nathaniel David Ryder the Third. Then, if you can believe it, they told me people call him the Preacher."

"You want me to arrest this man for beating your husband, yet you don't have a clue what happened, do you, Mrs. Richmond?"

"Aren't you listening? I just told you what happened. Are you going to go arrest him or not?'

"Mrs. Richmond, I was there. Your husband challenged the man to a fight, then got his bell rung. Now I've tried very hard to be polite to your family, but I am going to tell you the same thing I told your husband. Listen, because this could save you a lot of problems. Things are different out here. One has to earn respect by what they do, not by who they are. A fair fight is an acceptable way to settle differences. Your husband picked a fight and lost, so I am not going to arrest anyone."

"Young man, I will have your badge for this. *No one* speaks to me this way. *No one.*"

"Then let me make this as plain for you as I can. My name is Nathaniel David Ryder the Third. Your husband challenged me to a duel and got his fight. He lost. I am a preacher and I don't get paid for this job of sheriff because I am only the acting sheriff. If you cause me any more problems I am going to show you what else is different between the east and the west. I will pull you over my lap and whip your spoiled rear. Now go back to your husband and talk him into going back to Virginia before one of you gets your family killed."

When Nathan was done Pricilla's mouth hung open and she stuttered incoherently several times. "I..I..I.. You…You…You, well I never!"

"No ma'am, I am sure you haven't, but you need to get used to it. Next time it may not be someone as nice as me. Some of the people out here will shoot you for running your mouth. Now goodnight."

Nathan turned and walked away. Now he really needed to clear his head. If he didn't get away from people someone was gonna get hurt. All it would take was one more word before he lost it. He went into the stable, grabbed his saddle, and walked over to Lightning. "Hey boy, I think you and I need to go for a little run. I need to feel close to Nate tonight. Are you up for it?"

The horse snorted and bobbed his head up and down. "I swear, Preacher, the longer I work with horses the more human I think they is."

Nathan spun hand on his Colt.

"Whoa, there, didn't mean to startle ya. It's just me, Hank. I heard someone come in wanted to make sure they didn't need me."

"Sorry, Hank, just wound up tight tonight. I'm gonna take Lighting out for a run. Let us both burn off some energy and get some air."

"Sure thing, Preacher. I can see something's got a bee in your bonnet."

"Thanks. I'll bring him back when we're done, and groom and cool him myself."

"All right. Excuse me for askin', but seeing as how your filling in for the sheriff, shouldn't you tell me which way you're going, in case we need ya?"

"You're right, Hank. I'll ride out toward the mountains in the north. I won't go any farther than the foothills and be back before morning. I'm supposed to preach at the church tomorrow."

"Yeah, I heard that. I think just about the whole town is planning on being there."

As they chatted Nathan saddled up Lightning and led him out of the stable. He mounted up and headed out toward the mountains.

Abner saw Nathan head out of town, going north. He knew the boy was just trying to clear his head, but what he didn't know was those foothills were a breeding ground for outlaws. He needed to do something to help protect the boy. Then as quiet as the breeze, he heard the Holy Spirit whisper. "Got it God, and thank ya."

Abner headed to the hotel to get Bart. If anyone could back the boy up without getting on his nerves, it would be the gunhand. He asked Mark to get Bart and tell him Abner needed to talk to him in the saloon. Abner figured that with all the conversation in there they wouldn't be overheard.

*****

Slim and Shorty were trying to stay inconspicuous. They knew there were warrants out for both of them. They would have gone south and hidden, but first they had a score to settle. They just had to find that preacher who'd outwitted them on the train.

Last they had heard this was where that eastern preacher was headed. They figured as much of a busybody he'd been in their business, he'd made waves here too.

They sat at the bar nursing their drinks trying to stay sober, yet appearing to be unwinding. All the while they were listening for one name. Just as Slim was about to call it quits, he saw an old timer who motioned for a familiar looking man to join him. If the new fella had been dressed in black and wearing two guns Slim would have sworn it was Black Bart Cody.

Slim scooted a bit closer, as the younger fella got up to the oldtimer. "Abner, Mark said you need me to do something for you?"

"Bart. Not for me, for Nathan."

"What has that Preacher gotten himself into now?"

"Nothing yet, he just need to go for a ride to clear his head. Problem is he headed towards the foothills trail. You and I both know what might happen there."

Slim watched as Bart nodded. "Alright, I'll go change and ride out after him. I swear Abner, that man can be so smart one second and a real greener the next."

"Cut him some slack Bart. Miss Grace shocked him and we both know when the woman you love shocks you everything gets scrambled."

"Ain't that the truth."

Bart and the old man left. Slim slid back over to Shorty. "I told ya we would find that low down preacher here. Drink up and lets hit the trail."

They tossed back their drinks and started to stand when a man dressed like a bartender minus the apron stopped behind them. "Fellas, I couldn't help but overhear you conversation. I'm gonna offer you some free advice here, and I hope you'll take it. Ya'll best be fearing the Preacher. He'll either change ya with religion or send ya to hell hisself. One way or another, when you meet the Preacher you gonna be meetin' the Good Lord too, either in your heart or in person. Either way the choice is yours."

Slim looked at Shorty and then back at the fella. "Mister, I don't know who you are but we can handle the likes of him."

Joseph shook his head as the two headed out. "They're gonna wish they had listened to me."

*****

When Bart entered the room Nathan had gotten for Maryanne and him, he started to strip out of his normal western wear. He pulled a set of old saddle bags out from under the bed. He pulled his gunfighter rig out, laid it on the bed, and proceeded to put on his black outfit.

"Levi, what are you doing?"

Bart looked over at Maryanne, her eyes wide at what she was seeing. "Honey, Nathan's headed for trouble. I'm suiting up so that maybe I can head it off."

"Is it necessary for you to go as that gunfighter? I mean wouldn't you be able to help as Levi Cody just as well?"

"Not really, see Nathan is heading into outlaw territory without realizing it. If 'Black Bart' can catch up to him, my reputation may just keep him from getting a bushwhacker's bullet."

Maryanne struggled to understand what her husband was telling her. He had changed so much in the last five years and yet deep down he was still the same. Here he was, willing to risk his neck and the new life he was trying to build to help a friend.

She didn't understand everything about the west and how it had changed her man, but she knew now was not the time to ask for an explanation. "I see, then you do what you must, and I will pray you're successful. I'll also pray that you are both able to return safe and sound."

Bart strapped on the rig, quickly checked both six guns for full loads and tied them down low. He grabbed his black hat, strode over to his wife and gave her a kiss. "I know you don't understand. I'll try to explain after we get back, but right now time is important. I love you."

He strode out the door with the swagger of a gunfighter. Maryanne was amazed at the change in her man's entire demeanor. Where minutes before had stood her kind and loving husband, now walked a cold hard killer. If she was honest, she was a little bit frightened and a little bit excited at what lay under the surface of the man she loved.

******

Bart rode out towards the mountain pass praying he would be in time to keep Nathan from getting bushwhacked. He spurred his horse into a fast gallop. After about twenty minutes of hard riding, he saw another rider ahead. He knew it had to be Nathan and he was getting close to the foothills. Wanting to reach him before that happened, Bart gave his horse its head and spurred him to a full out run. He reached Nathan just as he reached the lowest of the foothills.

Nathan looked back at the sound of hoof beats and saw Bart in his gunfighter gear. The shock caused him to slow to a stop. "Bart? I thought you were putting all that behind you now."

"I was until some stupid eastern greener decided to ride into outlaw territory in the middle of the night to clear his head. Nathan, if you go forward anymore you're gonna get bushwhacked for sure."

"Why didn't Hank tell me that?"

"Preacher, you act so western people forget you've only been in the west for a few days. He probably figured you knew not to ride into the foothills."

"How did you know to come after me?"

"Abner saw you heading this way and was worried. He said Miss Grace shocked ya and figured you weren't thinkin' straight."

"Well, he was right on the first part. I don't know what to do. I love her. I really do, but it turns out she isn't who I thought she was."

"Does it change how you feel about her?"

Nathan thought about that for a minute. "You know, it really doesn't."

"Then what's the problem?"

"She misled me, that's the problem. How can I trust her?"

"I don't know, buddy, but I think if you really love her it won't matter in the long run. Now come on, we can continue this on the way back to town. I want to spend some time with my family, too, ya know."

Both riders turned and headed back to town. Never knowing just how close to death they had come.

*****

Slim and Shorty had taken a short, fast ride up into the foothills from a different direction than Nathan. They arrived knowing they were ahead of the Preacher. Carefully they got themselves hidden in the hills and set up crossfire to catch Nathan as he rode up the second hill. Then they settled in to wait.

After about ten minutes, they saw a single rider approaching the entrance to the mountain path. Just as the rider started down the first hill, a second rider came ridding, hell bent for leather upon him. The two stopped and sat just out of rifle range talking. "Come on, just a hair further."

As they continued to sit atop their horses and talk, Slim's finger itched to pull the trigger, but he knew he would never hit them. To make matters worse, after sitting there for several minutes, they turned their horses and headed back to town. Slim screamed and cursed his and Shorty's luck.

He decided right then and there he wasn't heading south until he had put an end to both the Preacher and Black Bart. If the news he'd heard in Franklin was right then he knew just the man to help them finish this. He motioned Shorty to cross over and once they were together, they headed toward the capitol city by the route they knew the prison wagon would have taken. With luck, they could catch up to it before it got there.

Chapter Thirty-three

As the dawn broke on Nathan's first Sunday in the west, he found himself in need of some time with the Lord before he preached at the church. He put on his go-to-meeting clothes, grabbed his Bible, and headed down to the lobby like normal. Once there, he settled into the high-backed chair he used every morning. He opened his Bible to the passage he felt he was to speak from.

Just as he was getting into the passage, a shadow fell across his light just like it had most mornings. "Good morning, Levi. I guess you're ready to get breakfast and talk about God like normal."

The voice that responded jerked Nathan's head up from his studies. "Levi isn't coming today. I thought, instead, you and I should talk."

Nathan looked up into the face of Maryanne Cody. "Mrs. Cody, you surprised me. You move as quietly as your husband."

Maryanne smiled. "I guess it is a family trait. Nathan, Levi told me about your problem, and I felt like I needed to talk with you about it, if you're willing?"

Nathan stood and offered her his arm. "Okay. Let us go across the street and get a bite to eat while we talk."

Maryanne took his arm and they crossed to the café. Once inside, Mrs. Sue took their order and brought their food. Nathan blessed it for both of them and then looked at Maryanne. "What did you want to discuss?"

Maryanne looked at the young preacher for a minute while she sipped her coffee. "I wanted to talk to you about your reaction to your young lady. He said that you were not sure you can trust her."

"That's true, Mrs. Cody. She lied to me. Well, she didn't exactly lie to me, but she led me to believe something that wasn't true."

"Yes, I believe I have the story straight. She didn't reveal her past to you when you first met. I imagine if she had it would have made a difference in how you handled the whole situation, wouldn't it?"

Nathan squirmed. "No, I still wouldn't have let the Kid drag her off against her will."

"Would it have kept you from falling in love with her?"

"No, I don't think it would have."

"Well, then, would you rather she hadn't told you and let you marry her thinking she had been completely innocent?"

"No, but…"

"Nathan, I assume Levi has done some things that I wouldn't be proud of while he was on the run, wouldn't you agree?"

"You know he has."

"Yet, here I am ready to start my life over with him. Do you think I am making a mistake?"

"No, but…"

"There are no buts here. Either you want to create a life with this woman or you don't. If you do, then it shouldn't matter. If you don't, and it is because of her indiscretions, which she has already told you are under the blood of Christ, then you need to put that Bible up and just be a cowboy."

Nathan started. She was right. If he didn't forgive and move on, then he really didn't have any right to be preaching about forgiveness and mercy. Then to make matters worse, a verse from Matthew Chapter Six sprang into his head. ***"For if ye forgive men their trespasses, your heavenly Father will also forgive you: But if ye forgive not men their trespasses, neither will your Father forgive your trespasses."***

Nathan knew exactly what he needed to do. If he hurried, he would have time before he had to get over to the church. "Maryanne, thank you. You're absolutely right. I need to go see Grace before church. Levi is a very lucky man to be married to such a wise woman."

"Oh, stop it. Go on, get out of here, and make things right with your woman."

Nathan went over to Sue and paid for their meal. Telling everyone he would see them at the church later that morning, Nathan left the café, headed for the Gundersons' place.

By the time he reached the stairs to the Gundersons' upstairs apartment, Nathan was practically running. He reached the door and began to bang on it frantically. After what felt like a lifetime he heard Abner bellowing, "Ok, ok, I hear ya. Hold yer horses."

Abner jerked open the door, giving Nathan quite a shock to see the old merchant in a half dressed state. He had on his pants and the red top of a pair of longjohns. He was still adjusting the straps on his suspenders as he looked into Nathan's face. "Nathan, you liked to tore my door down. What's wrong, boy? Do I need to get my scattergun?"

"What? No, of course not. Abner, where's Grace? I have to see her right away. I've made a terrible mistake."

"She's in bed, Nathan, where I'd still be if not for your infernal banging. I thought something was wrong. Can't this wait 'til a more reasonable hour?"

"Abner, please let her know I'm here and need to talk to her. I can't preach today 'til I make this right."

Abner took a step back, letting the Preacher into the house. "Came to your senses, did ya? Okay, Nathan, I'll tell her yer here and insisting on speaking with her, but the decision to see you or not is hers. Understood?"

"That won't be necessary, Papa Gunderson. I'll speak to him."

Both men turned at the sound of Grace's voice. Abner shook his head, and muttering under his breath, headed back to his bed. "Young love. I swear it'll be the death of me. Waking me up in the middle of my sleep...."

Nathan stood in the doorway, frozen by the whole situation. Until he saw her, he had known exactly how he would approach this situation. Now, standing in her presence, the fear that she wouldn't accept his apology kept him from doing what he had come here to do.

Grace looked at Nathan, as he stood speechless in the doorway. "Well, Nathan, you said you needed to talk to me. Here I am. Are you going to come in and talk, or am I going back to bed?"

Nathan stumbled into the apartment, pushing the door shut behind himself. Once he started moving forward, he found himself at Grace's feet, on his knees, and the words that just moments before wouldn't come past his lips began to tumble out faster and faster.

"Grace I'm so sorry. Nate was right, and your past doesn't matter. I, of all people, should have reacted different. I love you and that is all that matters. What you had to do to survive is just that, what you had to do. I don't care that you lived in a brothel. I don't care that you sang there or what you did there. If God can forgive you, then I have no right not to. I know my reaction last night hurt you, and I only hope that you will forgive me, and that we can move forward from here."

Grace looked down at the man at her feet. "Nathan, I do accept your apology. You say you love me, but I need to know; do you still want to marry me?"

Nathan grasped her hand in both of his, "Yes, Grace, I do want us to get married eventually, after we get settled in Redemption and you understand the life I'll be living."

Grace pulled her hand from his. "I'm sorry; Nathan, but I can't accept that. You seem to say one thing with your mouth but your actions scream something else. Either you want to marry me or you don't.

"If your answer is yes, then why wait? Why drag this out, saying you want to make sure I understand what I am getting into? If you want to marry me and I want to marry you, why can't we just get married and start our new life in our new town as husband and wife? Unless you aren't really sure you want to be married to me."

Nathan stood and stared at this woman, who had so captured his heart, with a look of surprise. He couldn't believe that she thought he didn't want to marry her because he had suggested that they wait. He truly had wanted her to understand the life she was agreeing to be a part of.

"I'm sure, Grace. Nothing will make me happier than to have you as my wife. I guess in a way it would make things less complicated for us to arrive in Redemption as husband and wife. I just didn't want you to regret your decision later when I'm away from home so much."

"Good, then that's settled. We'll get married now."

"You mean right now? As in today?"

Grace stamped her foot in aggravation. "No, not today, I'm not going to walk the aisle with my arm in this sling. We aren't leaving town for two weeks, right?"

Nathan nodded.

"Then next Saturday, after my stitches come out and I have time to get a dress made and you have time to get a new suit. I will not marry you in your cowboy gear, and for the ceremony, you will not wear those guns. Do I make myself clear?"

Nathan and Grace both jumped at the loud gaff that came from the other side of the kitchen. They both turned to see Abner laughing while trying to keep quiet. When he noticed them looking at him he came into the room. "Well, Nathan my boy, I can see that you're already learning a few things about married life. If the wife ain't happy you ain't gonna be happy. Have either of you thought about who will conduct this-here ceremony?"

Grace looked at the man who was quickly becoming like a second father to her. "Won't your town's pastor be back by then?"

"No, child. Pastor Barnes won't be back 'til the day before we are planning to leave."

"Well, then, Nathan will just have to do our wedding. He can, after all. He is an ordained pastor."

"True, he could, but I would suggest someone else. You don't want any hint of impropriety attached to your wedding. I could do it. I'm an ordained deacon. On the other hand, Sheriff Cole could do it, as well. He is not just the sheriff but also our Justice of the Peace."

"I want you to give me away, so do you think the sheriff will be able to officiate by then?"

"I think if Nathan asked him to he'd do it, even if he had to hop on one leg the whole time. He's convinced that the Preacher here saved our lives the other day. Can't say I disagree with him either. I'll ride out tomorrow and see if he will be able to be in town next Saturday."

Nathan nodded. "Thank you, Abner. I appreciate all you're doing for us."

"I told you boy, Wilhelmina and I have taken a real shine to this girl of yours. Now I am going to tell you something and I ain't gonna beat around the bush here. If'n you hurt this here girl again, you'll answer to me. Preacher or not, quick with a gun or not. You understand?"

Nathan smiled. "Yes sir, I believe your meaning is crystal clear."

"Good. 'Nuff said then. Now get out of my house and get yerself ready to deliver the sermon today. From what I understand, the whole town's a-plannin' to come see if you're really a preacher."

"Well then, I guess I'd better not disappoint them. I tell ya one thing, I can't wait to get to Redemption and just be Pastor Nathan Ryder, not this Preacher fella."

Nathan gave Grace a quick kiss and headed for the door.

Abner watched it all. and wondered how long it would take for Nathan to realize he was the Preacher and Pastor Nathan Ryder, and where he was physically wouldn't change that.

Chapter Thirty-four

Nathan retreated to the sheriff's office for a little bit of peace and quiet before time to preach. He took off his guns and laid them on the desk. He knew people were coming to see this person he had become; the gunhand known as the Preacher. Today they would only meet Pastor Nathan Ryder.

He pulled out his Bible and notes to look over one more time. After a quick word of prayer asking God to quiet and refocus his mind, Nathan went over everything he felt led of God to speak that day. As the time approached for the service to begin Nathan gathered the notes and Bible, put his hat on his head, and headed to the church.

At the church building, Nathan saw several men being directed by Abner to pull benches and chairs out of the building and set them up in rows in front of the church itself. Abner had a small portable pulpit sitting on the front landing of the church. Already more than half the benches and chairs were full of people from the town and surrounding countryside.

Abner, seeing Nathan, waved him onto the landing. "Well, Nathan, seems like we're gonna have to meet out here today. We already got more people here than will fit in the sanctuary. I got the benches from the picnic grounds moved around and Henry has a group of men with him raiding chairs from the café too."

"Abner, why are all these people here?"

"Seems like they's all curious as to if'n you's really a preacher or not."

Nathan shook his head in disgust and sadness. "But it's the Lord's Day. The focus should be on Him, not on me."

"Yep, reckon yer right Preacher, but maybe the Lord has allowed yer reputation to bring these people here to meet with Him. I say you just preach what is in yer heart to preach and leave the rest up to God."

"I don't see that I have much of a choice. Have you thought about what we're going to do for music? I mean, I doubt you want to drag the piano out here and back in afterwards."

Abner smiled. "I got that covered. Me and some of the boys brought our instruments, so it may be a fiddle, a guitar, and a squeeze box, but we can play them hymns about as good as we can trail songs, I reckon."

"Okay, I'll leave all this in your capable hands then. If you don't mind, I want to go inside and pray for a bit."

"You go right ahead, Nathan. I'll come git ya when it's time to start."

Nathan entered the sanctuary, walked slowly up to the altar, knelt down, and began to pray. "Father God, I don't know what You're up to today but I know You are doing something. Lord, please help all these people to see You today and not me. I don't want them to see the Preacher but to see Your servant the pastor. I stand on Your promise that Your word will not return void to You. Let my words be Your words and let the people's ears and hearts be receptive."

Nathan continued praying for several minutes until Abner came in, telling him it was time to start. As they walked out onto the landing, Nathan could see that the whole town was there. He also recognized several of the people from the wagon train that was set to leave the next day. He noticed all the available seats had been taken and several people were sitting in wagons that had been pulled up behind the chairs. There were even people sitting on blankets and quilts along the side. Nathan took a deep breath to calm himself as Abner walked forward to start the service.

"I declare, it is good to see so many people turn out to worship the Lord this Sunday. I figure some of you came to see if that Preacher fella is really a preacher and you won't be disappointed. First though, we are gonna praise the Lord Jesus by singin' a few hymns. So stand and sing with us, why don'tcha?"

He went on to lead a couple of hymns with him and his friends playing the music. Then Abner gave a few church announcements, like when Pastor Barnes would be back, and that there would be a dinner on the grounds that Sunday as well. He led the people in another hymn and then turned the service over to Nathan for the preaching of God's Word.

As Nathan stepped up to the pulpit he could see people shifting in their seats trying to get a better view of the Preacher who was a gunslinger. Trying not to show how uncomfortable he was with the fame his exploits had made for him; Nathan smiled out at the crowd. Placing his Bible on the pulpit, he began his sermon.

"Today we will be reading from the book of Matthew, Chapter twenty-five starting with verse fourteen. *'For the kingdom of heaven is as a man travelling into a far country, who called his own servants, and delivered unto them his goods. And unto one he gave five talents, to another two, and to another one; to every man according to his several ability; and straightway took his journey. Then he that had received the five talents went and traded with the same, and made them other five talents. And likewise he that had received two, he also gained other two. But he that had received one went and digged in the earth, and hid his lord's money. After a long time the lord of those servants cometh, and reckoneth with them. And so he that had received five talents came and brought other five talents, saying, Lord, thou deliveredst unto me five talents: behold, I have gained beside them five talents more. His lord said unto him, Well done, thou good and faithful servant: thou hast been faithful over a few things, I will make thee ruler over many things: enter thou into the joy of thy lord. He also that had received two talents came and said, Lord, thou deliveredst unto me two talents: behold, I have gained two other talents beside them. His lord said unto him, Well done, good and faithful servant; thou hast been faithful over a few things, I will make thee ruler over many things: enter thou into the joy of thy lord. Then he which had received the one talent came and said, Lord, I knew thee that thou art an hard man, reaping where thou hast not sown, and gathering where thou hast not strawed: And I was afraid, and went and hid thy talent in the earth: lo, there thou hast that is thine. His lord answered and said unto him, Thou wicked and slothful servant, thou knewest that I reap where I sowed not, and gather where I have not strawed: Thou oughtest therefore to have put my money to the exchangers, and then at my coming I should have received mine own with usury. Take therefore the talent from him, and give it unto him which hath ten talents. For unto every one that hath shall be given, and he shall have abundance: but from him that hath not shall be taken away even that which he hath. And cast ye the unprofitable servant into outer darkness: there shall be weeping and gnashing of teeth.'*

"Father God, I ask that You speak your message through me to these people. Open all our ears to hear what Your Spirit says to the church. Open our hearts to receive and accept what our ears hear. May we apply it to our lives to make us more like You want us to be. In Jesus' Name we pray, Amen.

"I want to start today by saying that when I came out west my only plan was to get to the territory and start my career as a pastor. I never expected to gain a reputation and certainly not before I even got to Redemption.

"This reputation as a gunslinger called the Preacher is not anything I ever wanted, and I have struggled with the fact that it happened. Then during my study times, I ran across these verses and realized that I, like all people, can gain some insight from them about how to live my life. That's what I want to share with you today.

"The first thing I realized is this: God gives all his followers gifts and talents. I know that in this passage talents are a form of money, but the idea still holds true. Every talent or ability that we have comes from God above. If you are an excellent cook, cowboy, farmer, or businessman, that talent, that excellence was given to you by God.

"The second thing I noticed is that God expects you to use what he gives you. The servants that he praised were the ones that took what he had given them and used it to make even more. The only servant he called wicked was the lazy or scared one, who took what he was given and hid it.

"God has given us these gifts, talents, and even our money to use for him. Yes, you take care of your physical needs, but then you help move God's kingdom forward with the rest. First Corinthians Ten thirty-one tells **us '*Whatsoever ye eat or drink or whatsoever you do, do all for the glory of God.*'** God expects you to use whatever you are able to do to bring Him glory.

"Some of you came here today to see if I was really a pastor or was I just the gunslinger known as the Preacher. Others of you have wondered how a man of God could be so good with a gun and be willing to use it? The answer to both is that I use the talents God has given me to help advance his kingdom. Yes, I am a preacher, as you are seeing today. Yes, I am a bit handy with a gun.

"Like some of you, when I first got out west I wondered how I could wear a gun and face men in the street knowing that if I won a shootout the other fella was bound for hellfire. Then I talked to a good Christian man in your community who lives by his gun.

"Sheriff Cole told me he had reconciled his job with his faith by realizing that, yes, he may send a few no-accounts to the hell fire, but in doing so he saved the lives of many others who would have a chance to come to God. He felt he saved more lives than he took. He was right. Yes, a few will die in their sin and spend eternity in hell. But it gives those they would have killed a chance to come to Christ. That's what Paul meant by *do all for the glory of God.* It's also what Jesus meant by this parable. If we don't use our talents then we are wicked servants, unfit to serve Him.

"The last thing I want you to notice in our text is that you must have a relationship with the Master to receive his gifts. Some of you are here today just to check me out. I hope through everything you've seen today and heard today you are now ready to check out God.

"Jesus wants to take away all the wrongdoing in your life. He wants to get to know you. If you want to get to know Him then I urge you to stand right now and walk down here to the first step, where Deacon Abner or I will meet you and tell you how to become a Christian.

"Don't wait; come right now. Those of you who are believers, maybe you need to come and ask God to forgive you for being a wicked servant. Now is the time, come right down here, get on your knees and ask God to forgive you and strengthen you to begin to use your gifts to bring Him glory. Come now."

Nathan moved to the bottom of the stairs, waiting to pray with those who came to meet Jesus for the first time. From all over the yard people began to make their way forward. Most went straight to a place in front of the landing and knelt in prayer.

One young man walked right up to Nathan his hat in his hand. Nathan recognized him instantly as the young man he had almost killed a few days earlier in a fit of rage. Lefty nervously looked up at Nathan. "Preacher, your words the other day and today have really grabbed me. I want to know this God of yers."

Nathan put an arm around Lefty and together they sat on the steps, where Nathan shared with the young man how to become a believer. After looking at scripture, Lefty bowed his head and became a servant of the Most High God.

As he did so, Nathan realized he was exactly what God had called him to be both a man of faith and a man of action. He realized he would always be both Nathan Ryder, pastor, and the Preacher, a fast gun for God.

As he looked out at the crowd of people, he saw his future bride sitting and watching him with a look of love and pride as her knight in dress clothes accepted his destiny. Nathan wondered what God had in store for them as husband and wife in this vast mission field called the Wild West.

Chapter Thirty-five

Once the service had come to an end several people came up to Nathan and told him how his sermon had awakened something in them. Nathan thanked each of them for letting him know. He encouraged them each to serve God with their gifts and talents from then on.

As the last of the well wishers left, just a small handful of people remained. Bart, Maryanne and young Levi, the Gundersons and Grace, and Lefty, whose real name was Timothy Dillon, were all seated, waiting for Nathan.

Nathan motioned for Bart and Maryanne to approach him. Once they arrived, Nathan looked at the few people still sitting and smiled. "Well, those of you who are gathered here are gonna witness one of the most joyous events a pastor gets to partake of. Levi Bartholomew Cody and Maryanne Cody asked me earlier if I would perform a marriage service for them. After a separation of five years, they wanted to renew their vows to each other before God. I thought it was a great way to begin their new life together here in the west. So Levi and Mary, if you will face each other and take each other's hands we will renew your marriage vows."

Bart and Maryanne turned toward each other and Bart took Maryanne's hands in his. Nathan faced them and smiled at the love he saw reflected in each of their faces. With one quick glance at the woman who would be joining him in this same ceremony later that week, Nathan began.

"Dearly beloved, we are gathered here today in the sight of God and these witnesses to join Levi Bartholomew Cody and Maryanne Cody in holy matrimony. Marriage is an institution ordained by God from the beginning. He himself preformed the first marriage ceremony between Adam and Eve in the Garden of Eden. Since then, scripture says that a when a boy becomes a man he will *'leave his father and mother and cleave to his own wife and the two shall become one flesh.'* In keeping with that, Levi and Maryanne are doing so again today.

Levi Bartholomew Cody, do you take this woman to be your lawfully wedded wife? Do you pledge to love, honor, and cherish her in sickness and in health, for richer and poorer, forsaking all others, 'til death do you part?"

Levi, with a big grin, looked at Nathan. "I do."

"Maryanne Cody do you take this man to be your lawfully wedded husband? Do you pledge to love, honor and obey him as Christ commands; in sickness and in health, for richer and poorer, forsaking all others,'til death do you part?"

Maryanne, with silent tears of joy running down her cheeks, squeezed Levi's hands. "I do."

Levi had indicated to Nathan earlier that he had never given Maryanne a wedding ring because he couldn't afford it. Nathan had a surprise for his friend that he had arranged with Abner Gunderson the day before. "Levi, please give me your hand."

Levi looked at Nathan with bewilderment on his face as he held out his hand. Nathan reached into his pocket, and pulled out a simple gold wedding band, and placed it in Levi's outstretched hand. "Place this ring on Maryanne's left hand and repeat after me. 'With this ring I thee wed'."

Now tears began to pool in Levi's eyes as he slid that simple circle of love on his wife's ring finger. His voice, filled with emotion, spoke. "With this ring I thee wed."

Nathan, with the biggest grin ever, placed his hands on the heads of these precious friends and prayed. "Father God, I ask you to bless the union of my friends Levi and Maryanne. Help their lives be centered on you as they raise their family to love and follow your path. In Jesus' name I bless them, Amen. Levi, Maryanne I now pronounce you husband and wife. Levi, you better kiss your bride."

Levi needed no further instruction, but wrapped his arms around the woman who had waited patiently five years for his return. As their lips met he crushed her to him, trying to convey without words that he was never going to leave her again this side of death.

"May I present to you all Mister and Missus Levi Bartholomew Cody."

Levi and Maryanne turned to be congratulated by those who had stayed and watched the service. Grace went up to Maryanne and asked her if she would stand with her the following weekend as she was married to Nathan. Levi and Maryanne both turned to look at Nathan, who was all smiles. Levi clasped him on the back. "So I see Maryanne talked some sense into ya this morning."

"Yes, between your counsel last night and hers today I was able to get Grace to take me back."

"How did you decide to get married? Last we talked you were adamant on waiting 'til after ya'll got to Redemption."

"Grace pointed out that if we truly loved each other and knew God wanted us to be married that waiting was just foolishness on my part."

Maryanne looked at Grace and giggled. "I bet that is exactly what she did."

Grace giggled too. "Actually I kind of insisted we quit playing at romance and start our lives together, before we traveled to Redemption. I think Nathan realized I was right, that if we were going to get married, then waiting was a waste of time."

All of them laughed together. Then Levi pulled Nathan away from the women for a serious talk. "Nathan, I be grateful for the ring. How much do I owe ya?"

"Consider it my wedding gift, Levi."

"No sir. If my wife is gonna wear a wedding band, then I'm gonna be the one who paid fer it."

Nathan nodded and then told Levi the price. Levi reached into his pocket, pulled out the money and paid for the ring. "Maryanne and I have talked, and we are gonna accept your offer to go to that ranch of yers. Maybe in a few years I'll be able to save up enough money to buy us our own ranch."

"I'm glad you accepted, Levi. I've come to consider you a close friend and would have hated having to leave you behind."

"Well, I told you that because I wanted to let you know something. Nathan, I can buy my own wagon and supplies."

"No, if you're gonna work for me, consider the wagon and team as part of your first pay. The supplies are my wedding gift to your family since you wouldn't take the ring as a gift."

"All right. I noticed Lefty come forward today. Did he accept Jesus as Savior too?"

"He did. Surprised me too. He wants to join our little band and follow us to Redemption. I offered him employment as well. He'll ride as a driver during the wagon train and then we'll figure out what job to give him when we get to Redemption. By the way, he said Lefty was the nickname your brother gave him and that his name is Timothy Dillion. He wants to go by Tim from now on."

"Preacher, you sure have a way of changing a man."

"Not me, Levi. God is the one that changes men. I just speak his word."

The two men walked up to the loves of their lives and the four of them and Levi's son headed toward the café to see what Sue and Henry had for lunch. As they were leaving, Wilhelmina Gunderson called out after them. "Preacher, don't you let that girl overdo it. Doc Soneman told her she needs to rest and let that wound heal."

Nathan turned to the woman who was becoming a surrogate mother to Grace. "I promise I'll see her safely to your door, Mrs. Gunderson, right after lunch."

"We'll be holdin ya to yer word, youngster," Abner shouted after them. "I'd hate to have to come horsewhip ya on the Lord's Day."

Everyone laughed and went their separate ways, realizing they were becoming more than a group of friends and traveling companions. They were growing into a family.

*****

After lunch Levi and Maryanne had taken young Levi and headed for the hotel so the boy could nap and they could spend some time together as husband and wife. Nathan walked Grace home to the Gunderson's apartment and had stolen a few kisses at the door before sending her to bed to rest and heal. It was only after he was heading down the stairs that he realized that he still didn't have his guns on. He decided that he would pick them up and go spend some time in his rooms with God before making rounds as the acting Sheriff that evening.

*****

As the sun was sinking behind the mountains to the west, Nathan was strolling through town doing his rounds as acting sheriff. His gunbelt was back in place and Jack's badge was pinned securely to his shirt. Everywhere he went people were greeting him and talking about how much they enjoyed and were touched by his sermon. Nathan thanked each of them. He was amazed at how quiet Franklin seemed tonight. After his first week being one full of excitement and danger, the peace and quiet of this day seemed almost unnatural to him.

He was almost done with his rounds checking each closed shop to make sure it was locked tight, when something caught his attention. In the shadows of the buildings on Main Street Nathan caught a fleeting movement. He stepped back into the shadows himself, watching for more. Just when he thought he had imagined it he saw a small movement across the way, down by the livery stable. As he watched, the movement became a person who opened the livery door just a crack. The shadowy figure was much too small to be Hank, and moved with too much stealth to be up to any good. Nathan, hugging close to the buildings, began to slowly work his way toward the livery himself.

When he arrived across from the stable, he quickly crossed the street and slipped in the slightly opened door. In the dim light, he saw what appeared to be a young boy leading his grandfather's horse, Lightning, out of his stall. Lightning was saddled and ready for riding. Nathan drew his gun, slipped up behind the boy, and placed the barrel in the small of his back. "Boy, I don't know what you think your doing, but horse thieves get hung around here."

The youngster stiffened as the barrel prodded him in the back and in a low whisper, a very young voice replied "I wasn't stealing him, mister. I was just gonna ride him a bit."

"Well, unless this horse belongs to you, that is stealing, son. Does this horse belong to you?"

"No sir, he's my friend's horse."

Nathan almost laughed at the young scamp. He had no clue the man he was talking to owned the horse he had chosen to ride.

"Is that so? What's your friend's name? Also, what's his horse's name? And does your friend know you're gonna ride his horse a bit?"

The boy slumped a bit and mumbled his answers.

"Turn around here so I can hear and understand ya, boy."

The youngster turned and Nathan was shocked. What he had taken for a young boy was actually Lucinda Richmond in a pair of buckskins and a denim shirt, with her hair tucked up into a Stetson. "I said I ain't no boy."

"Miss Richmond, what are you doing? Your parents would have a fit if they saw you dressed like this, let alone if they knew you were trying to steal my horse."

"That ain't your horse. That's Lightning. He belongs to Nugget Nate."

If Nathan had been floored before, he was completely flabbergasted by this statement. "What makes you say this is Nugget Nate's horse Lightning? What would a little rich girl know about Nugget Nate?"

"I ain't a little rich girl. I'm twelve years old. That's practically a grown woman. I know that horse is Lightning, because his picture is right here." She pulled a small dime novel out of her pocket.

Nathan looked at a well-drawn picture of his grandfather sitting atop Lightning. The title said, "Nugget Nate: Original Mountain Man of the West."

"Well you're right, Miss Richmond, that horse does look like the one on the cover of this book. However, that horse belongs to me, not to the Original Mountain Man of the West."

Nathan watched the emotions play across the girl's face; doubt, then fear, finally setting on defiance. "If'n that's your horse what's his name?"

Nathan knew what that piece of information was going do to this situation, but he wouldn't lie to the girl. "His name happens to be Lightning."

"I knew it, I knew it, you're Nugget Nate, aint ya?"

"No, I'm not Nugget Nate."

"Then whatcha doin with his horse?"

Nathan knew his answer was going to do nothing but increase her hero worship and alienate him with her parents even more. "Nate was my grandfather."

"What do you mean he *was* your grandfather?"

"Nate passed away not too long ago. He left Lightning to me in his will."

"That must have been something else, having Nugget Nate for a grandfather."

"It was fun, that's for sure. Now let's put Lightning up and get out of here. I have a deal to make with you before you go back to your family's rooms."

Nathan watched as Lucinda unsaddled Lightning and put all his gear back where it was. He was surprised at how much the old mustang took to the young girl. He was also impressed by how gentle and knowledgeable she was about caring for the horse. It just confirmed to him that the deal he was going to offer her was the right one. When she was finished, they left the livery together.

"Okay, Miss Richmond, I have a problem I think you can help me with."

"What's that?"

"Since Nate left me Lightning I now have two horses. I don't have time right now to exercise them both. I was thinking that since you like Lightning so much and since Lightning seems to like you, maybe you'd like to come by and ride him for me."

"Really? You want me to ride Nugget Nate's horse every day?"

"Well, only if you can ride, and think you can handle him."

"Oh I can ride, and I know I can handle him, Mister Ryder. Please let me exercise him for you."

"Tell you what. You get your father to come down to the livery with you tomorrow and tell me its okay for you to ride him. Then I'll give you a chance to show me you can handle him. If that goes well, then yes, I'll let you exercise him for me."

"Great! You got a deal." Lucinda spit in her hand and held it out to Nathan. Trying not to laugh at the girl, Nathan copied her and the two shook. "I guess I'll see you at the livery tomorrow morning then, Lucy."

"No one has ever called me Lucy before. I think I like it. It sounds like a good western name."

"Well then, Lucy you will be, and you can just call me Nathan."

"Okay, Nathan, see you tomorrow." Then the girl skipped away to get her father to agree to Nathan's deal.

Nathan watched her go and wondered what God was up to and just what he was getting himself into now.

Chapter Thirty-six

Nathan woke early Monday morning just as the sun was beginning to rise. He quickly dressed and threw on his guns. He had so much he needed to accomplish today. There was wiring his parents about his pending nuptials. He needed to go see Grace and make sure she had the funds she needed to get that dress she was talking about. On top of that, he still had to make his rounds as sheriff and meet with Lucinda Richmond at the livery. This was certainly no time for dilly-dallying.

Knowing how pressed for time he was going to be for this whole week, Nathan grabbed his Bible and headed down to his spot in the lobby to spend time with God first. He knew how important that time was to having a productive day. He settled in and spent some time both reading God's Word and just thanking his heavenly Father for the many blessing in his life.

Levi caught up with him there and the two of them continued their routine with one slight change. Instead of the two of them having breakfast together and discussing God's word, the entire Cody family came to breakfast with Nathan and discussed the things they were reading and studying together. As Nathan watched his friend lead his family deeper into a relationship with God, he suddenly realized that he had the same obligation with his bride too. *"I should make arrangements to have Grace join me for devotions and these breakfasts."* As the thought solidified in Nathan's head he realized here was one more thing to do today.

After breakfast, Nathan and Levi headed over to the jail to open the office for the day. Levi had agreed to take the first shift in the office, thus allowing Nathan to get some of his errands done. Nathan would take the evening shift so Levi could spend the evening with his family.

Once they arrived, Nathan headed over to the Western Union office. As he stepped through the door, he almost collided with William, who was headed out at a run.

"Oh, Preacher, sorry 'bout that. I was jest headed over to see ya'll. I got's an urgent telegram fer the sheriff's office. I figgered since Jack was still laid up that it was meant fer you and Bart."

"It's ok, William, you can let me have it. Also, I'm gonna need to send a couple of telegrams east here in a minute."

"Sure thing, Nathan. Here ya go."

Nathan took the telegram from William. The words he read sent a tingling of apprehension down his spine.

To Franklin Sheriff's office

From: Missouri State Prison

Prison wagon attacked Stop

Prisoners escaped Stop

Overheard heading your way to settle score Stop

Be on guard Stop

End Message

"William, those telegrams are gonna have to wait. I need to let Levi and Abner know about this, and probably Jack as well." Without waiting for a reply, Nathan turned and ran back across the street. He entered the jail and handed the telegram to Levi. Once Levi had read it he handed it back to Nathan. "Wonder who he's coming to settle the score with; you, me or both?"

"I don't know, but we all need to be ready. Make some plans to keep your family safe as well. I know he's your brother, but from the way he was talking the day he left I wouldn't put it past him to go after your family."

"So how do you suggest we handle this, Nathan?"

"I know you're not gonna want to hear this but, you need to put your other gun back on and start carrying your rifle with you. I'll do the same and we'll get Abner to start walking patrols as well. I'll see if James and Mark know how to shoot and get them to start carrying as well. Finally, I'll ride out later today to see Jack. I'm sure this isn't the only time the town has needed to be ready for war with outlaws."

"Okay, I'll go get armed. I'm also gonna tell Maryanne to keep Little Levi and herself in the room unless you or I are with them. Nathan, you got to know if it comes down to you or Kevin, you take him out."

Nathan looked at this man who was quickly becoming more than a friend. "Are you sure, Levi? This is your brother we're talking about."

"No Nathan, we're talking about Kid Cody. Kevin quit being my brother when he set me up to take the fall for the murder he committed. Trust me when I say, if he comes after me or mine, I'll plant him. You need to decide right now you'll do the same."

"I understand, and I won't allow him to harm me, Grace, or any of the people in this town whom I've promised to protect. Go see to your family and I'll go inform Abner, then I'll ride out and let Jack know what's going on as well."

Nathan and Levi headed out to take care of their preparations. Levi went to the hotel to talk to his wife and become Black Bart once again. He wondered why God kept having him step back into the reputation he was trying to leave behind. He kept hearing words from Nathan's sermon about God given talents and using them for God. He didn't have time to dwell on that now, but soon he was gonna have to stop and consider them.

Levi headed to the hotel. Nathan went toward the dry goods store to inform Abner of the telegram. Along the way, he saw Lucy and Reginald Richmond heading toward him and the livery stable. Lucy appeared to have decided to forsake woman's wear altogether. She was still dressed like she had been the night before, in buckskin breeches and a denim shirt, wearing a Stetson pushed back all friendly like, with her long blond hair done up in a braid running down her back.

Reginald approached Nathan with a set look upon his face. His eyes were still black from their fight and someone had taped his nose. "Ryder, my daughter seems to think that you need her help. I tried to tell her that you don't like us or want us to be anywhere near you, but she was insistent I come meet with you. So here we are."

"Mister Richmond, I don't dislike you or your family. As I've told both you and your wife the rules in the west are different than they are back east. I'm only trying to keep you from getting killed before you're here even a week. I did ask your daughter if she'd be willing to do a favor for me last night, but I also informed her that you would have to agree. I don't want to come between a father and his child."

Reginald looked skeptical, but after a few more minutes of conversation agreed to allow Lucinda to exercise Lightning. Nathan told her he would go to the livery as soon as he took care of an important piece of town business.

"Okay Nathan. I'll meet ya there so you can watch me ride."

Reginald looked at his daughter. "Lucinda, you will treat Mister Ryder with the respect due an elder and you will call him Mister Ryder."

"Daddy, I'm almost a woman. What's wrong with me calling my friend by his given name?"

"Young lady, I may have given in on this wardrobe phase of yours, but you will act like a southern lady still, or I will take you home, tan your hide, and allow your mother to dress you properly. Is that understood?"

"Yes, sir." The two of them walked on toward the livery, their conversation continuing on the way. Nathan chuckled and then headed in to the dry goods looking for Abner.

Nathan found Abner stocking shelves. When he showed him the telegram the old merchant walked up front, picked up his shotgun, and broke the barrels, making sure that they both had a load of lead in them. Then he walked back to where he was working, taking the gun with him. "I'll be keeping ol' Besty here with me 'til you or Jack tell me otherwise, Nathan. When I go upstairs tonight, I'll get Wilhelmina to start carrying her pepperbox too. Don't you worry none. We won't let nothing happen to our girl."

"I appreciate that, Abner. I'm gonna ride out to Jack's and let him know what's going on. After all, it is still his town."

As he was turning to leave he saw what Abner was stocking. He stopped and considered for a minute. He might just have found a way to mend some of the ill will with Mr. and Mrs. Richmond. "Abner, have you seen the Richmond girl?"

"Yeah, seen her when they was over at the café making a nuisance of themselves."

"What size would you guess she is?"

Seeing what Nathan was looking at, Abner rummaged around in the stack for a few minutes. "Reckon these ought to be about right."

"Put them on my account will ya? I'll settle up with you before the end of the week."

"Sure thing, Nathan, my boy. Let me give you a map out to Jack's place. Make sure you tell his missus I said hello."

With just a few more pleasantries and a promise to come by when he got back and spend some time with Grace, Nathan took his purchase and headed out the door to get Sunrise saddled and head out of town.

Nathan walked in to the livery to hear Hank talking to the Richmonds. "I understand yer telling me that the Preacher asked you to exercise this horse, but he ain't told *me* he wants ya to exercise his horse."

"I assure you, sir, my daughter may not dress decently, but she is not given to lying."

"I ain't sayin' she is, mister, but I can't let that there horse leave this stable without the Preacher's say so. You wouldn't want me ta let someone jus' walk in here and take a horse that belonged ta you, and I treat all my patrons the same."

Nathan came deeper into the livery to see Hank blocking the door to Lightning's stall, with Lucy inside and Lightning saddled. "It's ok, Hank. I did tell her I could use her help exercising Lightning. However, she and I need to come to an agreement. Lucy, I couldn't help but overhear your father say that they aren't happy with your choice of attire. To be honest, I'm not either. A young lady should dress like one, not like a mule skinner."

"Well, these clothes were good enough for Calamity Jane, so they're good enough for me."

"Lucy, you aren't helping your case. Jane was a friend of my grandfather's. She only wore breeches when she was mule skinning or buffalo hunting. Other than that, she dressed more ladylike."

Nathan held out the package that he had purchased at the dry goods store. "If you want to ride for me or with me, then you will take this package, go out to the outhouse, and change into them now. Otherwise our deal is off."

The girl looked like she might just walk out. Then Lightning butted her with his head. She looked at Nugget Nate's horse and the anger melted from her face. "Fine, give it here." Taking the package, she looked at Hank. "Where's yer outhouse?'

"It's around back, little lady."

The girl stormed out. Reginald looked at Nathan with gratitude on his face. "I don't know how you did that, but I thank you. Her mother and I tried everything we knew, but she insisted she was going to be a western woman."

Nathan smiled. "I have nothing against her wanting to be a western woman. She just needs to realize that western women are still women. For the most part they dress like a lady. When it isn't convenient, they modify their dress to make it convenient, but still as ladylike and modest as possible. You might want to visit the dry goods store and get her some more of those split skirts like I just gave her."

"Thank you, Mr. Ryder, I'll do that. You've actually kept me from having more of an issue with her mother."

"Look, Reginald, just call me Nathan, or if you really must, you can do like these guys around here and call me Preacher. But every time you say Mister Ryder I want to look around for my father."

"Of course. I'm sorry for the misunderstanding we had. I believe you're right, and I need to be a bit more learned about the life out here in the west." He rubbed his still bruised chin. "Just wish your lesson hadn't been so hard to take."

All three men were laughing as Lucy walked back in, wearing a split skirt in place of the breeches. "All right, I done changed. Can I ride Lightning now?"

"Well Lucy, I must say you're the spittin' image of a proper western lady. If you think you can keep up with me and Sunrise, then you can ride with me to the sheriff's farm just outside of town and back. That is, if your father approves."

Lucinda looked at her dad. "Please, Daddy?"

He nodded. "Just this once, Lucinda, but after this you must only accompany the Preacher if he can find a proper chaperone."

"Oh Daddy, he's too old for me and anyway I don't want no man. I want to prove a woman can make it on her own out west."

Nathan looked at the girl. "Lucy, your father is right. How about you run and get your brother. He can ride behind me on Sunrise."

Hank spoke up. "You headed out to Jack's, Nathan?"

"Yeah Hank, got an official telegram he needs to be aware of. Why?

"Doc Soneman and his wife are on their way out there in my buckboard. If'n ya'll give them two critters their heads ya should catch up with them in just a few minutes."

"Thanks, Hank, that'll do this time. Come on, Lucy, let's see if'n yer western enough to ride Nugget Nate's steed." With that taunt Nathan swung up into the saddle and took off out the back of the stable. Lucy mounted Lightning and, giving her best western whoop, took off after him.

Chapter Thirty-seven

The week flew by. Nathan had been busy from sunup to sundown every day. After returning from Jack's, he had put the plans Jack told him to into motion. Still no one had seen or heard anything from Kid Cody or the men who had helped him escape.

Nathan and Grace had kept busy planning their wedding. Grace had a new dress made and Nathan had a new suit. The church had been cleaned and decorated with simple wildflowers. Finally, the big day had arrived.

Nathan woke up on Saturday morning with a feeling of excitement and dread. He was excited that today Grace Hopewell would become his wife. However he couldn't get over the feeling of dread that something was wrong. Not being able to put his finger on what was causing it; Nathan got up and grabbed his Bible. When he needed comfort and peace, he knew where to go.

As he settled himself in the hotel lobby and opened Nate's old Bible, he bowed his head and went to God the Father with his concerns.

"Father God, I thank you that I can come to you with my concerns. I also thank you for the unexpected gift of Grace as my wife. Help us to keep you in the center of our marriage. We have agreed to stand upon your word that a three-stranded cord is not easily broken. We want to intertwine our two lives together with you as the central cord. Father, I know I should be the happiest man in the world today, but I can't overcome this feeling of dread. I give it to you, God. If there's something I need to do, show it to me. But no matter what, fill me with your peace that passes all understanding. I ask all this in Jesus' name, Amen."

Nathan looked down where the Bible had opened to and saw that God was already answering his prayer. Nate's worn old Bible had fallen open to Psalms 27. Nathan started reading, realizing that God was trying to tell him something.

"Ps 27:1 The LORD is my light and my salvation; whom shall I fear? The LORD is the strength of my life; of whom shall I be afraid? 2 When the wicked, even mine enemies and my foes, came upon me to eat up my flesh, they stumbled and fell. 3 Though an host should encamp against me, my heart shall not fear: though war should rise against me, in this will I be confident.

4 One thing have I desired of the LORD, that will I seek after; that I may dwell in the house of the LORD all the days of my life, to behold the beauty of the LORD, and to enquire in his temple. 5 For in the time of trouble he shall hide me in his pavilion: in the secret of his tabernacle shall he hide me; he shall set me up upon a rock. 6 And now shall mine head be lifted up above mine enemies round about me: therefore will I offer in his tabernacle sacrifices of joy; I will sing, yea, I will sing praises unto the LORD.

7 Hear, O LORD, when I cry with my voice: have mercy also upon me, and answer me. 8 When thou saidst, Seek ye my face; my heart said unto thee, Thy face, LORD, will I seek. 9 Hide not thy face far from me; put not thy servant away in anger: thou hast been my help; leave me not, neither forsake me, O God of my salvation. 10 When my father and my mother forsake me, then the LORD will take me up.

11 Teach me thy way, O LORD, and lead me in a plain path, because of mine enemies. 12 Deliver me not over unto the will of mine enemies: for false witnesses are risen up against me, and such as breathe out cruelty. 13 I had fainted, unless I had believed to see the goodness of the LORD in the land of the living. 14 Wait on the LORD: be of good courage, and he shall strengthen thine heart: wait, I say, on the LORD."

Nathan closed the Bible and stood. "I get it Lord. I will trust in you and wait on you. Thank you for your words." He walked over to Mark and reminded him that he would need bathwater sent up around noon so he could get cleaned up for his wedding.

"Yes sir, boss, I'll make sure it's done. wouldn't want Miss Grace to leave ya at the altar because you smell like Sunrise and gunsmoke."

"That's for sure, Mark. Feel free to leave a note telling everyone that rooms will be available after the wedding so you can attend if you want."

"Thanks Nathan. James has already told everyone the saloon will be closed 'til after yer hitchin'. From what he told me there were a bunch of toasts made ta ya'll last night. Better hope the Good Lord didn't approve all the blessings for children or you and Miss Grace'll be overwhelmed with young'uns."

Nathan laughed. "From your mouth to God's ears, about not approving them all. A few would be fine, but a passel of kids sounds kinda scary."

Nathan went to his room to drop off his Bible and lay out his clothes for the wedding later. He strapped on his guns and as he started out he remembered what Grace had told him the night before. "Nathan, you had better not show up for our wedding carrying those pistols. If you do I will make life hard on you for the foreseeable future."

He smiled as he left the room to get some food and check in with Jack. "I'll leave them at the jail for the wedding." He told the memory.

******

The day sped past for Nathan. After breakfast and a lot of good-natured ribbing from Mrs. Sue, he went to the barber and got a haircut and a shave. There, too, he was forced to endure the jests and japes of several of the town's menfolk, both married and single. Nathan tried to retreat to the hotel but there he faced the giggles and twittering of the chambermaids as they changed the linens in his room.

"We don't want your bride to sleep on dirty sheets now, Preacher," one of them commented.

The other laughed and winked. "Not that we figure she'll be getting much sleep." Both maids laughed at the blush which flooded Nathan's face as they made their way out of the room.

Now freshly washed and dressed in his wedding suit, Nathan strapped on his Colt but didn't tie it down. Yes, he had promised Grace not to come to the wedding armed, but he would carry at least as far as the jail. With his reputation and Kid Cody still on the loose, he wasn't taking any chances.

At the jail, Nathan met up with Bart and Jack. Bart had young Levi with him since Maryanne was helping Mrs. Gunderson get Grace ready for her big day.

"Well, Nathan, this is yer last chance to run, boy," Jack grinned at Nathan.

"Nope, Sheriff, I can't run. That girl would track me to the end of the earth. If she didn't, Bart's wife or the Gundersons would."

The three men laughed and Nathan took off his gun rig. "I promised Grace I wouldn't wear this to the wedding, Jack. Mind if I leave my gear here 'til afterwards?"

"Not at all. You got nothing to worry about, Nathan. Not all of us had to make that promise." Both Bart and Jack turned around and lifted up the back of their jackets to show they each had a hidden gun tucked into the small of their backs.

"If that no good brother of mine shows up at yer wedding, we'll handle him right quick."

Nathan clapped both men on the back. "Ya'll both be fine friends and I thank you for your caution. Let's just pray all this precaution is for nothing."

Jack and Bart nodded. "From your lips to God's ears, Preacher."

Jack took Nathan by the arm. "Best get you across to the church, Nathan. Wouldn't be good if the groom and official were late to this shindig. Might get ol' Abner's dander up. Then we would both be in for a world of hurt."

All three men and little Levi laughed as they exited the jail and headed to the church. There seemed to be a steady stream of locals headed that way too. Nathan just hoped there wasn't a repeat of Sunday's crowd. He didn't mind people wanting to wish him and Grace a happy marriage but the thought of so many coming just to glimpse the Preacher getting married, or to see if Kid Cody showed up, rankled at him. All the way up the street the feeling of dread that had so bothered Nathan all morning dropped heavy on his soul once more.

Jack led Nathan, Bart, and young Levi to the back door of the church. Once they entered Jack took a seat on the platform while Nathan and Bart went to front of the altar. Bart sat Levi in the first row where he could keep an eye on him, then stood beside Nathan.

Nathan looked out at the crowd in the church. There wasn't an empty seat to be found. Both side aisles were crammed full of people standing toe to heel. Several more tried to push in and crowd the center aisle but Jack's wife was having none of it.

She planted herself just inside the double doors and every time someone else tried to crowd in she could be heard to say, "You all will just have to stand outside and look in a winder. I'll have Jack arrest any one of you fool headed men who try to crowd the center aisle so the bride can't walk it."

Nathan was grateful for her help and tenacity. He knew she was a true western woman with a backbone made of steel. He wondered if Jack wasn't scared of crossing her by getting injured again. He knew he would be if Grace were like that. Who was he trying to fool? Grace *was* like that. How else did he end up at this altar today?

The pianist started playing and every eye turned to the doorway. Any moment now, the bride would enter and walk the aisle. Just when the wait was beginning to get uncomfortable there came a commotion from outside and the double doors of the church burst open.

In stumbled Abner Gunderson, half dressed. Nathan and Bart instantly noticed his Sunday go to meeting shirt was soaked in blood and he was holding a bloody towel to the side of his head. Abner's eyes searched the front and when they came to rest on Nathan, he held out his left hand, clutching a piece of paper. Without saying a word he collapsed, unconscious.

Both Doctor Soneman and Doctor Simms pushed through the crowd of people and got to the old merchant. Nathan, Bart, and Jack were just seconds behind. Luke looked up and said, "He's alive, just unconscious." Doc Simms gently waved some smelling salts under Abner's nose.

The old man jerked awake and frantically looked around. Seeing Nathan, he once again held out the piece of paper in his hand. "I'm sorry, son, that no good skunk got the drop on me and pistol whipped me. He's got our girls."

Nathan took the paper from Abner.

Preacher, I told ya you hadn't seen the last of me. I got me an Emerald that I hear you hold very dear, and imagine my surprise when I got my no account yellow brother's wife and that old gray haired biddy too. Ya'll want to ever see them alive again, you meet me in the street, in front of the church, just before sundown. If ya don't show I'll start killing everyone I see "til ya do. Today's the day, Preacher!

Kid Cody

Nathan looked at Bart and handed him the paper. "He's got the girls and Mrs. Gunderson." Searching the crowd, he saw Hank in the back.

"Hank, go saddle my horses and as many others as you can. We're gonna track him and finish this right now."

Bart reached out and snagged Nathan by the arm. "Nathan, yer not thinkin' straight. You can't go after him. He done told ya if you ain't here to face him he'll start killing people 'til ya are. You leave the girls to Jack and me. I think I know where he would have taken them."

"Jack isn't going anywhere." Mrs. Cole's voice came from the back of the crowd. "He still isn't re-covered enough to go riding around in those moun-tains chasing bandits."

Jack just nodded. "She's right and so is Bart. Nathan, no one here is fast enough to take the Kid ex-cept you, and I ain't able to ride them mountains just yet."

From the right side of the church came a voice, "I'll go with Bart."

Everyone looked right and saw Timothy Dillion step forward. "I figger between the two of us we know where the Kid's taken them and we can get them back."

Bart looked at the youngster for a minute before nodding. "He's right, Nathan, Timothy and I will deal with getting the ladies back and take care of the owl hoots watching them. You just deal with the Kid, and this time finish it once and for all."

Nathan looked at the two former bandits. "Bring her back to me and I'll be much obliged."

Bart and Timothy nodded. Bart looked at Mrs. Cole. "I'd be obliged if you would take care of young Levi 'til I get back, please, ma'am."

"Of course, Bart. You don't have to worry about him. We'll keep him safe."

The four men walked down the aisle and out the door: Bart and Timothy to get their horses, Nathan and Jack to get ready for battle with Kid Cody.

Chapter Thirty-eight

Nathan picked up his gunbelt and strapped it on. He turned to Jack and handed him the sheriff's badge. "This is yours, I believe. You'll be needing it."

Jack took it and reached into the drawer to pull out a deputy's badge to give Nathan. Nathan shook his head. "Not this time, Jack. This time it's personal all the way. The Kid wants to know which gunslinger is faster. Well he's gonna find out."

Nathan turned and walked out of the Jail, headed to his hotel to get dressed for the conflict at hand. Jack watched as he left, thinking he had never seen the Preacher so hard or cold. The Kid didn't stand a chance. "God have mercy on his soul."

Nathan went straight to his room. He undressed and laid his wedding suit on the bed. He prayed he would need it again later this evening. He put on his buckskins and opened Nate's trunk. He strapped on his gunbelt, grabbed his second gun, and slid it in place on the right side against his holster facing his left hand.

He slid Nate's bowie knife into the small of his back, adjusting it so that it was easy to reach and yet comfortable to wear. Finally, he picked up Ol' Davey's hatchet, as Nate had always called it, and slid it into place on the left side of his gunbelt. He turned and walked out, closing the door behind himself.

Mark looked up as he saw Nathan heading down the stairs. Nathan knew He was startled by what he saw. Cold determination was set on the face of the Preacher. He shuddered as Nathan exited the hotel.

Abner was pulling on a clean shirt when he looked out the window of the doctor's office to see Nathan stalking down the center of the street. Except for the hat, the old merchant would have sworn he was seeing Nugget Nate forty years ago.

Nathan looked just like his grandfather had the day he rescued that eastern girl by killing her abductors in the street. What was that girl's name again? Penny, that's what Nate had called her when he'd left her in Wilhelmina's care. Abner was chilled to the bone when he remembered what had happened that day. Quickly he prayed God would be merciful to the Preacher and spare him the burden Nate had carried after that fateful day.

******

Bart and Timothy lay prone on a flat rock overlooking a small shack nestled in the foothills just beyond Franklin. This was the last hideout the Missouri River Gang had used. They both were sure this was where the Kid had taken the women after kidnapping them from Abner's place. They were certain someone was here because of the thin trail of smoke rising from the shack's chimney.

Bart wanted to get as good an idea as he could of how many men his brother had watching the ladies. With no windows on the back of the structure and only two horses and a buckboard visible out front there was no real way to tell. Knowing his brother, there could be as few as one or as many as five. They knew the Kid had two of the gang with him when the prison wagon was attacked. They also knew only two men had attacked the wagon, thanks to the telegram sent by the warden to Franklin.

Bart motioned for Tim to slide back with him off the rock. "Ok, this ain't getting us anywhere, so I got another plan." He took of his long duster coat and gave it to Timothy. "You're younger and skinnier than me, so you slither down onto that roof and place my coat over the top of that chimney. When the place fills with smoke, they'll have to come out to try and un-clog the chimney. I'll be waiting along the side and we'll get the drop on them then. As soon as they come out, you remove that coat. If the girls are in there I don't want them choking ta death before we can res-cue 'em."

Timothy took the coat. "Got it. Just be careful. They're as likely to come out shootin' as to come out empty handed."

Bart smiled a smile Timothy had seen before. It looked friendly 'til you noticed it didn't reach to his eyes, which were as cold as steel. "Well if'n they do, that will make this so much easier. We can just leave their dead carcasses here for the buzzards."

Both men started moving slowly and cautiously down the mountainside, disturbing as little as they could. When they reached the shack Bart boosted Timothy up on the roof, then slipped around the side where he could see the front door. Timothy carefully and quietly approached the stone chimney and placed Bart's duster over the top, blocking the hole, causing the smoke to back up into the shack. Within a couple of minutes they could hear coughing coming from inside.

Bart watched as the door was thrown open and two men stumbled outside. Both had pistols drawn and were trying to clear their eyes and lungs of the wood smoke. "Drop them shooters, boys!" Bart yelled as he fired a round between them to let them know they were covered. Both men whirled to where they had heard the sound of his voice and aimed their guns. Three guns fired as one as both Bart and Timothy fired at the outlaws. Both men crumpled to the ground without getting a shot off.

Timothy quickly removed the duster from the top of the smoke stack as Bart rushed inside with both guns still drawn. Inside, he could make out the three women tied up and gagged, choking on smoke. He holstered his weapons, pulled a knife from his boot, and cut the cords holding all three to their chairs. As they exited the shack, both Wilhelmina and Grace grabbed him. "How's Abner?" "Where's Nathan?"

"Abner's fine. He was with both Doc Soneman and Doc Simms when I left. They were cleaning him up and giving him stitches."

Then turning to Grace, he said, "Nathan stayed in town to deal with my brother. He had threatened to shoot bystanders if Nathan didn't show."

"Oh, No! Bart, you have to hurry. Nathan isn't facing your brother alone. The Kid has three men with him. They were going to catch Nathan in a crossfire if The the Kid lost."

Bart looked at Timothy. "You bring the girls back to town in the buckboard. I'll try and get back to help Nathan."

Without waiting for a reply, Bart raced back up the mountain to where his horse was tethered. He ripped the reins free, vaulted onto its back, and tore off towards town as fast as he could go. When he heard the thunder of hoofs behind him he turned to see Grace on Timothy's mount riding hell-bent for leather after him. "You need to go back, Grace. It won't be safe to ride with me."

"No, Bart. I love him and I need to be there for him."

Without another word, the two raced to town, both praying they wouldn't be too late.

Chapter Thirty-nine

Nathan walked down the center of the street heading to the church. Several town people saw him and started to approach him to offer their sympathy or express their good will, until they took one look at his countenance. They might have thought he didn't notice or that he was lost in his own dark thoughts, but they would have been wrong. He was deeply aware of everything that was going on around him. He noticed the looks Sue and Henry gave him as they passed; looks of concern that turned to fear. He heard Sue tell Henry, "We needed to pray for that boy. He's on the edge again."

Nathan noticed some of those who got out of his way turned and walked along the boardwalk behind him, anxious to see the shootout. To him none of it mattered. He was in a place where the only thing that mattered was the man who had taken Grace from him. The one who had pushed and pushed until Nathan had surrendered to the violence that was in all men's hearts. He was so intent on everything that he saw her coming before he heard her. Even she didn't matter, not this time. He had been gentle but firm with her last time. This time he would not be.

"Mister Ryder, Mister Ryder, Mister Ryder, I need to speak to you. My husband said to leave you alone, but I cannot allow my family to stay over that saloon one minute longer." Priscilla Richmond was not going to be put off any longer. She had tried to talk to the new desk clerk but he told her that Mister Ryder was out and the desk was closed till further notice.

Yet here was that man walking up the street like he owned it. Well he would listen to her or face the full force of her wrath this time. He might intimidate her husband but she had brought two children into this world and worn corsets that would put most men in bed for a week. This man was nothing to her.

She rounded on him and got one look at his face. What she saw stopped her in her tracks. She slowly backed up away from the visage of cold hard death shining out of his eyes. "Umm ... Ahh ... Never mind. I think it can wait 'til you're in the office."

Priscilla made a beeline for the hotel. She needed a sherry to help steady her nerves and renew her courage. As a matter of fact, maybe Reginald should deal with the hotel owner from now on. Yes, it was a man's place to deal with these situations. She would just continue to look after the children.

Nathan never slowed his pace. As he reached the corner to turn to the church he slowed long enough to slip the hammer-thong off his Colt. Then he turned and continued towards the church.

He looked left as he caught motion coming toward him on that side. He saw Jack moving as fast as he could on his injured leg. He had his sixgun tied down just like Nathan. He stopped and faced his friend and former boss. He shook his head. "Not this time, Jack. This one doesn't end in arrest or surrender. Bart had it right. Kid Cody gets planted this time. I gave him every chance to come to God and turn around. He wants a showdown. He's gonna get one."

"I don't think you noticed Nathan, but I ain't wearing my badge either. I'm not here as sheriff. I'm here as your friend and to fulfill my debt to ya. I won't interfere, but I'm gonna watch yer back for ya."

Nathan nodded and the two proceeded up the street together. As they reached the open area in front of the church, Jack peeled off to the side and Nathan took his stance in the middle of the street.

He watched as the sun started to slip behind the foothills. The time the Kid demanded had arrived but there was no sign of the sidewinder.

"Kevin!! I'm here, ya yella-bellied lowlife. Just like ya wanted. Just me and my Colt. You wanted to know who's faster. You made big boasts about plantin' me, well here I am. Come and get some!!"

From the side of the church a shadow detached and slowly approached the Preacher. "Big words, Greenhorn. Let's see if ya have the sand to back them. Oh, but I gotta tell ya, boy. No matter what happens, you ain't never gonna see the girl again. I told the boys, win or lose, plant her lying tongue and plant it deep. As for my brother's fluff and that old biddy, they're all singing with the angels by now."

Nathan's heart froze and he silently prayed for Bart and Timothy to succeed in their mission. "Don't matter, Kevin. You're gonna be burning in hell before the night's done."

"I done told you MY NAME IS KID CODY!!!"
The Kid's hand streaked towards his sixgun. He
cleared leather and yet Nathan hadn't moved. As he
was bringing his gun up to bear on the Preacher it
looked like Nathan had just shrugged. A loud boom
split the air. Cody dropped his gun. His hand didn't
obey his commands anymore. Then, before he could
even realize he'd been shot, the light faded and he fell
to the ground dead.

Nathan walked up to the corpse and said, "Don't
matter what ya call yerself. Now it only matters what
God calls ya." He turned to walk away and felt a bullet burn across his cheek. He looked up and saw two
men, one on each side of the street, aiming rifles at
him. His sixguns both flew into his hand and boomed
again. The two outlaws fell dead where they stood.
Just as he started once more to walk away, he heard
another shot behind him and turned to see a man falling from the church bell tower. Then he noticed Bart
and Grace galloping past the church at full speed.

Before the horses had come to a complete stop,
Grace was throwing herself off her mount and into
Nathan's arms. Nathan grasped her like a drowning
man grabbed a life preserver.

"Thank God, you're alive," he said at the same
time she said, "Thank God we were in time." Then
there was no more speaking as their lips met and the
whole world dissolved around them. When they
parted for air, Nathan looked at the woman who
meant the whole world to him. "I'm gonna go get
changed so we can get married."

He started to turn when she grabbed him. "No, Nathan."

He stopped and turned. "No? You don't want to get married?

"No, we aren't waiting another minute. Jack's here. There are witnesses here. I want to marry you right now."

"But I'm armed and in my buckskins."

"I don't care. We aren't waiting not one more minute." Then in true western fashion, Grace turned to where Jack stood and yelled, "Get over here Jack Cole. I'm getting hitched right now."

Jack came running up as everyone laughed and gathered close.

No one cared that there were dead outlaws in the street. It seemed everyone wanted to see the Preacher get his happy ending.

Chapter Forty

Jack convinced Grace to move her impromptu wedding ceremony into the church. As they were entering the building, he sent his wife to get Abner Gunderson for him. Then he set some of the townsfolk to lighting the lanterns hanging from the ceiling.

While the preparations were being made for a nighttime wedding, Nathan took the opportunity to remove his weapons and place them on the front pew. Grace might not have allowed him to go and get cleaned up and into his new suit, but he could at least honor her original request and get married without being armed to the teeth.

As the last lantern was lit, the sound of a wagon arriving could be heard outside. Nathan, Grace, Bart and Jack all went outside to see Timothy arriving with Maryanne and Wilhelmina. Abner was also coming from up the street with a clean shirt and a bandage on his head. Wilhelmina and Grace rushed to the old man, relieved that his injury was not as bad as they had believed.

Maryanne was reunited with her husband and child. Everywhere people looked were signs of the love these people felt for each other and the closeness of their relationships.

"Well, since you're all finally here, maybe Jack will quit delaying my wedding now." Grace's impatience and determination caused everyone to chuckle as they re-entered the church.

Jack headed to the platform while Nathan and Bart took their places on the right side of the altar. Maryanne took her place on the left side of the altar. With every eye watching her, Grace took Abner's arm and they walked up the aisle. As Grace took her first step, the church's pianist began to play the wedding march.

Nathan looked at his bride coming up the aisle and thanked God for his protection and provision that day. It was as if everyone else had completely disappeared from their presence.

Every person in the church could see the love and complete devotion these two young people had for each other. It was obvious to everyone they only had eyes for each other.

As Grace arrived at the altar, Nathan stepped forward and took her arm from Abner. Together they turned to face Jack who, like everyone else, was smiling at the two of them.

Jack looked out at the crowd and began the wedding ceremony. "Dearly beloved, we are gathered here tonight in the presence of God to unite these two in Holy Matrimony. It has been a long hard road to get us here today, but with God's grace, protection and provision we have arrived, a little late and battle-worn, but we made it."

With that statement, spontaneous applause and cheers erupted all throughout the church. Jack smiled and continued. "So let us delay no longer. Who gives this woman to be married?"

Abner stepped forward saying, "Seeing as how the Hopewells have passed into Glory, Wilhelmina and I speak for them and give Grace to Nathan to be wed." Abner turned, walked back to his wife, and hugged the already-crying woman.

"If there is anyone here who has just cause why Nathan and Grace should not be married, let them speak now, and hope the Preacher don't ever find ya."

Everyone laughed, and the last of the tension of the day seeped away. Jack smiled and waited a good minute before continuing. "I see no one objects. Wise choice." Again, his words brought laughter. "Now, let us continue. David Nathaniel Ryder the Third, do you take this woman to be your lawfully wedded wife?"

Nathan looked deep into Grace's eyes. "I do."

Jack nodded. "Do you vow to love, honor, and cherish her, to protect and provide for her, in sickness and in health, in times of feast or famine, forsaking all others 'til death do you part?"

"I do."

Turning to Grace, Jack asked, "Do you Grace Lillian Hopewell, take this man to be your lawfully wedded husband?"

Grace lost herself in the love coming from Nathan's eyes. "I do."

"Do you vow to love, honor, and obey him in sickness or in health, in times of feast or famine, forsaking all others 'til death do you part?"

"I do."

"Nathan, you told me yesterday you had a ring to present to Grace. Will you take her hand and place the ring on it?"

Nathan took her hand, reached into his shirt pocket, and pulled out his grandmother's diamond wedding ring. He had found it the day before in Nate's trunk. He slipped it on Grace's finger.

"Now repeat these words after me. With this ring I thee wed."

Nathan looked deep into Graces eyes and let the depth of his love for her rise to the surface where everyone in the room could see it clearly. "With this ring, I thee wed."

Grace, overwhelmed by what she saw began to cry silently with tears of joy, and opened herself up to Nathan, also allowing everyone to see the depth of her love for this man before her. The sight was more than several of those present could stand and all around the sanctuary eyes began to leak with tears. Some at experiencing the feeling for those they loved again, others for sadness at never having experienced that depth of love.

"By the power invested to me by God and the state of Missouri, I now pronounce you man and wife. Nathan, you may kiss your bride."

Even before the words were completely out of Jack's mouth, Nathan had Grace in his arms and his lips crushed against her. Time seemed to stand still for both of them. Everyone and everything else disappeared as they lost themselves in the sensation of their love for each other. The passion built between the two of them until neither thought they were going to escape it.

Just when it seemed they would lose themselves in each other, Jack's voice interrupted them. "Uh-hum. I said you could kiss your bride, not devour her. Take a breather, Preacher."

Nathan pulled back as everyone in the church broke into laughter once again. From somewhere in the room a man's voice was heard yelling, "Let the honeymoon begin." The laughter increased and Grace turned almost as red as her hair. Jack stepped down from the pulpit and, turning the couple to face the audience, said, "Let me present to you Mr. and Mrs. David Nathaniel Ryder the Third."

The crowd erupted in cheers and several rebel yells. Nathan led Grace back down the aisle, getting stopped along the way with hugs and back-slaps. Everyone wanted to congratulate the happy couple. When they finally made it to the door, Nathan took Grace by the hand and headed straight to the hotel.

About halfway there, Nathan became aware of someone yelling his name. He stopped and turned around to see young Levi running toward them with Bart and Maryanne coming slower behind him. When the boy got close, Nathan could see Levi struggling to carry Nathan's gun rig. Nathan waited for Levi and his parents to catch up. He took his rig from Levi, and his knife and Ol' Davey's hatchet from Bart. Bart put his arm around Nathan and Maryanne put hers around Grace. Maryanne led Grace a little away from the men and began to speak quietly with her.

Bart led Nathan a little away from the women, and when Nathan started to object Bart interrupted him. "I know you want to be with your bride, but Maryanne and I both thought it might be best to speak with you first. I know you love her and can't wait to consummate your marriage, but we thought we should see if there were any questions you might have before you were alone with her.

Nathan looked at his friend, "I don't think that's necessary, Bart."

"Maybe not for you, Nathan. But I guarantee ya, the girl is anxious and needs some reassuring. So walk with me to the hotel, and let Maryanne settle her nerves."

Nathan nodded and the two friends continued to the hotel. When they arrived, Bart led them up to the desk. "Mark, did ya do as I asked before this all started?"

"Yes sir, Mister Cody, the girls are filling the tub now. We heard the shouting all the way from here and figured it was time."

"Good. After they get the Ryders' filled, will you have them fill the one in my room too? I am sure Maryanne will want a bath after today's ordeal."

"Of course, sir. Mister Ryder, allow me to offer my and the whole staff's congratulations to you and Mrs. Ryder."

"Thank you, Mark. Will you see to it that no one disturbs us in the morning? I think we will both want to sleep in after today."

"Certainly sir, I will see to it personally."

Just then, Grace and Maryanne entered the hotel. Grace's face was once again lit with an intense blush. Apparently, Maryanne had indeed answered some questions and explained what was to come to Nathan's bride. Nathan walked to the two women and held out his arm to Grace, who took it. Together they headed up to Nathan's room.

As they reached the door, Nathan opened it, then scooped Grace into his arms. "I know this isn't our home, but it is for the next week, so I thought carrying you across the threshold would be appropriate."

"Thank you, dear." Grace laid her head on his shoulder. Together they crossed into the room. Nathan kicked the door shut and Grace slipped the lock in place. Their lips met again and the whole world disappeared.

When they came up for air, Nathan carried his wife to the washroom where a full tub of steaming water awaited her. "Levi and Mark thought you might enjoy a bath after your ordeal this afternoon."

Grace nodded. "That would be wonderful. Remind me to thank them later."

"I will."

Nathan put her down and turned to leave. "I'll wait for you in the other room."

Grace reached out and stopped him. "Why? Aren't you going to help me out of this dress? Plus, if you leave, who will wash my back?"

Nathan looked at his wife. "Are you sure?"

"Nathan Ryder, we are husband and wife. In just a bit we will be in bed together. Now is not the time for you to be shy. Not only that, but you smell like gunsmoke. You need a bath as badly as I do."

As she was speaking, she began to undo the strings of his buckskins, removing his clothes. She ran her hands over his shoulders and chest, marveling at the man God had given her. Slowly she turned around, indicating the buttons of her dress. "My button hook is still at the Gunderson's. Will you undo these for me?"

Nathan started as if spooked, then reached out and undid each of Grace's buttons. When the last one was undone Grace turned toward him and let the garment fall to the ground. Quickly she shed the rest of her garments and without a word, she took his hand and led him to the bath. Together they got clean from the day's trials, marveling at the gift of the spouse God had given them.

Much later as they lay in bed with Grace cradled in his arms, Nathan watched as his wife slept peacefully. Silently he thanked God for keeping her safe that day, and for allowing him to prevail in the battle with the Kid and his gang. He asked God to bless their marriage and to complete the plans he had for both of them.

Nathan didn't know what the future held, but he was grateful God was allowing him to face them with Grace at his side. He kissed her forehead as she slept, then whispered, "I love you, Grace Ryder. I can't wait to settle in Redemption with you."

"I love you too, Nathan," came her sleepy reply. Their lips met again and sleep was the last thing either of them thought of for quite a while.

Epilog
Eight Days Later.

The week since Nathan and Grace's wedding had flown by. Everyone thought it was sweet that Nathan wasn't seen without Grace the entire week. They had stolen what time alone they could, and did everything else together. They retrieved their wagon and team from Hank, and Nathan had settled up with him for Sunrise and Lightning. Then they had gone to the dry goods store and collected the supplies Abner had reserved for them. They met the new owner, settling their account and loading their supplies.

Later in the week, Nathan's final employee arrived in Nate's private Pullman set up. The Pullman and cattle car were unhitched and Nathan arranged to have them stored on the sidetrack until the railroad made it to New Mexico. He introduced Grace to their lawyer and business manager, Justin Smythe. Throughout the week, Justin kept Grace entertained with stories of Nathan's past and their trips west with Nate.

Before long the time had come and everything was set. The Gundersons' wagon was at the staging area along with the Codys' and the Ryders. Doc Soneman had his wagon ready as well, having been left behind by the last wagon train. Timothy was driving the chuck wagon. Abner had decided since they were all going to the same place they would just cook together. Justin had picked up a smaller wagon for himself and had it outfitted at the dry goods store. Everything was ready. Monday was here and they were all mounting up, ready to pull out.

Those who had become close friends with them had come to see them off.

Sue and Hank wished them luck. Hank called, "Ya'll take care of each other on that trail. Oh, and whatever ya'll do, don't let that Abner Gunderson cook anything. Ya'll die of food poisoning if'n ya do."

They all laughed, giving the old southern cook and his wife a hug. As Sue hugged Nathan she told him, "I'm proud of the man yer becoming, Preacher. Take care of that gem of a wife God gave ya."

"I will, Sue. Thanks for yer friendship and wise counsel."

"Ah y'all, go on now before ya get's me ta bawling."

Next Jack Cole said his goodbyes to everyone. "Abner, I'm gonna miss ya around here. Ya been a faithful member of our town and we are gonna be the worst for yer leaving."

"Jack, I thank ya. Now you get to fill in fer the pastor when he's on circuit. I be thinking you'll find it ain't as easy as Nathan and Pastor Bryce make it seem."

Jack nodded and turned to Nathan and Levi. "Well, gentlemen, I think our town will be a bit duller without ya. I, for one, am looking forward to it."

Everyone laughed, and Jack shook each man's hand. "Seriously, ya both are welcome here anytime. If either of ya decide to get into lawman work, let me know. I'll give ya a good recommendation."

Nathan and Levi thanked him and told him how much they had enjoyed his friendship while in Franklin. Nathan looked around and saw Timothy saying goodbye to what had to be his family. The woman who Nathan was sure was Tim's mother walked over to him. "Preacher, thank you for leading my boy to Christ. You were the answer to a mother's prayer. I also want to thank ya for getting him out of the gunslinger life. You take care of him for me, please."

Nathan smiled. "I will do so, ma'am, and I promise, Mrs. Dillon, Grace and I will keep him fed and dry. Plus, we'll try and remind him to write you and let ya know how he's doing."

"I'm much obliged."

With the last of the good-byes said, Nathan indicated that everyone should mount up. Just as he was getting ready to move out, four more Conestoga wagons pulled in to the yard. Mr. Richmond jumped down from the first one and yelled at Nathan. "Glad we caught ya. I didn't think the servants were gonna get here in time, but luckily they did."

"Reginald, are all these wagons yours?"

"Yes, Nathan. I told you our servants were bringing our belongings. You told me we could travel with you if they got here in time."

"Yes, but I figured a couple of guys and one wagon. What in the world did you do, bring your whole plantation with ya?"

"No, these are just the important furnishings from the main house, and supplies."

"Okay, well, as long as you have what you need to provide for everyone and ya'll pull yer own weight, I don't see why ya'll can't join us. Just pull in the line before Timothy there, as we ride out."

"Sure thing. Thank you again."

"No problem, but Reginald, I want to be plain here. If you or your people give me any trouble, we'll leave ya'll at the next town along the way. Do you understand? Ain't nothing personal, but everyone's gotta pull their own weight on the trail." Nathan pointedly looked at Prisicilla, sitting under an umbrella and fanning herself in the second wagon.

"I understand. Our part will be done, I assure you."

"Ok, get ready to head out then."

Nathan walked back to Timothy and told him to hold back 'til after the four Richmond wagons had filed into line. Then Nathan walked to his wagon and climbed up beside Grace.

"Nathan, are you sure about this?"

"Not really, but I can't let them go on their own. They'd be dead in less than a week. Let's just pray they're ready for this and keep their word about pulling their own weight."

"And if they don't?"

"Then I guess I'll just have to teach them how."

"So you let them come so you could beat him up again?"

"One must find their entertainment where they can, my dear. Besides, this time, maybe I'll let Abner or Levi do the honors."

"Oh, you." Grace slapped her husband on the arm, then leaned against him, laying her head on his shoulder for just a minute before sitting as close as she could get.

Nathan took one last look at Franklin and, tipping his hat to those watching, stood up and yelled in a loud and clear voice, *"WAGONS HO!!!"*

With the creek and groan of the wagons and bawling of the beasts, the wagon train headed out of Franklin, Missouri onto the Sante Fe trail, heading to Redemption in the New Mexico territory and adventure along the way.

The End

About The Author

George McVey is an ordained pastor who has worked in several different types of churches. He lived in several different states, but has finally settled in his home state, West Virginia. George is married to his high-school sweetheart, Sheri. The two have been married 26 years. Together they have 3 children now, Valerie, George Jr., and Alfred. Valerie has given them one grandson, Nathan.

PG, as his friends call him, has always been a storyteller. As a teen he used to create and tell stories to his friends and family. As a pastor he makes up stories to illustrate the points of his sermons and Bible study lessons.

Two years ago God moved PG to begin to write. He has written several Bible studies and short stories. His first two books are non-fiction Bible studies. One day he woke up with several characters in his head trying to tell him their stories. He began writing them down.

One of the stories is this book. He is currently working on the sequel entitled *Redeeming Trail.* PG is also working on another non-fiction book entitled *The Weapons of Our Warfare.* You can find all PG's books on his Amazon Author page: Pastor George H McVey Sr. Several of his short stories are on his short story blog: http://georgesshorts.wordpress.com/

If you wish to contact PG you may do so on face-book at https://www.facebook.com/pastor.mcvey?ref=tn_tnmn or email him at pastor.george.mcvey@g-mail.com. He looks forward to hearing what you think of *Redeeming Reputation.* Also, go to Amazon.-com, leave a review and tell your friends about PG's books.

Be on the lookout for Book Two of the
Redemption Tales Series

Redeeming Trail

Avalible March 1, 2013

Continue reading for an exciting preview of
Redeeming Trail.

.

Chapter One

Diamond Dale Cavanagh sat in the saloon in Independence playing Five Card Stud like he did most nights. Only tonight he was having trouble concentrating. There was a guy from the current wagon train who claimed there was a new gunslinger in the territory. Joe was telling his tale and garnering free drinks with every repeat. "I tells ya the Preacher reaches out and beats him to his own gun and pistol-whips him on the head. Kid Cody falls to the ground, out before he even realized he'd been outdrawn with his own six-shooter. Then the Preacher walks over to the desk clerk, breaks open the shooter and drops all the cartridges in his hand, then gives him the gun. Then he tells him to send someone to get the sheriff so the cowboy can sleep it off. Then he turns like an eastern gentleman, offers the school marm his hand, and escorts her to dinner, purty as ya please."

Dale tried to ignore the drifter, but the tales just kept coming about how this Preacher took out three more men that night in a fair fight. How he faced down the Kid's brother, Black Bart, the next day; then later in the week took on the rest of the Missouri River gang, killing all but two of them.

Dale folded his hand and walked over to the storyteller. "Now I think yer just spinning tales, fella. Ain't anyone that fast or that good."

Joseph looked at the gambler with the diamond buttons on his shirt. "Lookie here, mister, I'm a tellin' ya straight. The Preacher's quick as a greased pig, and faster than lightnin' on the plain. Why iffen an owl hoot meets the Preacher he's a gonna meet God, either on his knees in prayer or face ta face."

Dale looked the drifter in the eye and saw that he believed every single word he was saying. Just then the Western Union agent came in a shakin his head. "Well boys, who's buyin' me around? I just delivered the most interesting piece of news to the marshal not five minutes ago. Seems like Kid Cody done went and got himself killed."

"What you talkin' 'bout, Rusty?"

"According to the sheriff in Franklin some feller named the Preacher just out drew him and shot him dead."

With those words Dale downed his drink and motioned to the rest of his boys that they were leaving. If there was new talent in Franklin and the Missouri River Gang was gone, then it was time for the Cavanagh Gang to expand its territory a bit to the east. Besides, Dale needed to see this Preacher fella for himself and maybe add to his own reputation. "Mount up, boys; it's time to head out to Franklin. I think we need to see this Preacher for ourselves and test his resolve."

Twelve men climbed into the saddle and turned east. In a cloud of dust and the sound of thundering hooves the Cavanagh Gang set out for Franklin and a chance to see Diamond Dale brace the Preacher.

*****

The wagon train was in sight of Boone Lick as Nathan halted the train to rest the teams, water them, and allow the wagoneers a chance to grab a bit of lunch and stretch the kinks out of the drivers. Nathan and Abner walked a bit away from the group to talk about the rest of the day.

"Abner, I don't want to drive them too hard to-day. Where's the best camping point for us to stop tonight without pushing too hard? I mean, besides you, Tim, Levi and me, most of these people are used to the easier livin' in the east."

Abner Gunderson took off his hat and scratched at the stitches on the side of his head. "I reckon yer right, Nathan. Let's see." He pulled a map out of his breeches pocket and looked at it for a minute. "I fig-ure we ought to be able to make it ta Arrow Rock 'round five tonight. That'd be the best place to make camp. It's got a stream that runs down off the rock and a wide space we can circle the wagons."

Nathan nodded. "Sounds good. Let's put some grub in our stomachs and then round 'em all up. Once we get there I want us to all eat together and make some decisions. Also, I want to make sure the Rich-monds and their servants understand what's expected on this trip."

"I was a might surprised when ya let that tinhorn and his four wagons join the line. Are ya sure that was wise? That woman's gonna right drive us crazy, I'm a thinkin'."

Laughing, Nathan nodded. "Yer probably right, ol' timer, but I'll tell ya like I told Grace this morning. If worse comes to worse I can always administer another lesson in life in the west or let you or Levi administer it."

"That sounds right fun. I wouldn't mind seeing that dandy try them there Queensbury rules on ole Black Bart, fer sure."

"Levi, Abner. Call him Levi."

"Oops, I plum fergot."

Then the two men went and got a bite to eat. After they were both satisfied Nathan looked at his wagon drivers and yelled "Wagons Ready?"

From up and down the line came the answer, *"All Set!"*

Nathan and every other driver mounted up. Nathan, grabbing the reins in firm hands, bellowed, "Wagons *Ho!*" Snapping the reins set Tiny and Mouse to pulling the Ryder wagon westward once more. Nathan had no inkling that trouble in the form of Diamond Dale Cavanagh and his Cavanagh Gang was heading toward Franklin with bloodlust for the Preacher, David Nathaniel Ryder the Third, in their hearts. Trouble was gonna find them soon enough, and it would dog them this whole trail.

*****

Levi Cody walked along with one hand on the harness of his lead ox. He was leading the team from the ground, allowing his wife Maryann to get used to the feel of the reins in her hands. He kept sneaking a glance back at her, thanking God repeatedly for a second chance to be a husband and father. No sooner had that prayer winged heavenward when he felt the small hand of his son slip into his. Young Levi was trying so hard to be a man like his dad, the dad he hadn't even known until a week ago. Levi let go of the ox, reached down, snagged the five-year-old-boy and swung him up on the back of the ox. "Well, son, why don't you ride Ol' Blue here a while so we can talk, and rest yer legs a might?"

"Ok Daddy. What ya want to talk about?"

"Tell me about your life in Philadelphia. Did you have many friends there?"

"Not a lot. I spent most of my time with mama, listening to her talk about you and how we were gonna find you someday. But I did have one friend. His name was Joel Jensen. His daddy said you used to work fer him as a policeman. Is that true?"

"Yes, I did, until your uncle tricked me into thinking I was gonna be hung as a killer. Then I didn't listen to your mama, Captain Jensen, or God and I ran off to hide. What lesson do you think that should teach us, little Levi?"

"I don't know, Daddy, what lesson should it teach us?"

Reaching up and tousling his son's auburn hair, Levi smiled. "Always listen to yer Mama cause she is one smart lady."

Little Levi smiled back at his papa and nodded his agreement.

The two Cody men went on in silence for a while. One was grateful to finally meet and get to spend time with his daddy like other boys he'd known. The other was lost in his thoughts of the new life he was going to carve out of the New Mexico Territory for himself, his wife and son.

******

Nathan kept stealing glances at his wife sitting beside him on the wagon seat. It seemed almost like a dream. He had this beautiful woman beside him and she was his wife. *Lord, how things have changed in the short time I've been out west. You've blessed me with friends, more money than any one man has a right to and the most beautiful wife I could have ever imagined. Thank you for all that you have given me. Lord, help me be the type of godly husband who always loves his wife like you command, just as your Son loved the church.*

He reached out his right arm, put it around his wife, and drew her in as close as he could. Grace looked at him with her emerald-green eyes and Nathan felt his heart skip a beat. *I wonder if I will ever get used to how beautiful she is?*

Grace smiled and laid her head on his shoulder, content with what God had provided for her in a husband. She felt her husband squeeze her even closer and whisper, "I love you Grace Ryder. You definitely are flesh of my flesh and bone of my bone."

Grace sighed, and exaggerating her Georgian accent, answered, "Why I do declare Mister Ryder, you sure know how to flatter a girl. Why if you keep this up I may just need my salts to keep from swooning."

Nathan chuckled, pulled his arm back, and concentrated on keeping Tiny and Mouse reined in. No sense letting those two big beautiful Swedish plow horses set a pace the mules and oxen couldn't match. The miles melted beneath their hooves as they drew nearer to their first night on the trail, heading for their new lives in Redemption.

For more of this exciting story look for Redeeming Trail book two of the Redemtion Tales Series

Avalible March 1, 2013.

And if you enjoyed this book you may wish to check out the following books as well.

 <u>Healing Love</u> by Sophie Dawson

Lydia Walcott is on the run.. Seeking shelter from an ice storm in a livery stall, Lydia goes to sleep hoping that in this small town of Cottonwood she'll find a job, a place to live and friends.

Dr. Sterling Graham, having just delivered a baby, rides back to town over the ice covered roads. Exhausted from the long night, he decides to sleep on the cot in the livery.

Sterling's reputation and career, along with Lydia's hope for a new life, are put in jeopardy when gossips spread the news that, "Doc spent the night in the stable with a woman."
The story grows as 'facts' are added. Something needs to be decided that will repair the damage to Sterling's career and give Lydia the home and safety she needs.

The unwelcome solution is that they marry. How do they learn about each other and mesh two lives into a successful marriage which honors God, while coping with issues of trust, pride, epidemic and injury, and the fear that Lydia's brother will find her?

 Lord's Love by Sophie Dawson

Cottonwood 1875

Out from under her domineering mother and into an apartment above her workplace, Maggie Taylor finally blossoms into the woman she feels God wants her to be. She revels in her independence and doesn't want any sort of entanglement with a man.

Forced by his father to leave England, Sinjon Lytton arrives in Cottonwood only to find he's to work as a stable hand.

Maggie's mother would love nothing more than to see them married. Maggie worries if their faiths are too different to get what her heart desires. Sinjon wants what Sinjon wants and nothing is going to stand in his way.

When all options seem wrong, can they learn to trust God and see that he will make a way? Even when it seems impossible?

 Giving Love by Sophie Dawson

'The Lord giveth and Lord taketh away. Blessed be the Name of the Lord.'

The verse has special meaning to Drew Richards and Katie Reed. Both are reeling from the worst loss they have ever known. Drew lost his wife, Rachel, in childbirth. Katie, both her husband and infant son in a fire.

Now, to save Drew's newborn daughter, he has to ask Katie to do the unthinkable; nurse his daughter knowing each time will be like an arrow to her soul. Katie knows the pain of losing both spouse and child at the same time. She will do anything to keep Drew from experiencing that same pain.

Can love grow from the giving of themselves for each other? Will a rash of petty thefts and an interfering know-it-all cause more problems than they can overcome? Will they live their lives in a loveless marriage?

Chantal's Call by Traci L. Bonney

Chantal Atherton grew up sharing her last name with her hometown, and as the oldest daughter of the founding family's current generation, she chafed under the expectations of her parents and their country club set.

Everything quickly changes when Brigitte, Chantal's younger sister and the rebel of the Atherton family, joins a new religious organization and starts pulling away from her parents and sister. As Chantal investigates the group's leader and finds out he is not who he claims to be, she turns to the newest member of the sheriff's department, Deputy Marc Thibodaux, for help in reaching her sister.

Chantal's lukewarm faith is challenged as she looks for answers. At the same time, her heart hears a call of another kind, but a recent heartbreak has her questioning whether or not she is willing to risk love again.

Can she answer the call, and can she find a way to help her sister before it's too late?

<u>Brigitte's Battle</u> by Traci L. Bonney

Thanks to her family and friends, Brigitte Atherton is free from Roger Forrester, the felon who posed as a spiritual leader named Joseph Zacharias and seduced her into his cult. But while she escaped the bondage of his control, she is haunted by the fact that he eluded capture and is still at large.

As she enters a new year with her sister and parents, she bears the physical and emotional scars of his abuse. She also bears another consequence of their relationship: an unwanted pregnancy.

She battles the trauma of her victimization and struggles with what to do about the unborn child. And she soon discovers that she isn't the only Atherton woman whose past is filled with heartbreak.

Can Brigitte learn to trust again - to trust not only herself, but the men in her life? And will the man who scarred her so deeply be brought to justice?

Made in the USA
Lexington, KY
07 January 2016